FROM CHAOS BORN

IN HER NAME: THE FIRST EMPRESS, BOOK 1

Michael R. Hicks

This is a work of fiction. All of the characters, organizations and events portrayed in this novel are products of the author's imagination or are used fictitiously.

ISBN: 978-0988932104
FROM CHAOS BORN (IN HER NAME: THE FIRST EMPRESS, BOOK 1)

Copyright © 2012 by Imperial Guard Publishing, LLC

All rights reserved, including the right to reproduce this book, or portions thereof, in any form.

Published by Imperial Guard Publishing
http://AuthorMichaelHicks.com

ACKNOWLEDGEMENTS

As always, I have to give a lot of thanks to the editorial team for this book who spent a great deal of time and probably took a lot of aspiring while splashing the manuscript with red ink.

From Norway, and knowing my native language better than I do (well, maybe that's not saying much), we have Frode Hauge and Marianne Søiland. They've brought some unique perspectives to critiquing my writing that I think has been extremely helpful, and Frode has taught me everything I know about hunting trolls.

I'd also like to thank long-suffering Mindy Schwartz, who has a mind like a steel trap and catches bloopers that I had no idea I'd even written. Sometimes I wonder if she writes them in on purpose, but I've decided I'm not going to test that theory.

My heartfelt thanks also go to my wife Jan, of course. This year's been a wild whitewater ride in many ways, and I never would have been able to stay in the boat without your strength, faith, and love.

Most of all, however, I'd like to thank you, dear reader. Your interest in my books has allowed me to live my dream of writing full-time, and I cannot thank you enough.

FOREWORD

While this book is part of the *In Her Name* series, it represents something a bit different from the previously published novels. Those volumes tell of the century-long war between the human race and the ancient Kreelan Empire and that conflict's eventual resolution.

(Note: If you're reading this and have absolutely no idea what I'm talking about, press the pause button and go get the lead novels of two of the other trilogies on my web site - free.)

With *From Chaos Born*, we're about to turn back the clock roughly *one hundred thousand* years, focusing our attention on the Kreelan Homeworld and its handful (at that time) of interstellar Settlements. There are no humans in this story: here on Earth, our *homo sapiens* ancestors shared the world with the Neanderthals, and stone-tipped spears were still a rather novel invention.

The Kreelan race, by contrast, was already ancient, with the rise and fall of countless civilizations dating back a further four hundred thousand years, divided into four distinct Ages. After a terrible war, even by their savage standards, that took their entire race to the very brink of extinction in the Second Age, a balance of power emerged among the seven ancient martial orders, the priesthoods, that allowed a race uniquely tailored for war to survive against itself. Their people were born, lived, and died in a path of life, the Way, that was defined and taught by the warrior priests and priestesses. There were no gods, for they had been cast aside after the race had nearly perished. War was life, even as it brought death. The race survived, but it was a time of chaos without end.

In what later would be the singular event that would determine the end of the Fourth Age, a girl child was born to the master of a great city and his consort. The child was unlike any other who had ever been given birth, for instead of black hair and black talons, her hair was white as pure snow, and her talons, the long and sharp nails at the ends of her fingers, were a fiery crimson.

Her name was Keel-Tath, and, as foretold in an ancient prophecy, she was destined to unite her race and found an empire that would, at its height, span ten thousand suns across the galaxy.

From Chaos Born is her story. But it is only the beginning...

CHAPTER ONE

The sun was just rising over the mountains of Kui'mar-Gol, painting the magenta sky in hues of flame above the three warriors as they rode along the ancient road toward the city of Keel-A'ar, leaving a long trail of dust in their wake.

Kunan-Lohr rode at the lead, periodically lashing his animal to keep up the brutal pace. The beast ran on two powerful rear legs, the taloned feet tearing into the worn cobbles of the road. Its sides heaved with effort, the black stripes over the brown fur rippling as it panted for breath, the small forearms clutching at the air, as if begging for respite.

Not given to cruelty, Kunan-Lohr drove the beast mercilessly because he had no choice. Bone weary himself, he had already killed four other animals by running them to death in the two months he had been traveling. The seven braids of his raven hair were still tightly woven, but like the rest of his body were covered in dust and grit. His silver-flecked eyes were sunken in the dry, cracked cobalt blue skin of his face. His armor, a gleaming black when he had set out two months ago, was beyond any hope of repair by the armorers. The breast and back plates were pitted and creased from battle, and the black leatherite that covered his arms and legs had been cut open and stained with blood. Some was his own. Some was not. His right hand clutched the reins, while his left hung limply at his side, broken. Two of his ebony talons on that hand had been snapped off, and the others, like his armor, were scratched and pitted from desperate fighting against bands of honorless ones who preyed upon travelers in these troubled days.

Of sleep, he had allowed himself precious little. It was a luxury he had not been able to afford. During the fifty-six days that had passed since he had begun his journey home from the east, he had slept only eight times. He had stopped no more than once a day to eat and let his animal graze for the short time he would allow. Every other waking moment had been in the saddle, riding hard.

His pace had been too much for all but the last two warriors who now accompanied him. The rest of the three hundred with whom he had begun this journey had either perished in the battles they had been forced to fight along the way, or were somewhere behind him, making their own way home.

Even with the wind whipping past from his mount's furious pace, the sour reek of his body odor still reached his sensitive nose. Normally fastidious in his grooming habits, he had only allowed himself the luxury of bathing when he had been forced to stop and barter for fresh mounts. It was not the way in which the master of a great city such as Keel-A'ar should arrive home, but time was his enemy now, and he knew he had very little left.

He could feel her more clearly with every pace the *magthep* took toward home, could sense her with every beat of his heart. His consort, Ulana-Tath. They had once been *tresh*, joined in the path of life that was simply called the Way, when they had first entered the *kazha*, or training school, overseen by the great warrior priests and priestesses of the Desh-Ka order.

Despite Kunan-Lohr's discomfort and desperation to return home, he could not help but grin, his white fangs reflecting the fire of the sunrise as he recalled those days. Ulana-Tath had bested him in everything for most of the early years at the *kazha*, beating him soundly in training nearly every day. Be it with sword or dagger, spear or unsheathed claws, she had beaten him. She was the finest warrior among their peers through her fifth Challenge, when at last he had become her equal. While he bested her in the sixth and seventh Challenges before they came of age as warriors, he had always suspected that she had let him win. And he had loved her all the more for it.

While they were already bound, body and soul, as *tresh*, there was no question when they became warriors that they would be consorts, a mated pair. It was often the case with male and female paired as *tresh*, for a deep bond already existed. While the Way did not demand monogamy, *tresh* who mated as a pair typically did so for life.

And so it had been with them. They loved and fought together, seeking perfection and honor on the battlefield and in their lives.

One enemy, however, remained steadfast in its refusal to yield to their most determined efforts: they had been unable to bear children.

Kunan-Lohr's smile faded as he thought of the sad and frustrating cycles they had endured in that singular pursuit. Many times had they tried, and every time had failed to conceive. The healers were confused and frustrated, for they had determined that both he and Ulana-Tath were fertile and entirely healthy. It was a confounding mystery, as if some dark magic had cast a veil between their two bodies, denying them what they most desired.

While it had been a most bitter disappointment, despair was not the way of their kind. The intensity of their love for one another remained undiminished. Indeed, if anything, their bonds grew stronger, matched only by their lust for battle. In the perpetual wars that raged across the face of the Homeworld, the two made their mark in service to the great warrior who was the mistress of Keel-A'ar, and who in turn served the King of the Eastern Lands of the continent of T'lar-Gol.

Over the cycles that passed and the many battles that were fought against opposing kings and roving bands of marauders, Ulana-Tath and Kunan-Lohr rose in the ranks of the peers until Kunan-Lohr won the leadership of the city of Keel-A'ar in a Challenge, defeating the mistress of the city. As had long been customary in their city, the Challenge had been to first blood, not to the death. For the Way, as taught by the Desh-Ka priesthood, held that there was great honor in victory, and no shame in defeat. The only shame for those who lived by the sword was not to step into the arena to accept the challenge of combat. Aside from the non-warrior castes, who lived by a code that was less bloody but just as difficult, the only path to leadership was through the clash of swords in the Challenge.

After that, Ulana-Tath had challenged him, and he had bested her, drawing a thin bead of blood from her shoulder with his sword. She had bowed and saluted his victory, but the smile in her eyes and the joy that echoed from her spirit in his blood told him that, as he had suspected, she had not entered the arena with the intent of winning the contest. She had already won his heart, and had no interest in becoming the mistress of the city.

But she would be his First, his most trusted lieutenant, the sword hand of her lord and master.

Those had been the good days, he thought now, before the rise of the Dark Queen, Syr-Nagath. An orphan and survivor from the Great Wastelands beyond the Kui'mar-Gol Mountains, she had come to their lands wearing armor she had taken from the dead, with the eyestones of a *genoth*, a great dragon that lived in the wastelands, around her neck. Young, little over the age of mating, she had walked the many leagues to the king's city and challenged him the day she arrived. The right of challenge belonged to every warrior, and the only thing anyone had questioned had been her wisdom in choosing such an opponent.

No one had expected her to win. For the king, while growing old, was still a formidable and ferocious opponent.

But against this demon, as Kunan-Lohr remembered all too well, having presided over the Challenge himself, the venerable warrior had stood no chance at all. Syr-Nagath had toyed with the older and much more powerful-looking warrior just long enough to pick apart his weaknesses. Then she killed him.

To fight to the death in a Challenge was an ancient right. But it was relatively rare, and usually occurred only in cases where serious offense had been given. Every group, from the small bands of honorless brigands who haunted the mountains and forests, to the most powerful nations, needed their warriors in order to survive. It was an unwritten code of the Way that mercy was acceptable, even preferable, in the arena.

That changed under Syr-Nagath. As Kunan-Lohr had feared after she had slain the king, warriors had gathered to challenge the young mistress from the wastelands. He would have challenged her himself, had he not known what these new challengers did not: he had seen her fight the king, and knew that she was by far the superior warrior. Those that chose to fight her believed that the old king had lost the Challenge simply because he was old. In that, too, Kunan-Lohr knew they were wrong. Unlike these challengers, he had sparred many times with the king, and knew just how good he had truly been.

Ten of the kingdom's best warriors died at the hands of Syr-Nagath in the day that followed the king's death. By the time the sun had set, she was covered in blood that was not her own.

"*Ka'a mekh!*" Kunan-Lohr had himself given the command for the thousands who had watched the gory spectacle to kneel and render a salute to their new leader.

Their new queen.

Since that day, over ten cycles ago, the continent of T'lar-Gol had run red with blood, more than had been spilled in millennia. Syr-Nagath was bloodthirsty, even for a race that lived for war.

During most of the time since the Dark Queen had risen to power, Kunan-Lohr and Ulana-Tath had been away on campaign, leading their warriors into battle after battle. He would not have thought it unnatural, save that Syr-Nagath demanded that her vassals strip their cities and lands of most of their warriors, leaving the other castes nearly defenseless against the bands of honorless ones who had become bold enough to strike out of the forests and mountains for the rich plunder of the cities. Keel-A'ar had survived unscathed because its ancient walls could easily be defended by a small garrison against anything short of an army, but many other cities and villages across the land were not so fortunate.

Unlike those who followed the Way as taught in the *kazhas*, the honorless ones had no taboo against the ill-treatment or killing of non-warrior castes. Healers, armorers, builders, and the many other castes that were the foundation of life as defined by the Way were murdered or, worse, taken as slaves. It was unthinkable to warriors such as Ulana-Tath and himself to leave the other castes unprotected; it was tantamount to throwing one's own children to the *ku'ur-kamekh*, the ravenous steppe-beasts, to be torn apart and eaten.

But, as Syr-Nagath herself was fond of pointing out, she was not of their Way. No one knew anything of her past, but it would not have surprised Kunan-Lohr if she was one of the rare rejects from one of the ancient orders such as the Desh-Ka. That was the only explanation for her extraordinary fighting skills.

He knew with the same degree of certainty that she was not descended from the Desh-Ka, for he could not feel her, could not sense her emotions. Their race was descended from seven ancient bloodlines, each of which could be traced back over many thousands of years to one of the seven original warrior sects. The descendants of each of those sects had an empathic sense for the others in their bloodline. Those whose blood was mixed were empathic toward all their relations, but the intensity of the sensation was reduced as the bloodlines became diluted. Ulana-Tath and Kunan-Lohr were both pure descendants of the Desh-Ka, and could sense each other over hundreds, even thousands, of leagues. Others from their city, by contrast, were only distant whispers, fleeting sensations that formed an emotional tide in one's blood.

And it was that sense that had brought him home. Ulana-Tath had been summoned back to Keel-A'ar eight months earlier from the bloody campaign in the east to face a set of challengers for her place in the city's hierarchy of peers. To forbid her return was something that was not even in Syr-Nagath's power, much as the Dark Queen would have liked to try. Even honor-bound to her as they were, warriors such as Ulana-Tath and Kunan-Lohr, who were also masters and mistresses of their cities, would not fight if they could not defend their honor at home.

Kunan-Lohr, who had remained with the queen in the east, knew something momentous had happened with Ulana-Tath. It had been three months since she had departed for home, and he sensed a fountain of joy and wonder from her such as he had never before felt. The intensity of the feeling ebbed over time, but was always there, a constant in his heart. Three more months passed when a messenger arrived, sent by his wife with the news: she was with child.

He remembered the moment as if it were yesterday. The courier had arrived in the midst of a major battle, and the young warrior waded through the enemy to Kunan-Lohr's side to tell him that his wife was expecting a girl-child. Overhearing the news, the warriors who had just been trying to kill him lowered their swords and stepped back, rendering him a salute. Kunan-Lohr had a fierce reputation, and fighting him was a great honor for any enemy warrior. Allowing him the privilege of stepping away from the battle to attend to his child had been an even greater honor.

The Dark Queen, however, did not see things that way. After quickly cleaning the blood of the day's fighting from his body and armor, he sought an audience with her. Kneeling before her in the great pavilion that served as her palace, he had begged her to grant him leave, but she had refused.

"I must grant your right to return to defend your honor," Syr-Nagath had told him, her voice as cold as her eyes, "but this trifle is another matter. I command you to stay, and so you shall. Your child shall be given over to the wardresses in the creche, as custom demands. You may see it — her — if you are challenged for your lordship of your city, or when my conquest has concluded and I release you from my service."

To hold him in such a manner was her right, but few sovereigns in living memory had chosen to enforce it. Warriors who were allowed to return home to visit loved ones returned to war refreshed. Those who did not fought on, but with hearts heavy with yearning.

For five days, he begged her to give him leave to return home, pushing to the very brink of challenging her to fight in the arena.

On the sixth day, she had relented, but her promise of his release had come with a price: to mate with her. While

Kunan-Lohr had been disgusted at the prospect, at that time he would have done anything in order to return home.

While it was unusual for a king or queen to demand such a thing, it was not unheard of. There was no dishonor or taboo in doing so, for there were few taboos or strictures in Kreelan life regarding mating.

But mating with Syr-Nagath was a cold, loathsome union that left him feeling soiled, and he carried away long gashes in his back from where her talons raked him in her ecstasy. Unlike the cuts and stab wounds he had received in the fighting on the way home, he would have the healers remove any trace of Syr-Nagath's marks upon his flesh. Not to hide them from Ulana-Tath, but to cleanse himself of the Dark Queen's stain.

Rounding a bend in the road through a stretch of forest, his heart lifted as Keel-A'ar finally came into sight.

"At last," he breathed. His tired *magthep*, as if sensing the end of their journey was near and that food and rest would soon be at hand, quickened its pace.

Keel-A'ar stood at the center of a great plain that was bounded by forests to the south and east, and the mountains of Kui'mar-Gol to the north and west. It was among the oldest and greatest cities of the world. A great wall surrounded it, the seamless surface a tribute to the builders who had created it many generations ago. The walls reflected the sun rising at his back, the light rippling along the serpent-hide texture of the ancient fused stone. The height of six warriors and as thick as three laid heel to toe, the walls had withstood many assaults over the ages. Like everything in the city, it was carefully tended and maintained by the builder caste, so much so that it looked new.

A branch of the Lo'ar River ran beneath the walls through the center of the city, but it was not for the sake of beauty or idle pleasure: in times of siege, it provided fresh water and fish to sustain the defenders. While there was need for vigilance, lest a foe mount an attack from under water, the fish that provided much of the city's food were also part of its defense. The vicious *lackan-kamekh* were bountiful and lethal, with rows of needle-sharp teeth. The wall was surrounded by a moat that could be flooded with water and a host of the terrible fish if the city were attacked. Only in winter, after the river had frozen over and shut away the light of the sun, did the *lackan-kamekh* sleep, hibernating on the river bottom.

Above the wall, he could see the golden domes and spires of the taller buildings rising above the walls to catch the sun's rays. They were a beacon of welcome to his weary eyes.

As he and his two companions drew closer, he looked again at the sun, which rose steadily in the magenta sky behind him toward the great moon. On this day there would be an eclipse of the sun by the moon, an event that only took place every fifteen thousand and seven cycles. It was a momentous omen, and even in his weariness, the thought lifted his spirits. He knew in his heart that today was the day his daughter would be born.

"Faster!" He whipped the *magthep* to a sprint toward the waiting gate, leaving his two companions fighting to keep up.

* * *

Like the *lackan-kamekh*, the killer fish, the city's defenders never slept, particularly in these times. With most of the city's warriors away on campaign in the service of the queen, the small garrison Kunan-Lohr had been allowed to retain never relaxed its guard.

They had been attacked several times by bands of honorless warriors, and had easily defeated the disorganized mobs. But their master and his master before him had taught them well: overconfidence was as much an enemy as those who would destroy the city. They were charged with protecting that which was most precious to those who followed the Way: the children in the creche and the non-warrior castes.

Anin-Khan was the captain of the guard. Aside from Ulana-Tath and Kunan-Lohr, he was the most senior and skilled warrior, having challenged them both to contests in the arena. After they had drawn first blood in the contests he had fought against them, he had accepted with great honor the responsibility of the city's defense. It was a measure of Kunan-Lohr's trust in him and his abilities, for while the city's master was away, it was the most important role a warrior could fulfill.

He spent most of his time on watch, which was nearly every moment that he was not asleep, in the barbican, the defensive structure that jutted out over the city's main gate, or the watchtowers that rose at key points along the wall. From those vantage points, he had a view over the open plain between the city and the surrounding forests.

He happened to be standing watch on the barbican when he caught sight of a trail of dust from the main road leading from the east. His bloodline was not pure Desh-Ka, and so his empathic sense was not terribly strong, but he could always tell the approach of his lord and master.

"Alert the mistress," Anin-Khan told one of the guards. "Our master returns."

The guard saluted and set off at a run for Ulana-Tath's chambers.

While he was certain in his heart that Kunan-Lohr led the trio of approaching warriors, Anin-Khan waited until he could clearly see his master's weary face. Parties of warriors and non-warriors were often welcomed at Keel-A'ar on their travels, but never before Anin-Khan himself had given his approval. The honorless ones had been growing bolder, and had tried to gain entry under the guise of honorable travelers.

Sure now of the approaching warriors, he called to the gatekeepers below. "Open the gate!"

The guards below him shouted their acknowledgement before turning a set of great wheels in the thick walled guard house, grunting and straining with the effort. The massive metal gate, thicker than a warrior stood tall, slowly rose, driven by the wheels and supported by a complex set of thick chains, counterweights, and pulleys.

Kunan-Lohr and his two escorts thundered through, ducking their heads under the ancient metal as it rose.

"Close it!" Anin-Khan favored his master with a salute as the trio of riders sped through the courtyard behind the gate and on into the city proper. He very much wanted to greet his master in person, but would not leave his post. There would be time for that later.

For now, he and the other guards would continue to attend to their duties.

The trio hammered along the streets, which were now lined with thousands of people, kneeling and rendering the *tla'a-kane*, the ritual salute, with their left fists over their right breasts. All but a handful were of the non-warrior castes. Armorers, porters of water, healers, seamstresses, builders, and many more, the colors of the simple robes that defined their castes creating a vibrant rainbow along the gracefully curved streets of inlaid stone.

Ignoring the pain of his broken left hand, Kunan-Lohr returned the salute, holding it as he rode past his people. His eye caught the glint of the armor of the soldiers on the battlements, who were also kneeling.

He ground his teeth together in frustration, not wanting to show his concern on his face. There were so few warriors, now. Too few to properly defend the city from anything more than the most half-hearted attack by anything other than the honorless ones. And how long would it be before they had grown enough in numbers to pose a credible challenge?

May the Dark Queen's soul rot in Eternal Darkness. The curse was one he had thought many times in the cycles since Syr-Nagath had risen to power, but he had never given voice to the thought. His honor would not permit it.

They flew by the central gardens that formed the green, open heart of the city. The main garden, set deep in the earth compared to the surrounding land, was surrounded by terraced levels that were open to the sky above. Unlike most days, it was empty, for the people who would normally be there, enjoying a contemplative moment or tending the garden were lined along the streets to greet him.

Glancing up, he saw the sun and the moon rapidly converging, and felt a quickening of the urgency in the empathic link with Ulana-Tath.

There was little time, only moments, remaining.

He beat the straining *magthep* savagely, at the same time murmuring his apologies to the beast for inflicting such cruelty. He silently promised that the creature would receive every comfort the animal handlers could give as compensation for its valiant service to his cause.

The beast responded, its exhausted legs stretching farther, its taloned feet striking sparks from the stone of the streets as it dashed forward.

After one final, skittering turn, the citadel came into view. At the center of the city, it was a fortress within a fortress, the home of the city's master or mistress. While it was the final defensive structure of the many that had originally gone into Keel-A'ar's design, it was also one of beauty. The walls, which rose even higher than the defensive walls around the city, were of glittering granite, black with white and copper veins, and polished to an exquisite sheen. Like the other structures in the city, it was not a regular shape, formed by mere triangles, circles, or rectangles. It was a work of art in itself, the smooth lines making it look as if it could sail away upon the wind, pulled toward the stars by the great golden spire that rose from its apex.

Home, Kunan-Lohr thought as he brought his exhausted mount to a skidding stop just inside the gate in the wall surrounding the citadel. He quickly slid to the ground among the crowd of retainers who had gathered, filling the courtyard. As one, they knelt before him.

The two other riders arrived just a moment later, barely bringing their beasts to a stop before dismounting.

Many hands, eager to help, reached out to take the reins from the riders.

"Tend them well!" Kunan-Lohr ordered as the animals, gasping for breath, were led off to the corrals where they could rest.

Other hands offered food and drink to the riders, and words of welcome to the lord and master of the city.

Gratefully accepting a large mug of bitter ale, Kunan-Lohr drank it quickly to help slake his thirst. His party had run out of water the day before, giving the last of it to the *magtheps* before making the final run for home.

"My thanks." He handed the mug back to the young porter of water, who bowed, greatly honored.

Then, willing himself not to run, he took long, urgent strides toward the entryway, where stood the housemistress, who was also the senior healer.

"Where is she?"

"In the birthing chamber, my lord." With a look upward at the impending eclipse, the housemistress turned and led him inside through the tall arch and thick, iron-reinforced wooden door of the entryway.

Kunan-Lohr's footsteps echoed in the stone corridors as he followed her to the infirmary wing where the sick and injured of the city were treated, and where the young were brought into the world.

He restrained his urge to sprint to his consort's side, forcing himself to keep pace with the housemistress. To his pleasant surprise, she was moving faster than he would have believed possible without breaking into a run.

Upon hearing a cry up ahead, unmistakably Ulana-Tath's voice, he put paid to decorum and ran, his good hand clenching tightly around the handle of his sword as he sensed her pain.

He skidded to a stop in the birthing room, which had several large stone basins. Only one of them was in use now.

Ulana-Tath, nude, was leaning back in the basin, which was filled with warm water. One of the healers, her white robes bound close to her body while she was in the water, attended her. Two other healers stood close by, should they be needed, along with the wardress who would be responsible for the child in the creche until she was old enough to enter the *kazha*.

"My love." Ulana-Tath reached out a hand for him, and he took it. He hadn't realized it was his left hand, the one that was broken, but ignored the pain as her powerful grip squeezed it. He kissed her briefly, ashamed that he was so filthy from the long, hard ride. His shame quickly receded as he was overwhelmed with her beauty and the miracle of what was taking place before his very eyes.

She cried out again.

"Push, my mistress!" The healer in the basin moved in close between Ulana-Tath's legs, spread wide and trembling. "She is almost here..."

With one final grunt of effort, Ulana-Tath gasped in relief as the baby was finally released from her mother's womb into the healer's gentle hands.

As the midwife held the child under the water, one of the other healers leaned over the basin and carefully laid on the water what looked like a thin layer of dough, whose surface was swirling with blues and purples. It was living tissue that she held in place as the midwife gently brought the child up underneath it. The tissue, healing gel, wrapped itself around the infant's body, completely covering it.

The adults watched intently as the gel disappeared, absorbed into the child's skin as the midwife lowered the child back into the water. Moment's later, it began to ooze out the nose and mouth, and the healer gently gathered it up as it left the girl's body.

The healer closed her eyes as the oozing mass was absorbed into her own skin. With senses developed over thousands of generations, the healer "listened" to what the healing gel, which was in fact a living symbiont, told her of the child's body.

The healing gel was not only a diagnostic tool for the healers, but their primary instrument, as well. Through the healing gel, the healer could visualize and repair any injury, even replace lost limbs, and cure any ill. The infant now had full immunity from every strain of disease on the planet, and any errors in her genetic coding that would have posed a threat to her health would have been corrected.

After a moment, the healer smiled and opened her eyes. "The child is perfectly well, mistress."

All breathed a sigh of relief. While problems with birthing and newborns were very rare, their health was never taken for granted.

The healer carefully lifted the child from the water, placing her in Ulana-Tath's waiting arms. After only a few moments, the infant began to cry, her tiny voice echoing through the birthing chamber.

"She is beautiful, my love." Kunan-Lohr, master of a great city and a veteran of many terrible battles, highest of warriors among those beholden to him, knelt by his consort's side like a child himself, utterly humbled by the miracle before him. His ears could hear his daughter's cries of life, but his heart could also feel the tiny voice that had joined the murmur of souls that bound together the descendants of his bloodline.

Looking up at the wardress, he asked, "What is to be her name?"

Tradition held that the wardress who would be responsible for the child from birth until she was ready to enter the *kazha* would also name her. "In honor of the city whose master is her father, and the family bloodline of her mother, the child will henceforth be known as Keel-Tath."

"An honorable name," Kunan-Lohr told her, "well-chosen."

As if sensing that she was the center of the entire city's attention, Keel-Tath's tiny hands waved in the air, groping blindly. After one of the healers quickly cleansed his free hand, Kunan-Lohr offered his daughter his little finger, careful that she reached only for the flesh, and not the sharp talon.

She wrapped her fingers around his, gripping it with surprising strength. Her own nails, which someday would grow long and sharp, glittered in the steady glow of light that fell from the walls.

He frowned. "Her talons…"

The senior healer bent closer to see, and with a subtle gesture of her hand the light in the room brightened.

"What is wrong?" Ulana-Tath gasped as she saw her daughter's fingers.

Among their race, the nails that grew from their fingers, eventually to form talons, were uniformly black, both on the hands and the shorter nails on the feet. Unlike some of the animal species on the Homeworld, which sported startling degrees of differentiation, there was very little among their race. Black talons, black nails on the toes, cobalt blue skin, and black hair were features of every child born since at least the end of the First Age, four hundred thousand cycles before.

Keel-Tath's tiny nails, both on her hands and feet, were a bright scarlet.

"And her hair!" Ulana-Tath's view was closer than that of the others, and her eyes widened as she looked closer at the wisps of hair on her daughter's head, clear now in the brighter light. She had seen enough newborns to know what she should be seeing. And what she should not. "It is white!"

Without a word, the senior healer held out her hand, and the healing gel materialized out of the skin on the arm of the healer who had wrapped it around Keel-Tath. She wrapped it around the forearm of the senior healer, and the mass sank into her flesh. Closing her eyes, the senior healer focused on the story the symbiont had to tell.

After a long breathless moment, she opened her eyes, focusing on the squirming child. "She is healthy, my lord. Extraordinarily so." She reached out a hand and gently brushed the snow-white wisps on the child's blue-skinned crown. "I have no explanation, but there is nothing amiss. Of that there is no doubt." She paused. "As with your difficulties in conceiving a child before this, I have no explanation."

Ulana-Tath exchanged a look with Kunan-Lohr. Among all else that had ever been accomplished in the ebb and flow of their civilization over the long ages, the art of the healers was without doubt the most advanced. If the healers said the child was healthy, then she was. Clearly different, perhaps, but healthy.

Breathing out a sigh of relief, Ulana-Tath kissed her daughter on the head, gently nuzzling the white hair.

Kunan-Lohr set aside his apprehensions as he gazed with rapt love at his daughter, who still clutched his finger. "A child unlike any other, born under a Great Eclipse, can only be destined for greatness," he said softly. "May Thy Way be long and glorious, my daughter."

CHAPTER TWO

A month's ride from Keel-A'ar to the northwest, beyond the mountains of Kui'mar-Gol, the temple of the Desh-Ka stood upon a great plateau. The oldest and most powerful of the seven ancient martial orders, the Desh-Ka taught the Way to the young through the *kazhas* near each city on the continent of T'lar-Gol, but otherwise kept to themselves. Revered and feared by their blood and kin, the high warrior priests and priestesses had ages ago removed themselves from the affairs of the world beyond the great temple's walls, just as had their counterparts in the other six orders. This had long ago been decided by a great conclave of the seven orders.

Four of those orders remained on the Homeworld, while the other three had migrated to the stars in generations past. Maintaining the balance of power had become the function of the orders, ensuring that armies from the Settlements, the colonies among the stars, did not destroy the Blood of the Homeworld, and vice versa. All the planets upon which the Kreela lived and breathed were worlds at war. So had it been, and so many believed would it always be, a stasis of bloodshed until the end of time.

One who questioned both the wisdom and the truth of that ages-old premise dreamed as he slept fitfully in his small chamber within the stone barracks of the Desh-Ka temple. Ayan-Dar's sleeping mind listened to the ebb and flow of the souls that whispered in his blood, sensing — *knowing* — that something had just changed. His subconscious sifted through the strands of emotions that he thought of as voices in the great song of his people, searching, searching...

There! A tiny voice, barely a ripple in the river of emotions that flowed through his mind, cried out. The voice was clear and pure, more than any other he had sensed in his long life.

His good eye snapped open and he stared up through the clear crystal dome at the roof of his chamber. Overhead, the great moon was sliding across the face of the sun, casting the world into an eerie darkness. It was his habit to sleep during the day, for he had long ago chosen to spend most of his waking hours in the quiet of the night, where he could enjoy the most solitude.

He frowned at the sight in the sky above him. There had been much pomp and to-do about the Great Eclipse, of course, but Ayan-Dar had not been overcome with excitement and awe as had the peers and acolytes. He knew they thought him little short of a heretic, but such spectacles held little interest for him now, in what he considered the sunset of his life. Unlike most of the peers, he had traveled among the stars during the last great war with the Settlements, and had seen such sights that froze him with awe and amazement, or made him tremble in fear. For him, the Great Eclipse was little more than a novelty of nature.

He focused his attention on this new voice that cried out in the Blood. He was better attuned to this sense than most, as his lineage was completely pure back to the original founders of the Desh-Ka early in the Second Age. The new voice, that of a newborn, was not the only one to appear under the Great Eclipse, of course. But there was something different about this one. He could sense it just as surely as he could smell the smoke of the celebratory pyres lit by the acolytes in the temple's arenas. They celebrated because tradition held that the Great Eclipse was a good omen for all who witnessed it.

Ayan-Dar did not believe that the spiritual voice that had begun to sing as the great moon passed over the sun was a coincidence. He had long prayed to the Ancient Ones, the warriors of the spirit, whose voices he could hear whispering in the depths of his soul, for something to change the equation of his race, to take them on a path to the greatness he believed his people could achieve.

He wondered now if his prayers had been answered. For the first time in many cycles, Ayan-Dar felt the stirrings of a sense of purpose. It was a welcome feeling, for many cycles had passed since he had done anything that he considered truly worthy. How could he? The great challenges of his life, both those of the sword and those of the spirit, had already been fought and won. He went through the motions of life with little enthusiasm, for he had seen all there was to this existence. There were some days when he longed for an honorable death to take him from this life, but he knew he would fulfill his duties as a priest to the last.

With a groan, he rose from his bed of old animal hides and knelt on the cold stone floor. As with everything in the life of those taught to follow the Way, there was ritual to all things, even dressing oneself. In Ayan-Dar's case, certain modifications had to be made, for he only had one arm. His right arm, and the eye on the same side, had been lost in battle many cycles before during the last incursion from the Settlements. The healers could, of course, repair such trifles, but Ayan-Dar had enjoyed the notoriety his wounds had given him. As any warrior, he treasured his battle scars, and no priest or priestess could boast more scars than did he.

His scarlet lips peeled back in a half-grin, half-grimace, revealing his worn-down and yellowed fangs as he began to strap on his armor. Unlike the other high warriors, he no longer had any acolytes, his last having mysteriously disappeared months before. There was no one to assist him in the daily ritual of donning his armor.

Not that I need anyone, he thought with a quiet huff. As a high warrior priest of the Desh-Ka, he was not limited by the frailty of his body.

Relaxing his mind, he focused on the armor and the straps, and the armor quickly wrapped around his torso and limbs, buckling itself into place as if guided by invisible hands. The gleaming black breast and back plates rose from their place on the floor, and he held out his arm as the metal clamshell closed around his barrel-chested torso.

The breast plate bore the cyan rune of the Desh-Ka, which matched the rune on the sigil device affixed to the front of his Collar of Honor. All who served the seven martial orders, from the lowest acolyte to the high warrior priest or priestess who guided the temple's affairs, wore the same fashion of collar, a gold-trimmed band of living metal, black as his talons. But only the members of the priesthood wore the sigil device. And from their collars hung rows of pendants, starting with the Line of Stars that inscribed the wearer's name. Below that hung pendants, formed of precious metals and stones, proclaiming the deeds and accomplishments of the wearer. While Ayan-Dar had long since fallen from grace among the other priests and priestesses for his heretical views, none could deny his legacy as a great warrior. From his collar hung more pendants than had been bestowed upon any other warrior in living memory.

He rose to his feet, and his leg armor levitated from the floor and attached itself like an outer skin around the black gauze-like undergarment his people wore. Stepping into his sandals, the leatherite straps wrapped themselves around his bulky calves. He was shorter than most of his peers, but of stocky build. And despite his age of one hundred and fifteen cycles, he could still defeat most of the young acolytes in any test of strength, even without using his powers.

His armored gauntlet rose from the floor and slipped over his left hand, his ebony talons fitting through the holes in the metal and leatherite as the clasps closed around his wrist. Three *shrekkas*, deadly throwing weapons with several curved blades around a central hub, whirled from where they had been stacked on the floor to snap into place on the right side of his breast plate. The weapons were traditionally carried on the left shoulder, but since Ayan-Dar had no right arm, a different arrangement had been required.

At last, his sword rose from a cradle next to his bed, the scabbard securing itself to the leatherite belt around his waist on his right side. Gripping the swirling gold handle, he pulled it a hand's breadth from the gleaming black scabbard. The blade was as long as his leg, the living metal shimmering in the dark light of the eclipse. The sword's handle molded itself to his palm, and he could sense the will of the blade, just as he knew it could sense his. While his weapon did not have a mind, he believed with all his heart that it was an extension of his soul.

With a deep breath, he stepped toward the thick wooden door of his room. Turning the ancient latch, he pushed it open, emerging into the main hallway of the barracks. Heading toward the open arch that led outside, he passed many other such doors, all standing open, the rooms empty.

Stepping outside, he heard the singing of the acolytes from the direction of the arenas. Grimacing, he moved toward the sound. He had once reveled in the ancient chants that were so soothing to the ears, but the sound now was wreathed in the same stifling sameness that permeated the rest of temple life, and it no longer brought him any pleasure.

He passed by the *Kal'ai-Il*, an enormous stone construct that was a fixture of every temple and *kazha* on the

Homeworld and throughout the Settlements. Known as the Stone Place, it was a place of public atonement where punishment was delivered to those who had fallen from grace. It was very rarely used, for few strayed far from the Way once they first set foot on the path, but the imposing structure in the midst of their lives loomed over them all as a warning. The last time anyone had been unfortunate enough to find themselves shackled and whipped here had been fifteen cycles ago. Life in the temple, as it was outside, was harsh and often cruel, but Ayan-Dar would be quite content to meet his end not ever seeing such a punishment again, let alone experiencing it.

The thousand members of the priesthood and their acolytes stood around the five arenas at the center of the temple complex, singing as the celebratory pyres sent flames upward toward the darkened disk of the moon that now fully blocked the light of the sun. Despite his cynicism, Ayan-Dar had to confess to himself as he strode across the sands of the arenas toward the dais in the center of the main arena, that it was an impressive sight and sound. More than that, the power that resonated here was out of all proportion to their number: the five hundred priests and priestesses alone could destroy entire armies. And, in times past, the Desh-Ka had done just that.

He bowed his head and saluted T'ier-Kunai, the highest of the high among the priesthood as he took his place to her right.

With a tightening of her lips, she returned the salute, fixing him with a frigid glare. "I tolerate your intransigence because you have earned your honor, Ayan-Dar. But you need not set such a poor example for the acolytes."

Ayan-Dar cast her a sideways glance as he observed the celebration around him. The acolytes and the priesthood, all in their ceremonial armor, made a magnificent display against the backdrop of the massive and ancient buildings of the temple. The magenta sky was ribboned with clouds that reflected the strange light that poured from the Great Eclipse.

He did not bother responding to her rebuke for being late to the ceremony. He rendered few apologies in these days. It was unkind to her, he knew, and he felt a faint shred of shame that he quickly pushed aside.

"You have sensed it." He spoke loudly enough to be heard over the crooning of the acolytes, but not so loud that any others could hear. T'ier-Kunai did not hold him in high regard in many ways, but more than any other in the temple, he trusted her.

She paused before answering. "It is a cry upon the wind, Ayan-Dar. Nothing more. The song of the child's soul stood out because we are all more attuned in the fleeting darkness of the Great Eclipse. Such has been recorded in the Books of Time in ages past. You know this."

"Indeed, my priestess, which is why I know this is different. I feel it in my bones."

At that, T'ier-Kunai offered him a rare smile, baring her long and brilliantly white fangs. "And how, great warrior priest, could that be? Your bones are so old they have turned to stone."

He bared his own fangs, engaged by her humor, even at his own expense, as T'ier-Kunai sang the chorus, the priesthood answering a verse posed by the acolytes. Out of habit more than anything else, Ayan-Dar joined in, his deep baritone blending into the harmony.

When the chorus was over, he leaned closer to T'ier-Kunai. "With your permission, my priestess, this ossifying old priest would like to pursue the matter." His voice turned serious. "I believe we dare not do otherwise."

Sparing him a look, she sighed. "You know that you need not ask my permission to undertake such quests of curiosity,

Ayan-Dar. You have spared me consideration enough times in the past." She leaned closer. "But do not embarrass me by again making your way across the arenas as you depart."

"As you command, my priestess." Ayan-Dar saluted, bowing his head. "It shall be so."

With a gentle rush of cold air, he vanished as the edge of the sun reappeared behind the dark disk of the great moon.

* * *

After leaving T'ier-Kunai's side, Ayan-Dar had reappeared at the entrance to the stables where the *magtheps* were kept. He saddled up one of the beasts and bridled two others as pack animals. This was a task normally appointed to acolytes, but all of them were free of their duties for this day as part of the celebrations. Ayan-Dar did not begrudge them their temporary freedom from toil, for he preferred to do such things himself, without the over-eager help of the well-intentioned younglings.

Next to the stables was one of the temple commissaries, and he took for himself bags of water and ale, packages of dried meat, a shelter, and a few other items that he thought might be useful. He was not sure yet where he was going or how long he would be away. The first part of his quest would be to find a place of quiet solitude where he could seek out the voice, to learn the location of this child among all who had been born that day. All he knew now was that the child, whom he believed to be female from the tone of her spiritual voice, had been born of Desh-Ka lineage. Most likely she was here on the continent of T'lar-Gol, but she could as easily be among the stars. The Bloodsong, as some called it, knew no bounds, was not constrained by any distance or laws of physical reality.

Having strapped the various bundles to the snorting *magtheps* and tying off the reins of the pack animals to his saddle, he took one last look at the sky, which was now an ugly blood red as the eclipse ended.

With a quiet *humph*, Ayan-Dar mounted the lead animal and headed toward the winding path that led down from the plateau to the valley below.

After two days of easy riding, he arrived at a hilltop he had visited long ago. It was not a great mountain, and did not have a view of endless vistas. Its appeal for him lay not in such things, but in the ancient ruins that lay there. Among the withered granite bones of the buildings that had once formed a small village was a circular structure not unlike the *Kal'ai-Il*. Its true purpose he did not know, for there were no records of this place in the Books of Time, so ancient was it. Unlike most habitations from olden times, which had either been destroyed and rebuilt countless times, or obliterated from history forever, this place had somehow survived. The endless wars that swept over their world like waves of blood had always parted around this place, as if it possessed a secret magic all its own.

Relieving the *magtheps* of their burdens and freeing them to graze, Ayan-Dar built a small fire at the center of the circular structure amid the shattered and eroded remains of the columns that had once surrounded it. He liked to think it was a temple to ancient gods in a time when his people still had gods in which to believe. But the only god his people worshipped now was war. It was the only god that could hope to survive in a crucible of endless bloodshed.

With a mirthless smile, he knelt by the fire, holding his hand out to the warmth as night's chill began to set in. His race was born and bred for war, and he would be the last one to say otherwise. Even the non-warrior castes were tailored for war in their own way, each of them occupying a niche in a system, an ecology, that had evolved over millennia to support the warrior caste. It was a perfect symbiosis of intelligent beings working in harmony in the ultimate endeavor.

But the Way, the code that defined the system by which all but the honorless ones lived, was a closed loop. His race had stopped evolving in the cataclysmic First Age of their recorded history, four hundred thousand cycles ago. The Books of Time from that period were, not surprisingly, fragmentary, but the glimpses he himself had seen showed that very little had changed in all the ages since the first titanic upheavals of those ancient civilizations. For better or worse, they remained the children of their ancient forebears.

In his heart, he wished for more. He felt his race could achieve greatness on a galactic scale, reaching outward for conquest and dominion, rather than continually gutting itself, spilling its own precious blood. He knew that his quest now was not unlike others he had undertaken in the past, seeking some way to upset the ages-old balance. Others, such as T'ier-Kunai, saw his journeys as flights into fantasy. And it was these journeys of foolish self-indulgence, looking for the answer to a question that no other dared ask, that had eventually brought him to his current questionable status within the order.

"There must be more." His whisper was lost in the darkness beyond the fire as he closed his eyes.

Focusing on the tiny voice that had awakened him that morning before he began his quest, he cast out his second sight, searching the world, and the stars, if need be, with the eyes of his spirit.

* * *

Ayan-Dar sensed them in his mind and blood long before he could smell or hear them. A group of *kurh-a'mekh*, honorless ones, had surrounded the hilltop, no doubt drawn by his fire.

It had been many cycles since he had ventured beyond the confines of the temple, but he had heard tales from acolytes and his fellow priests and priestesses of a growing number of marauding bands that terrorized the villages and smaller cities of T'lar-Gol. It was a phenomenon that was as easily calculated as the date of the Great Eclipse. When leaders such as Syr-Nagath, the Dark Queen as she was often called (although not in her presence, he surmised), became bent on conquest, they always stripped their vassals of warriors, leaving their homelands nearly defenseless to those not of the Way, or who had strayed from the path.

Ayan-Dar lamented that it was happening so soon after the last great collapse, just after the war with the Settlements in which he himself had fought over seventy cycles before. Their civilization ebbed and flowed in a pattern that stretched back to the First Age, with continents and even entire worlds rising from prehistoric savagery to a certain plateau. Then, like a great tree, it rotted from within as cities and nation-states began the inevitable conquest of their neighbors. Eventually, the fragile system would collapse back into chaos.

The rise of *kurh-a'mekh*, like maggots on carrion, was a flag that the next collapse would occur soon. Food supplies would dwindle as the non-warrior castes were ravaged, the armies that grappled in their pointless struggles would starve, and whatever progress had been made in crawling out of chaos would be wiped away. Some of the cities would survive, as would the orders like the Desh-Ka, who would resow the seeds of civilization for the next rise.

Civilization had not had much time to rise again since the last collapse. On the one hand, that usually meant that the next collapse would not be so catastrophic, for they did not have far to fall. On the other, it was highly unusual that the honorless ones had arisen so quickly, and in such numbers.

But that was a mystery beyond his desire to contemplate.

"Leave now, and I will spare your lives." Ayan-Dar's deep voice boomed across the hilltop, startling the *magtheps*, who had moved close to the fire after grazing, fearful of the predators that roamed the wilderness. They, too, were another sign of the coming fall, for there were too few warriors to police the edge of the Great Wastelands, and the wicked beasts that lurked there were expanding their territories into the western realms of T'lar-Gol.

His warning was met with a round of hisses.

"And we will spare yours, if you drop your sword and armor, then walk away."

Opening his eyes, Ayan-Dar stared at what he took to be the leader of the thirteen brigands who now surrounded him. The female was younger than the others and badly scarred. But they were not the proud scars of battle that warriors had the healers carefully preserve as living trophies. They were simply the legacy of her butchery of unfortunate warriors and, no doubt, those not of the warrior caste, as well.

"Do you know what I am, daughter?" Ayan-Dar did not need to gesture at the rune on his breastplate, for it gleamed in the flickering fire light like a thing alive. While he did not fear them, he was surprised that they did not fear *him*. It was nearly unheard of for honorless ones to attack a warrior they knew to be of the priesthood.

"I know that you will be dead, old priest, if you do not do as I say." She stepped closer, a glittering sword in one hand.

Looking closer, his eyes widened with recognition. Every weapon was unique, hand-crafted by the armorers, and he knew this one quite well. It was the object of the final quest of a promising young acolyte, Ria-Ka'luhr, whom Ayan-Dar had sent into the mountains of the north several months before. It was the last thing he had to complete before he would have been selected to become a priest. And a fine priest he would have made, Ayan-Dar knew.

Ria-Ka'luhr had disappeared without a trace. And yet, here was the sword.

The girl, for she was little more, by age, looked down at the sword she held. "He died bravely. He killed four of us before he fell."

He suspected her words were a lie. Ria-Ka'luhr had been a skilled swordmaster, and would have killed more than four of these vermin before falling to their ill-treated blades.

"And how many of you will die at the hands of his master?" Ayan-Dar, the fire of bloodlust rising in his veins, stood, his left hand clenching tightly at his side.

"None."

Many cycles of training, even before he had become a priest, had given Ayan-Dar an exceptional sense of hearing. Behind him was a soft whine and click, that few other than a priest or priestess would have heard.

In a blur of motion, he whirled toward the brigand who stood behind him, holding a projectile weapon. It was ancient, a relic from before the last fall, a type of weapon that was regarded with contempt by the warrior caste. But it was quite effective at its intended function of killing.

Before the brigand could pull the weapon's trigger, the hilltop was bathed in a searing flash of cyan as a bolt of lightning shot from Ayan-Dar's outstretched hand, vaporizing the brigand with a deafening boom.

Continuing the turn of his body, he took the three *shrekkas* in turn, hurling them at the three opponents who were farthest away. The whistling blades took the heads from all three. The bodies, fountaining blood from their severed necks, collapsed to the ground and twitched.

Coming back around to face forward, Ayan-Dar's sword sang from its sheath. With blinding speed he lunged forward and first cut the hand from the girl that held his acolyte's sword, then he took off one of her feet.

Disarmed and immobilized, she fell to the ground, screaming.

Five of the remaining honorless ones charged him, while the other three ran away. Or tried to.

Flinging his sword into the air to momentarily free his hand, Ayan-Dar leaped in a somersault far over his attackers' heads, stretching out his arm toward the three who were attempting to flee. Bolts of lightning erupted from his palm, and the three *kurh-a'mekh* vanished in clouds of white ash.

He caught his sword in mid-air before landing in the midst of the five surviving brigands. In a single breath, their bleeding corpses lay at his feet, their armor hacked and pierced by his great sword.

Flicking the blood from his blade, he sheathed it before returning to the fire and the young female who lay writhing there. The burning in his blood cooled to melancholy sorrow as he watched her agonized struggles.

"It did not have to be this way, young one." He knelt beside her and put his hand on her forehead. He was not a healer, but with his powers he could ease pain. In a moment, her thrashing ceased, and her breathing slowed. She stared up at him as he removed his hand. "You could have walked away, and I would have shown you mercy."

"I could not. *She* would have known."

Ayan-Dar shook his head slowly. "I do not understand, child."

The girl's eyes had a haunted look. "I am bound to the Dark Queen." She held up her remaining hand, and Ayan-Dar saw a deep, ugly scar across the palm.

He narrowed his eyes in shock and anger. The Desh-Ka and the other orders had an ancient ritual. It was known as *drakash* in his own sect, and by different names among the others. It was the blood bond, when an acolyte was accepted into the priesthood. Blood was shared through cut and bound palms of master or mistress and acolyte in a very sacred ceremony. It was the ultimate act of acceptance. Part of its purpose was also to bridge the void between the seven major bloodlines, for none of the orders demanded that acolytes be from their particular bloodline, but any member of the priesthood must be able to sense those of their own order.

It was a way of accepting a new priest or priestess into the body of the priesthood, but there were also ways it could also be used to bind a servant to a master. Those ways were beneath the contempt of the ancient orders, but there had always been those rogues beyond the temples who would use it to their own ends. Once such a bond had been made, the Dark Queen could not see the greater bloodline, but would be able to sense the feelings of those who were bound to her in such a manner.

It was the ultimate act of control.

This young female who lay dying could not have let him go, even had she wanted to, for the Dark Queen would have known. From what he had heard, Syr-Nagath would not have turned a blind eye to such a transgression.

Far more troubling was that these brigands served her at all. The queen should have been hunting down such bands, not employing them for her own unfathomable purposes.

The dying girl answered his unspoken question. She raised her hand to his chest, brushing her talons over the gleaming rune of the Desh-Ka. "This is what she seeks."

Before Ayan-Dar could ask her any more questions, her eyes closed and her hand fell to her side. He felt her spirit pass from her body, and whispered a prayer of mercy, that she might find peace in the Afterlife.

For a long time afterward, he sat next to the child's lifeless body, staring into the glowing embers of the dying fire and wondering at the meaning of her words.

This is what she seeks...

CHAPTER THREE

Syr-Nagath, the Dark Queen, brooded in the great pavilion that served as her home while on campaign. The enormous white stretch of canvas of her palace sat on a hill overlooking the battlefield, and the city of Taliah-Ma'i beyond. She was covered in blood, for she always fought at the head of the growing horde of her army, to satisfy her own bloodlust as much as to inspire fear in those who served her. Crimson spatters and streaks covered her face and armor, and dripped from her talons to the floor. She breathed in the heady scent, the fire in her blood momentarily rekindling as her right hand strayed to the hilt of her sheathed sword.

The army defending Taliah-Ma'i had fought bravely, but had fallen in a day. After a brief but brutal fight, she had offered the right of Challenge to the master of the city, to allow him to die with honor and spare the destruction of his lands and people, who would then be honor-bound to serve her.

Luckily for them, he had accepted. But he had not died quickly. Few of the many who had been forced to face her in the arena did. It was his blood that stained the animal pelts at her feet. Every Challenge she fought was yet another example to instill fear in those bound to her. For fear was one of the few emotions that she truly understood.

She turned, taking in the panorama of her army. Over thirty thousand were encamped here, with another four hundred thousand arrayed to the north and south as her warriors swept across T'lar-Gol toward the great Eastern Sea.

And every city and village that was taken added their warriors, their resources, to her campaign. It was part of the Way, a code of life and honor that she so fervently wished to destroy.

But to do so would take more than armies of warriors. That was the simple part, and one that many leaders in the past had used to control a continent, or even the entire Homeworld, if only briefly. A very few had even reached toward the stars in the time since the Settlements had first been founded, seeking to unite their race under the Way.

Unification was not Syr-Nagath's dream. She did not want her race to rise to something greater, but wanted to utterly destroy it. She wanted to sever it completely from its past in an orgy of destruction, before rebuilding it according to her own design. The conquest of T'lar-Gol was only the first part of her plan. But before she could span the stars, before she could fulfill her desires, she would need more than mere warriors. She would need to control the powers of the ancient orders.

To do that, she would have to destroy them.

"My mistress."

Syr-Nagath turned to find her First kneeling at the entryway, sensing the excitement in her First's blood. The Dark Queen flicked a velvety tongue over her lips, tasting the blood of her last victim. "Bring him."

With a quick salute, the First stood and disappeared.

A few moments later, Syr-Nagath heard the clank of chains and watched as a prisoner was led in, escorted by six warriors and the First. Bound by the hands and feet, badly beaten, the captured male was forced to his knees before her, cursing with anger at his captors through swollen, bloodied lips.

"Leave us."

The guards and her First saluted before marching from the room.

Stepping forward, Syr-Nagath took hold of the prisoner's hair and forced his head back. One of his eyes was swollen shut, while the other was blood-red, staring up at her with undisguised hate.

Ignoring his baleful gaze, she looked at the Collar of Honor around his neck. There was no sigil, but she saw the outline of the Desh-Ka rune on his breastplate. An acolyte.

"What is your name?"

He only glared at her.

"There is no point in denying me that much, acolyte of the Desh-Ka." Kneeling before him, she reached out and drew the tip of one of her talons along his face, from his ear to the tip of his mouth.

He made no reaction beyond the glare with which he favored her as blood welled up from the wound.

She sat back, licking his blood from her talon. It had taken all this time, over ten full cycles, for her to capture one of them, an acolyte, alive. She could not confront the Desh-Ka directly, but she had bound an army of honorless ones to her. Setting them to cause the mayhem expected of their kind had merely been cover for their true purpose, which now knelt in chains before her.

The young acolyte spat on her, the blood from his mouth mixing with the stains on her armored breast.

She entwined the talons of one hand in his hair. As with all who followed the Way, it was carefully braided into seven braids, each representing a different covenant. The two most important were the first, the Covenant of the Afterlife, and the third, which was the Blood Bond. His third braid had been severed, the roots of it bound in a black ring. He had been cut off from the empathic link to his bloodline, and could not sense those who shared the blood of his forefathers. Nor could they sense him. To all who had known him, he had simply disappeared.

With a snarl, she took hold of his hair, her talons tearing into his scalp, and hauled him up by his braids. Her grip was far more powerful than seemed possible for her lithe frame.

As the acolyte opened his mouth in a gasp of pain, she brought her lips to his. He clamped his mouth firmly shut until she sank the talons of her free hand deep into his side.

His mouth flew open, screaming at the pain, and her tongue darted in to tease and violate him, retreating as he tried to bite it off.

He shoved himself against her, trying to throw her off balance with the mass of his body in an attack born of pure desperation.

With a snort of contempt, she deftly stepped aside, allowing his momentum to carry him into a thick wooden table. His face struck the smooth, polished surface, and he slid to the floor, dazed.

"A priest, you clearly are not." She stripped out of her armor, letting it fall to the floor beside her in a bloody heap before kneeling, nude, to straddle him. As he groaned, she began to unfasten his armor. "Not yet. But you shall be."

"No!" He struggled against her as she stripped him of his armor, then his clothing, just as she had already stripped him of his dignity.

She kept him pinned, her knees on his shoulders, as she undid the third braid of her own hair. While she despised the Way and all it represented, the hair of the Kreela was more than a mere adornment or vestige of evolution. The bonds were real, even among the honorless ones. With her talons, she severed a lock of hair from the braid, close to her scalp, grimacing at the unpleasant sensation that ran through her core.

What she was attempting was something that none had dared do since early in the Second Age. It was dark knowledge that had been buried deep in some of the most ancient Books of Time, kept in the mountain fortress of Ka'i-Nur in the heart of the great wastelands to the west. It was guarded by the seventh of the ancient orders. Unlike the other six, it had fallen from grace long ages ago. Few, even among the other orders, even remembered it. Only a handful of the curious or unlucky were foolhardy enough to try and cross the wastelands to find it. Fewer still ever returned.

Syr-Nagath had been born there. While she had been raised as a warrior, she had spent many an hour poring over the ancient tomes and pulling secrets from the tongues of the keepers. Vast riches of powerful knowledge were to be found. Much of it was dark, forbidden to the world beyond Ka'i-Nur's walls. In past times, many had sought to destroy those Books of Time, which is why the surviving texts and keepers had been cloistered away in the ancient fortress.

Her mother had been the high priestess, although the title rang hollow. Unlike the other six orders, the Crystal of Souls that had once belonged to Ka'i-Nur had disappeared. None knew the fate that had befallen it. Without it, none who followed the order's ancient ways could ever inherit the crystal's special powers, as did the priesthoods of the other orders.

Syr-Nagath had been born of a Ka'i-Nur mother, but her father had been an Outsider, a pilgrim from the far southern lands of Ural-Murir on a quest for knowledge. He had met the fate of all but a few unfortunate enough to reach Ka'i-Nur: he had never been allowed to leave. The high priestess, on a whim, had taken him as a lover, and Syr-Nagath had been the product of the forced union. He had died in an attempt to escape soon thereafter.

When Syr-Nagath had been born, she had created something of a stir, for in appearance she was like the outsiders. This had given her mother the opportunity to attempt something that she and her forebears for generations had sought, the destruction of the outsiders.

Born of Ka'i-Nur, trained in combat and steeped in their ancient form of the Way, Syr-Nagath was sent out into the world of outsiders to wreak havoc.

And so she had.

With dawning horror, the acolyte began to snap his torso back and forth, desperately trying to throw her off.

She bared her fangs, an expression of humor, at his pathetic attempts to escape.

Using his own twisting motion against him, she easily flipped him over on his stomach before slamming a fist against the back of his head, stunning him. Then she removed the ring binding the stump of his third braid and carefully began weaving in her own hair.

When she was done, she drew a talon across her right palm, dripping the blood across the hair she had just weaved into his. Then she wrapped her hand around the splice, gripping it tight as the acolyte moaned beneath her. The binding grew warm, hot under her palm, just as her own body warmed, aroused by the young warrior pinned beneath her. Her breathing quickened as she anticipated the next part of the ritual, which demanded a more energetic consummation of their union.

The heat under her palm peaked, then began to cool. Removing her hand, she saw that her hair had been fused to his. She brushed away the blood, which was now dried. It flaked away. The hair she had spliced in had multiplied, and it continued to do so, growing longer, as well, before her eyes.

In but a few moments, his hair appeared normal under even the closest inspection.

And now she could sense him, as clearly as if she were looking in a mirror of her own feelings. She sat up, straddling his back, and shivered at the sensations of pain and despair that welled up from his heart. She could not sense the others of the Desh-Ka bloodline, for that had not been her intention. In fact, she did not desire such a union. Not yet. This ritual bound him to her alone, made him a slave to her will.

But the true test was not in what she could sense from him. Releasing him from his bindings, she rolled him over on his back before she straddled his waist, her heart beating quickly with anticipation.

His good eye flickered open, and he looked up at her, an expression of unutterable misery on his face.

"Tell me your name," she asked again.

"Ria-Ka'luhr." He closed his eye in shame.

"Love me," she commanded, knowing that it was the most loathsome thing she could demand of him.

He tried to resist, but could not.

Reaching up with trembling hands, he took hold of her shoulders and pulled her down to lay on top of him, his lips parting to kiss her.

Syr-Nagath sighed with pleasure as their bodies became one, knowing that she now had the key that would help her destroy the Desh-Ka and upset the balance of power forever.

* * *

"You are bound to me now."

Syr-Nagath's whispered words burned Ria-Ka'luhr's soul like acid, and he flinched as he felt her graceful talons drag gently down the skin of his chest in the aftermath of their union, the final consummation of the ritual she had performed. He could feel the hair of his third braid like a parasite on his skull, its teeth biting into his flesh, into his soul. His will was no longer his own.

He cursed the misfortune that had landed him here. He had been on his way from the lands of the far north, of eternal snow and ice, after fulfilling the last quest Ayan-Dar had set before him. He had been tasked with reaching a temple to the ancient gods that stood upon the tallest mountain at the top of the world. It was the greatest physical and mental challenge Ria-Ka'luhr had ever faced, and Ayan-Dar had warned him that few of the acolytes sent upon this particular challenge survived.

Undeterred, Ria-Ka'luhr set out on his mission, traveling north from the Desh-Ka temple. It took him over four months to reach the mountain on which the temple stood. There, he was forced to turn his *magtheps* free and continue alone, on foot.

After braving the frigid winds and climbing the seven thousand steps to the top of the great mountain, Ria-Ka'luhr finally reached the temple. Every moment of the four days it took him to climb to the top, the wind howled, spearing him with tiny daggers of ice as the cold sapped the life from this body. The air was so thin that he wheezed and gasped for every breath as he dug his feet and the talons of his hands into the frozen snow, forcing himself onward.

Freezing and near death, he reached the summit. There stood the temple, shrouded in blowing snow. Staggering to the white-crusted doorway, he had to use the handle of his sword to hammer the ice from the hinges and latch of the door. Just as he was about to give up, he was finally able to pry it open and crawl inside. With the last of his strength, he managed to close the door behind him, locking out the shrieking wind.

His skin blackened and frozen, he lay on the frost-rimed stone floor, shivering uncontrollably. The temple was little more than a circular room topped by a domed crystal ceiling that let in the milky light of the fading day. Ancient runes that he could not decipher were carved into the stone of the walls in orderly rows. Between them were faded frescoes depicting what he thought must be the gods of old.

But those were all things he noted subconsciously as he stared at what was in the center of the room. On a raised stone dais lay a sword that was the object of his quest.

"In the temple," Ayan-Dar had told him, "you shall find a sword. Take it, and leave your own in its stead. Do this, and you will survive."

With a groan, Ria-Ka'luhr had pulled himself along the floor, digging his scratched and frayed talons into the stone for purchase. The temple was small, perhaps four or five warriors heel to toe, but crossing the distance to reach the dais seemed as difficult as the climb up the mountain.

His sword was already in his hand from hammering the ice from the door. But it took some effort to free it, as it had frozen to his gauntlet.

Levering himself up on one elbow, he shoved his sword upon the dais before taking the other one.

Then he collapsed.

When he awoke, the temple was no longer freezing. It was warmed by glowing coals in a hearth that ran all the way around the base of the wall.

On the dais, the sword was gone, replaced by fresh meat, water, and a large flask of ale.

Peeling off his gauntlets, he looked at his hands. The flesh was no longer blackened by frostbite. Running his fingers over his face, his skin felt normal. On further reflection, after taking inventory of his body, he realized that his injuries had been healed.

At his side was the sword he had taken from the dais, the true object of his quest. There was nothing sacred about it, save that it had been left here by Ayan-Dar as a token of success, and as a reward. It was a fine sword, one crafted by the master armorer of the temple, a prize worthy of the hardships endured to take it.

He meditated on these things as he ate and drank, wondering how long he had been in the temple before he had awakened.

After one more night's sleep, he began the perilous descent. While it was terribly difficult, he knew that he was stronger now, that he would make it home.

He had just emerged from the mountains, leaving behind the bitter cold, when he came upon a group of unfortunates, victims of a raid by honorless ones. He stopped to render what aid he could, not realizing until it was too late that he had been deceived.

The young female warrior he had knelt down to tend to reached out to hold his hand and thank him. One of her talons grazed his skin, and he instantly felt a numbness that quickly began to spread.

She had smeared some venom from a small predator on her talon. In sufficient quantity, the venom quickly killed. Used in just the right amount, it would merely paralyze.

Ria-Ka'luhr realized that he had been baited into a trap. He fought as long as he could, and killed over ten of them before the venom overcame him.

Still conscious, he could only scream in his mind as they stripped him of his armor and took the sword, the precious sword. They bound him in chains, hand and foot, and forced a device into his throat that would prevent him from swallowing his tongue.

They cut the third braid from his hair, severing his emotional tie to his bloodline. It was a cruel, horrible act that left a sudden stillness in his soul. The emotional song of the others of his bloodline had been with him since birth, and to have it suddenly cut off was like being rendered deaf.

That was when he realized why they had done it. With the link severed, he would have simply disappeared, his own emotional song would have stopped in the perceptions of others. Ayan-Dar and the others of the priesthood would likely think him dead.

They tossed him into a wagon and covered him with a fetid tarp. And that is how they delivered him to the queen's First.

With a groan, Ria-Ka'luhr pushed the shame of his capture from his mind.

Beside him, Syr-Nagath propped herself up on one elbow, tracing circles on his chest with her index finger, the talon scoring the skin deep enough to draw a thin thread of crimson.

"Your cares will soon fall away, acolyte of the Desh-Ka." She smiled, fresh blood staining her teeth from having bitten him in her passion. Her face was still covered in the blood of the opponent she killed earlier that day. "Soon you shall know my will. You will live for that, and nothing else. And what others shall sense of your heart, your emotions, shall be what I will." She leaned toward him, and her lips brushed his ears as she whispered, "I shall sing the song of your blood, and your soul will be linked to the Afterlife only through me."

He raised a hand to her, willing it to claw out her eyes, but he could not. His body was no longer his to command.

She reached out and closed his fingers with her own and pressed his hand back to his chest.

He stared up at her, his heart pounding. What she had done to him was so alien, so unspeakable, that he could not comprehend it. Syr-Nagath was nearly the same age as he, but she seemed so much older, an evil relic from some long-ago age. And should the Desh-Ka or any of the other orders learn of what she had done, they would descend upon her like a raging pack of *genoths*, great dragons that would destroy her, body and soul. The ancient orders had isolated themselves from the affairs of the race beyond the temples and the training grounds of the *kazhas*, but for an abomination against the Way such as this, they would act.

If only they could be warned.

* * *

Finished with Ria-Ka'luhr, Syr-Nagath got to her feet and poured herself a mug of ale. The dark blue skin of her body glowed in the fading light of the sun that shone through the opening of the pavilion that overlooked her newest city.

Her First appeared in the entryway to the chamber, kneeling and rendering a salute.

"Take him to the healers, then the armorers." Syr-Nagath gestured at Ria-Ka'luhr. "Once he is cleaned up, provide him with a mount and sufficient pack animals to reach the Desh-Ka temple. Then release him."

The First glanced up, surprised, before she remembered her place and returned her eyes to the floor. "Yes, my mistress." She turned to beckon the guards.

"They will not be necessary." She looked at Ria-Ka'luhr. "Will they?"

"No...my mistress." He rose unsteadily to his feet. Turning to her, he lowered his head and saluted, his body moving in jerky motions as if controlled by an invisible puppet master.

Nodding in approval, Syr-Nagath turned away as the acolyte followed the First from the room.

The Dark Queen thought of the life that she sensed growing in her womb, and reflexively brought a hand to her belly. Having a child had also been part of her plan, but she had been forced to wait, for not just any male would do. How surprised Kunan-Lohr would be, she thought, showing her fangs in a wicked smile, to know that he had sired the child that would lead their civilization to its undoing?

The fire that lit the sky as the sun fell toward the horizon blended into the Dark Queen's vision as she imagined her world, the Settlements, her entire ancient race roiling in flame, to be remade by her own hands.

* * *

Ria-Ka'luhr rode the *magthep* along the ancient road that led west. Behind him, the three pack animals plodded along, occasionally bleating in complaint at their lot in life.

A part of his mind that seemed to think on its own, as if his head was now occupied by two brains, was focused on how to explain his extended absence.

Perhaps, he thought, the best lie would be one founded on the truth. He would tell Ayan-Dar that he had been captured by honorless ones and taken to the east, for what purpose he could not discern, and that he had escaped. It was a rare thing, but had been recorded in the Books of Time. Ayan-Dar would no doubt welcome him with open arms and praise him for escaping an unworthy fate. The newly cleaned armor and his fresh mounts could be easily explained away, for even the smallest village of T'lar-Gol would provide whatever was needed to an acolyte of the Desh-Ka.

He clenched his hands so tightly that his talons pierced his palms, drawing blood. While his body had been healed and cleansed, and his armor and clothing made new, he felt unutterably soiled and wretched. He was worse than a traitor to his honor. He was a parasite the Dark Queen was injecting into the temple, the carrier of her plague of hatred. His only hope was that the priesthood would be able to recognize him for what he was and kill him quickly, before he could carry out her will.

Before he could become a priest.

He leaned over, spewing vomit to the ground as he thought of the evil that Syr-Nagath could do through him. His becoming a priest was only a question of when, not if. He knew that Ayan-Dar would almost certainly consider his final quest successful, even if based only on Ria-Ka'luhr's word. Beyond that, only the formalities had to be observed. As the temple's senior acolyte, he would soon face the cyan fire of the ancient crystal that was the heart of their order. If he survived that final trial, he would be a member of the priesthood.

Then, all would be lost. And he was utterly powerless to save himself or those he held most dear.

He brought his *magthep* to a halt and turned around to look back the way he had come. Night had fallen and the stars now reigned supreme in the sky, the great moon not yet having risen. He could see the flickering torches of the pavilion and the glow of fires in the valley beyond from the Dark Queen's army, a pox rapidly spreading across the lands of T'lar-Gol. He imagined the world opening up, a great maw that would swallow whole the Dark Queen and her dreadful ambitions.

For the thousandth time since he had lain with her, he brought his claws to his throat, desperately seeking Death's embrace and release from whatever the evil harlot might have in store for him and his temple.

And for the thousandth time, he could not. He could sense her will like a serpent coiled in his mind, an undeniable force that was devouring him. He could not even speak of the horror he carried within him, even to himself. He could give no warning of what he had become. It was as if his soul had been torn in two, with his true self locked into a rapidly shrinking cage, while the other part, the Dark Queen's puppet, roamed free and grew ever stronger.

He threw his head back and screamed, a soul-wrenching cry of anguish that tore the stillness of the night.

* * *

Ayan-Dar's eyes snapped open. He had been in a state of deep meditation, his mind's eye cast far away, when a tremor of such pain and dread echoed through his blood that it broke even his tremendous concentration.

It had been three weeks since he had encountered the group of honorless ones and had heard the young warrior's troubling words about the Dark Queen. The thought worried him, but it did not occupy his full attention.

That was reserved for his search for the child. Each night had brought him closer to her, and he knew that he was close now, very close. He would have found the child long before, were it not for the epic tides of pain and fear, of agony and ecstasy roiling the waters of the bloodline from the Dark Queen's campaign to the east.

Each night he swept the world around him, looking for the child. Each day he rode in the direction from which the tiny voice was strongest, when he could hear it during the ebbs in the great tide of emotions from the queen's war.

What he heard now, this piercing wail, was something else, something that set every one of his senses afire. It was a bone-chilling keening that erupted above the momentarily quiet war, voicing a depth of despair the likes of which Ayan-Dar had never known. He sought to grasp it, to seek out the poor soul to which it belonged, but it faded too quickly.

Then it was gone.

Deeply troubled, Ayan-Dar rose to his feet, his eyes peering through the darkness around him as his spirit looked far beyond.

As if in sympathy with the terrible cry he had felt in his soul, the song of the child he sought rose, so clear and pure that he instinctively turned to the southeast.

Toward the city of Keel-A'ar.

CHAPTER FOUR

"We can tarry no longer." Kunan-Lohr stood on the balcony of the chamber in the citadel that served as the sleeping quarters for himself and Ulana-Tath, watching the sun rise over the great forests and plains to the east.

The Dark Queen had granted him a cycle of the great moon to greet his newborn child and attend to any affairs of the city, but then he and his consort were to return to the war that continued to rage ever closer to the Eastern Sea.

He felt the roar of those of his bloodline who fought the raging battles that would soon leave Syr-Nagath the undisputed ruler of T'lar-Gol. The thought had left a deep sickness in his heart.

He felt Ulana-Tath's nude body press up against his back, her arms wrapping around his waist. Her recovery from birth had been rapid, as was the nature of their kind. Since then, they had spent every possible moment together, much of it in bed. "Why does despair fill your heart, my love?"

He covered her hands with his own, grateful for the warmth of her body against the chill morning air. It took him a moment to speak, for the words were little short of heresy. "I feel as if we have bound ourselves to one of the evil gods of old. We live for war, for that has been the Way since the First Age. But this..." He shook his head slowly. "This is something different."

"How is it different from any other great war from the Books of Time?" Ulana-Tath rested her chin on his shoulder as she, too, watched the sun rise. "Syr-Nagath will unite T'lar-

Gol for the first time in a thousand cycles, and will no doubt force a crossing of the Eastern Sea." She paused. "Are you sure that what troubles your heart is not envy, great master of Keel-A'ar?"

With a snort, Kunan-Lohr shook his head. "I envied the old king, for he was a great warrior who followed the Way, whose path was dictated solely by honor. Syr-Nagath follows her own path, a twisted road with its mysterious roots in the Great Wastelands from whence she came. And no one can sense her spirit, to know what she feels."

"There are many we cannot sense. Even some few of our own city, and beside whom we have fought."

"You do not understand me, my love: *no one* can sense her feelings." He turned around to face her. "I spoke, in private, to many of the other senior warriors of her army about this. Between them flow all of the bloodlines. None could feel her song in their blood. None."

Ulana-Tath made to speak, to protest. For to do such a thing, to question the one to whom their honor was now bound, could easily lead Kunan-Lohr to be bound to the *Kal'ai-Il* for punishment.

He put a finger to her lips. "I know, my love. I did not do this lightly. In truth, most of those to whom I spoke approached me for counsel in the matter. Her soul is shrouded in shadow like no other, and I believe there is dark knowledge at work here. But what it is, and what we may do about it, I do not know."

"We can only do what the Way demands of us." She held his gaze firmly. "The path of honor is ours, and it is a path we will follow to the end of our days." A gentle smile suddenly graced her lips. "We may do no less for our daughter."

"Indeed." The mention of their daughter, Keel-Tath, banished his dark thoughts. She was a full moon cycle of age now, and had been peered at or held by nearly everyone in the city, or so it seemed. He knew that, as a father who thought he could never have a child, he was grievously biased, but the child was beautiful by any measure. She stood out like a beacon among the other children of the creche with her lush white hair and red talons. Keel-Tath was boisterous at play and a vision of peace when asleep. The healers kept close watch on her, but so far she was nothing more or less than an extraordinarily healthy female child, the visible and unexplainable genetic anomalies notwithstanding.

The wardresses had already determined that she would be a warrior. Just as the healers knew the intimacies of the body, the wardresses keenly understood all the traits in young children that determined caste. Caste was determined purely on ability and affinity, not on the caste or status of the parents. A mated pair of warriors could produce a healer or porter of water, just as builders could give birth to warriors. It was a complex dance of genetics that the wardresses instinctively understood, just as the skygazers understood the movements of the stars and planets across the heavens, and the healers understood their symbionts.

The proud parents had looked in on their daughter at every possible opportunity, making the most of the time that Kunan-Lohr's pact with the Dark Queen had given them. Time that had been all too fleeting.

That thought brought a heavy sigh to his lips. He again looked out beyond the walls of the city, contemplating the unpalatable task of preparing for the long return journey to the East.

His silver-flecked eyes were drawn to three dark shapes, *magtheps* trotting along the eastern road, approaching the main gate.

He gasped in surprise when a banner suddenly rose from the barbican. It was black with a single cyan rune in the center, the sigil of the Desh-Ka.

"What would one of the priesthood be doing here?" Ulana-Tath wondered. The priests and priestesses were rarely seen outside the *kazhas*, and few ordinary followers of the Way ever had reason to visit the temple.

Yet every city worthy of the name had pennants such as this one to herald the arrival of any member of the priesthood of the seven orders, even though one of them, the Ka'i-Nur, had never been used in living memory here in Keel-A'ar. Acolytes, which were seen somewhat more often, were not accorded the same honor, although they were always greeted with the greatest respect.

Frowning, Kunan-Lohr could only recall two such visits by the priesthood to Keel-A'ar in his lifetime, and that was when he had been very young.

"I cannot imagine," was all he could think of to say. He returned to their bed of hides and knelt, quickly donning his armor. Ulana-Tath did the same.

Regardless of the purpose of the visit, the priest or priestess would want to meet with the master and mistress of the city.

* * *

After being hailed by the captain of the guard and granted entrance to the city, Ayan-Dar was greeted by a mob of well-wishers. His mounts were whisked away to be fed, watered, and groomed. Armorers quickly polished his armor to a gleaming luster and through some means he could not fathom caused the dust to fall away from his cloak. Others pressed a mug of ale into his hand, which he drank greedily, parched from the long last leg of his ride. As he finished, it was whisked away, to be replaced by a platter of food that he happily sampled, savoring the excellent cuts of meat.

When he was sated, the group around him knelt and rendered the ritual salute, *tla'a-kane.*

Anin-Khan, the captain of the guard, then stood. "This way, priest of the Desh-Ka." He led Ayan-Dar to a small but exquisitely kept garden that stood off to one side of the entry courtyard. "My master, Kunan-Lohr, will be here momentarily."

Ayan-Dar bowed his head as Anin-Khan saluted, then left him in peace.

Standing there amid the blooming flowers, breathing in their heady scent, Ayan-Dar could hear the child's spiritual voice now as clear as if he were holding her and she was singing to him. He had been on many a fool's errand in the past, and would not be surprised if this turned out to be another. But he knew he would never regret having made the trip to see any child who had such a voice in her heart.

He sensed a pair of warriors approaching, and turned to face them as they entered the garden. They knelt and rendered a salute

"Greetings, priest of the Desh-Ka," the male warrior said. "I am Kunan-Lohr, master of Keel-A'ar."

"And I am Ulana-Tath, his First and consort."

Ayan-Dar returned the salute, and the two warriors rose to their feet. "My thanks for your hospitality, my lord. Your welcome was most gracious."

Kunan-Lohr glanced at the first row of pendants that hung from Ayan-Dar's collar, proclaiming his name. "We are humbled and honored by your visit, Ayan-Dar. May I ask what brings you here, great priest, and how we may serve you?"

"I seek a child."

Kunan-Lohr and Ulana-Tath blinked at his words, unsure how to interpret them.

Ayan-Dar bared his fangs in a smile. "Fear not, master of Keel-A'ar. I do not come to rob your creche, but to pay homage to one who inhabits it. You see, a female child was born here a single moon cycle ago under the shadow of the Great Eclipse, a child whose voice echoed in my blood like no other. It is that child I seek, simply to pay my respects and rejoice in the purity of her spirit. It is a personal quest, a simple whim of an old fool. Nothing more."

For a moment, neither warrior spoke, but looked at him with expressions that betrayed surprise and bewilderment. Ayan-Dar could sense a tremor of excitement in their souls. And of fear.

"Our daughter was born just as the great moon darkened the sun." Kunan-Lohr told him, a tinge of uncertainty in his voice.

"And she is…different." Ulana-Tath added.

"I would see her, if you and the wardress would permit."

"Of course, Ayan-Dar." Kunan-Lohr bowed his head. "Please, forgive us. It is just that our child, Keel-Tath, is special to us in a way that few would truly understand. Come, we will take you to her."

Kunan-Lohr and Ulana-Tath walked on either side of Ayan-Dar through the city, with a small group of retainers following behind. Keel-A'ar's inhabitants lined the streets, kneeling, their left hands over their right breasts in salute. All had seen a Desh-Ka priest or priestess at the *kazha* that stood not far away, but very few had ever seen one within the city walls.

Ayan-Dar suspected that a Desh-Ka priest walking the streets of Keel-A'ar was as much an event for these kind folk as the Great Eclipse had been.

Beside him, Ulana-Tath's fear had broken and fallen away. A smile now graced her beautiful face.

"Does my presence entertain you?" Ayan-Dar asked with good humor.

"It does, my priest." Ulana-Tath had no qualms in answering so, sensing the playful nature in the priest's heart even as Kunan-Lohr shot her a look of disbelief. She ignored him. "You also greatly honor all who dwell here. Many cycles have passed since any of the pennants have been raised, least of all that of the Desh-Ka."

"Then my trip has been worthwhile." Looking around, he nodded in approval. "Your city is beautiful. I was the master of the *kazha* some cycles ago, likely before either of you were born, but never set foot inside the city walls." He snorted. "Such a pity."

"The city would be more beautiful still if the builders were able to focus more on what lay inside the walls, rather than on simply maintaining the defensive works." Kunan-Lohr had long had visions of making Keel-A'ar the jewel of all T'lar-Gol. But it would never be anything more than a dream.

They walked in silence for a moment before Ayan-Dar asked, "And what of the war, my friends? I have heard little news of the world beyond the temple's boundaries. I can sense the fighting to the east, but it is little more than an endless song of struggle and death."

"Syr-Nagath will soon control all of T'lar-Gol," Ulana-Tath told him without preamble.

"You do not sound happy that your sovereign has met with such great success." The priest's remark carried more than a hint of irony.

"We are bound to Syr-Nagath by honor, Ayan-Dar, but I fear that darkness clouds our future." Kunan-Lohr spoke quietly as they strode down the lane.

"So has it always been, master of Keel-A'ar." The priest turned to him. "Every great war precedes the next collapse. It is only a question of how high Syr-Nagath can climb before the foundation crumbles beneath her feet. The darkness you see beyond the horizon in your mind is what all great warriors see before the coming fall." He offered a grim smile, gesturing at his eye with his good hand. "We may only hope that the fall will be confined to the Homeworld, and that the Settlements do not again come calling. I enjoy the thrill of battle, the fire in my blood, but carnage on such a scale..." He shook his head.

"I fear worse than that."

Before Kunan-Lohr could say more, Ulana-Tath announced, "We are here."

They stood before the entrance to a large circular building of shimmering stone, with many crystal windows to let in the light of the sun and sky.

Three wardresses stood waiting, and after saluting, gestured for them to enter.

The creche was a study in organized pandemonium, or so it seemed at first glance. The older children, up to six or seven cycles of age, were divided up into groups that played a variety of games that challenged their bodies and minds. They were a boisterous lot this morning, filling their part of the creche with recitations of the *Se'eln*, the orthodoxy of the Way that governed etiquette and behavior. At a whispered command from the wardress leading their lessons, they instantly fell silent and, as one, knelt and rendered a salute to the visiting dignitaries.

Kunan-Lohr and Ulana-Tath returned the salute. Ayan-Dar stepped forward, looking more closely at the children, who were clothed in the gauzy black fabric that all who walked the Way wore under their robes or armor.

"May thy Way be long and glorious, my children." Then he returned their salute and bowed his head. He could not help but smile as he sensed their pride soar at his words.

The wardresses led them through the chamber where the toddlers played, attended by a small army of wardresses. The wardresses knelt and saluted, and the three dignitaries returned the honor as the children stilled, watching the great warriors pass through their chamber.

"Even now do they sense us in their blood," Ayan-Dar marveled. In all his travels, he had never visited a creche, even the one at the temple, for he had never found a need to. *Old fool,* he chided himself. *What else have you missed in your misspent life?*

"In here." The senior wardress passed through the portal leading to the chamber that belonged to the infants.

Ayan-Dar stopped dead in his tracks as he caught sight of the child, who was being held by her wet nurse. Keel-Tath was bound gently in a warm blanket, her white hair and crimson talons clearly visible.

"My priest?" Ulana-Tath asked him. She was clearly disturbed by his open-mouthed stare and sense of utter shock.

He said nothing. After a moment, he stepped forward to look closely at the child, who stared up at him, reaching with her tiny fingers.

"Who knows?" Ayan-Dar turned to Kunan-Lohr. "Who knows that she is born of white hair and crimson talons?"

With a gesture around him with both hands, Kunan-Lohr told him, "All of the city, of course."

"Nearly everyone has come to see her." Ulana-Tath moved closer to her daughter, her hand instinctively wrapping around the grip of her sword.

"And you have hosted travelers from afar who have seen her?"

"Of course," Ulana-Tath told him. "Some had come just to see her, others were passing through to or from the campaign in the east, or were engaged in trade. What of it?"

"Ayan-Dar, what is it?"

The old priest could sense Kunan-Lohr's heart thudding in his chest. Following the instinct of his consort, he, too, now gripped his sword, no doubt fearing that Ayan-Dar had, despite his earlier words, come to do their daughter harm.

"You need not fear me, my lord. But I would ask this of you: post a guard, your most trusted warriors, to protect her.

From this moment onward, let no one see her unless you would trust them with your daughter's life. *No one.*"

"But why?" Ulana-Tath stepped closer, fixing his good eye with her frightened gaze.

"Because, mistress of Keel-A'ar, she is, as you told me, different." Ayan-Dar turned back to look again at the child. "And in a civilization that has existed in equilibrium for hundreds of thousands of cycles, things that are different tend to not long survive." He put his hand on Kunan-Lohr's shoulder. "Swear to me that you will do as I ask."

"We can do nothing else, my priest." Kunan-Lohr answered, bowing his head. "We are bound by honor to answer to those of the ancient orders as we would any mistress or master."

"Do it not for honor and the Way, but for the life of your daughter."

"Would someone threaten her, a child? Here?" Ulana-Tath shook her head in disbelief. "Even the honorless ones do not harm children."

"I do not know, my child. But I also do not wish to take any chances." Ayan-Dar frowned. "There are too many coincidences here. I have many questions, but only one place to turn for answers, I fear."

"What do you mean?"

Ayan-Dar ignored Ulana-Tath's question. Instead, he whirled on his heel, his cloak fluttering in his wake. "I must leave at once." Calling over his shoulder, he told them, "Do as I bade you. I shall return as soon as I can."

In mid-stride, he vanished, leaving nothing but a brief, chill wind behind him.

Keel-Tath clapped her hands together, as if amused by the spectacle. The wet nurse held her closely, eyes wide with fear.

A brace of warriors led by Anin-Khan charged into the chamber, swords drawn.

"My lord!" He looked around a moment, confused. He had sensed the alarm of his master and mistress and had come at once. Now, he found that the priest was gone, and there was no threat that he could see.

"Your sense of timing is without fault, as always." Kunan-Lohr had known Anin-Khan since childhood, and they had both become warriors in the *kazha* of the Desh-Ka that lay in the forest not many leagues distant. "The priest of the Desh-Ka...suggested that we put a guard on our daughter, Keel-Tath. She could be in danger."

Anin-Khan's face twisted into disbelief before settling into an expression of outrage. "Not while I live and breathe, my lord."

"Then I will ask you to see to it, captain of the guard. Choose only your most trusted and capable warriors, those you can spare from their duty defending the city."

"It shall be done." Anin-Khan saluted, then turned to the six warriors who had accompanied him, quietly laying out his orders to form a guard on the master's daughter.

"Come, my love." With a caress of Keel-Tath's cheek, Kunan-Lohr led Ulana-Tath from the creche.

As they made their way silently along the streets to the citadel, he worried over not only the priest's words of warning, but the timing of the strange affair. He and Ulana-Tath had no choice but to return to the East, where war awaited them, leaving their daughter behind.

He felt Ulana-Tath's hand on his arm as fear took root deep inside him.

CHAPTER FIVE

T'ier-Kunai stared out the crystal window that overlooked the arenas that were at the center of the Desh-Ka temple. It was a physical arrangement that mirrored the importance of the arenas in their lives, which was itself a reflection of what her race held dear. The thrill of battle, the carnage of war.

As high priestess, her quarters had the benefit of such a view, although by any other measure they were the same as those of the other members of the priesthood here. The stone walls glowed, casting light into the chamber where she spent the few hours each day that she was not out and about in the temple. Here is where she slept on the thick bed of animal hides on the floor, or sat at the ancient wooden desk, preparing correspondence with ink and parchment. Aside from that and a few savored trophies from long-ago battles, the room was bare.

Those who chose the life of the priesthood and could survive its many trials were not tempted by or interested in material things. Their lives were dedicated to purifying the spirit as they perfected the art of war.

"The Ka'i-Nur do not welcome visitors, least of all from among the other orders." She turned to face Ayan-Dar, who had materialized, unbidden, in her quarters, to announce his latest self-appointed mission. Anyone else would have taken it for what his appearance had been, a serious breach of etiquette, but T'ier-Kunai had only sighed in resignation. She made allowance for the old priest's eccentricities, but she hoped that he understood that not everyone would be so tolerant. And she would not be high priestess forever, in a position to indulge him so. She frowned. "What could possibly tempt you into going there, Ayan-Dar?"

He bared his fangs in a toothy grin. "Another of my fool's errands, priestess." At her stern look, his smile faded quickly. "T'ier-Kunai, I have come simply to inform you that I am going, that in case I should not return, you will know what has become of me. I do not seek your leave or approval, not because I do not wish it, but because if something does go wrong, you will stand above reproach in the eyes of the peers."

"I will not be shackled to the *Kal'ai-Il* if you start a war, you mean."

Ayan-Dar made a dismissive gesture with his hand. "The Ka'i-Nur are bound to their fortress and have not strayed from it for many thousands of cycles. You have told me this yourself, high priestess. No. The worst they may do is kill me. They will not come seeking battle with the host of the Desh-Ka."

At that, T'ier-Kunai stepped closer, placing a hand on his breastplate over the cyan rune of their order, her eyes filled with concern for her old mentor. "Have you ever been there, Ayan-Dar? Have you ever seen them?"

Slowly, he shook his head. "I know only what you have told me, and what I have learned from the other keepers of the Books of Time since my return from Keel-A'ar." He paused, and she could sense a deep foreboding within him. "More important is what I have not learned, and that is why I feel compelled to visit Ka'i-Nur. If there are answers to my questions, they will be found there."

"After the Crystal of Souls bound to their order disappeared, they lost the powers such as we possess." She leaned closer. "But they are not to be underestimated. And dying is not the worst fate that could await you there. There is dark knowledge in that place from the early ages that is best left undisturbed."

"That is exactly why I must go."

"And you will not tell me of what you seek?"

"I dare not, T'ier-Kunai." His voice was a whisper now, his body tense, as if he was reflexively preparing for an enemy to attack. "All I can tell you is that this may be what I have been looking for."

"A means to unbalance the Way, to destroy the equilibrium that has maintained our civilization for the last three hundred thousand cycles?" Her incredulity was mixed with disgust at the thought. "You would cast aside all that we are and plunge us into an abyss from which there would be no return. You are mad, old friend."

"I know we have spoken of this many times before," he replied, and she could easily sense his frustration. "I know that you and the others consider my thoughts as heresy, and that you only indulge them because of my past glories, that you tolerate my quests because you believe they are in vain. I also know that I am not the first such heretic." He shrugged. "Many have come before me over the ages, and many of their names are inscribed in the stone walls of each *Kal'ai-Il* that stands brooding in every city and *kazha* across the Homeworld and the Settlements. And like those unfortunate seekers, I have a vision of something greater for our kind than simply maintaining an endless balance that leads us precisely nowhere."

He watched the acolytes and their mentors in the arenas as they sparred. Then he said, "Many, especially those of the ancient orders such as ours, would resist such change. Their positions have been assured throughout history as protectors of the Homeworld against the Settlements, with the orders that live among the stars doing the same, in their turn. The orders also preserve the Way, the priests and priestesses teaching all the young in the *kazhas*. And no single order is sufficiently powerful that it could ever overcome the others, or so we have always assumed." He turned back to her. "No high priest or priestess has ever tested the theory since the murky times during the terrible upheavals early in the First Age. Every night that I look up and see the stars, T'ier-Kunai, I see an infinite domain that would be ours for the taking if we would just reach out and take it in our hands. We could be masters of the cosmos."

"We already are," she told him crossly. "We attained the stars long ago and founded the Settlements." She gestured at the stump of his arm. "Or have you forgotten?"

"I do not speak of a handful of worlds that constantly war with one another! Think of the riches, by any measure, that are to be found beyond the narrow realm to which we have confined ourselves. The challenges to face and conquer, perhaps even races not our own against whom we could prove our mettle in war."

"And this, every great leader who has arisen has sought." T'ier-Kunai gestured toward the east. "Even now, Syr-Nagath follows the same path that you describe…"

"No! She follows the same path as have all who have come before her, a path that will eventually lead to the next fall. What I speak of would take us beyond collapse." He gently placed his hand on her arm. "Imagine no more falls. Imagine if we rose as high as our spirit and will could take us, limited by nothing but the number of the stars."

She could only offer him an indulgent smile. "It is a great dream. But it is still a dream. For it to become a reality, the ancient orders would either have to be united or be destroyed, which would lead to a war such as we have not seen since the end of the Second Age. As high priestess, even if I believed in your dream, that is something I simply could not allow." Placing a hand over his and giving it a gentle squeeze, she said, "Go now on your foolish quest. But heed my words about the Ka'i-Nur. Keep your wits about you, and your sword at the ready."

"Always, my priestess." With a breath of cold wind, he was gone.

T'ier-Kunai shivered, but not from the chill air of his passage. Even the thought of Ka'i-Nur left her heart cold with dread.

* * *

Ayan-Dar stood on the ancient road that wound through the Great Wastelands like the discarded skin of one of the great reptiles that dwelled here. Far beyond the white-tipped peaks of the Kui'mar-Gol mountains, this dangerous land was one of extremes. Blistering hot in the day, all year round, and deathly cold at night, an unprepared traveler would be doomed to burn or freeze to death.

Assuming of course, he was not first taken by a *genoth* and torn limb from limb.

Dark gray rock, razor-sharp, rose from the earth like gigantic teeth in a maw that spanned the horizon. There were no emerald trees, no ferns or lichens, no streams or pools of water. There were only the titanic gray knives of rock that seemed to bleed even the magenta sky of its color.

The formations were broken only by a single promontory, a long-dead volcano, atop which squatted the temple of Ka'i-Nur. Hewn of black stone from within the remains of the ancient caldera, the temple was the dark master of the bleak landscape. Nothing could be seen beyond the great wall that had been built to enclose the temple. No spires or domes, turrets or poles from which banners might fly protruded above the defensive works. Ayan-Dar had a sudden vision of there being nothing behind the massive walls but black doom.

His hand clenching the handle of his sword, he strode forward along the road, his second sight cast around him to keep watch for the unexpected.

While he might have considered materializing inside the temple itself, T'ier-Kunai had told him that to do so was impossible. Some unknown force protected the fortress from that particular power. She had once visited here during the last war with the Settlements, the same war in which he had lost his arm and eye. She was young then, but even so a very powerful priestess. The high priest had sent her to seek the support of the Ka'i-Nur against the invading armies from the Settlements, which were on the verge of defeating the defenders of the Homeworld.

T'ier-Kunai had never told him what had happened to her there in the short time she had spent behind those looming walls, but she had vowed that she would never go back, and would never send another. Her mission, such as it was, had failed, the Ka'i-Nur refusing to send aid.

Fortunately, the tide finally turned against the invaders, who in the end were destroyed.

As he approached the fortress, Ayan-Dar could discern nothing within. Even his second sight seemed blind beyond the black stone ramparts. He found it difficult to believe that not a single inhabitant of this malignant fortress carried blood of the Desh-Ka in their veins, but their spiritual voices were silent in his blood.

The dry gravel crunched under his feet as he made his way closer to the fortress, climbing the winding switchback in the road that led toward the massive gate, more foreboding by far than even the main gate of Keel-A'ar.

The sun blazed down on him, the heat so intense that the air shimmered above the worn cobbles of the road. He ignored the discomfort, focusing instead on the gate that now loomed above him. While the fortress walls were smooth and bare, the metal of the gates had been cast with intricate scenes of death, no doubt as a final warning to any souls foolish enough to seek entry.

He was certain that he had been closely watched since his arrival, and was no doubt being observed by many curious and hostile sets of eyes now.

And so, standing before the grisly tableaux that adorned the gate, he looked up toward where he suspected covered murder holes must be and grinned. "Greetings to the great warriors of Ka'i-Nur, and the keepers of the Books of Time whom they protect. I am Ayan-Dar of the Desh-Ka, and have come to..."

A spinning circular blade nearly as big around as he was tall sailed from the wall on his right from a slot thinner than his palm. Flying through the air at incredible speed, it hit him at waist level...and passed right through as his body momentarily merged with the passing metal. It disappeared into a slot on the far side of the entrance with a heavy *thunk*.

Ayan-Dar was impressed with the engineering of such a weapon, but disappointed that they had bothered using something so primitive against a priest of the Desh-Ka.

He looked up as small ports in the barbican over his head hissed open. Hundreds of small, wriggling creatures poured out, falling toward him.

The deadly spines and tail stinger of the *churr-kamekh*, a denizen of the wastelands that was just as deadly in its way as the giant *genoth*, were easily recognized. The stinger was as sharp and hard as a crystal needle, and the tail was strong enough to thrust it through metal and leatherite armor. Worse, the small beasts, about the size of his palm, attacked their prey in packs. It was not unknown for a hive to bring down a small *genoth* that was unwary enough to stray too close to the misshapen mounds the *churr-kamekh* inhabited.

He gave the Ka'i-Nur credit: it was an extremely effective way to dissuade unwanted visitors. The deadly little creatures were quite fast, and this many could easily kill an entire cohort of warriors in but a few moments. Had he been a warrior caught in such a trap, his only option for survival would have been to run.

But he was far more than a mere warrior, and it would take something a great deal more threatening than a pack of wasteland vermin or a spinning blade to kill him or make him flee.

Raising his hand above his head, lightning crackled from his palm. It did not shoot out in bolts as when he had killed the honorless ones on the hilltop some weeks before, but was cast as a net that spanned the space under the barbican.

The *churr-kamekh* squealed as they hit the web of tiny but intense electrical discharges. Their dark gray segmented bodies vaporized in bright flashes, sizzling and popping as they were reduced to a rain of white ash.

When they were gone, Ayan-Dar closed his palm and the electrical display ceased.

Lowering his arm to his side, his hand came to rest on the hilt of his sword. "I am happy I could assist you with your *churr-kamekh* infestation, but that is not why I have come." He could not help but smile as he imagined how difficult it must have been to collect the creatures. They could not be bred in captivity, but had to be caught in the wild. He suspected that replacing them would be a most dangerous task. "Could we please dispense with these games? I have come here only to ask the keepers of the Books of Time a single question. Then I will take my leave of your gracious hospitality." He made no attempt to keep the sarcasm from his voice.

"One question." The disembodied voice came from somewhere above him, echoing in the space under the barbican. It was a female voice, and sounded quite old to Ayan-Dar's ears.

He tried to cast his second sight beyond the stone and metal, to glean something about what lay on the other side of the gate, but again his efforts were thwarted. "One question is all I ask. If..."

"Enter, priest."

Snapping his mouth shut, Ayan-Dar stood there, waiting for the gate to open. But it remained shut, and there was no sound of gears or chains.

Another silly test, he thought. Tightening his grip on his sword, he stepped forward, right into the gate. He felt a chill as his flesh momentarily merged with the metal, which was as thick as he stood tall. Moving through it was like walking through cold water. In three long strides he was through, his body emerging from the metal on the far side.

He found himself in a courtyard of sorts, with two rows of warriors lining a path from the gate to a squat, windowless construct at the center of the fortress.

The warriors at first looked like any other, but upon closer inspection, he saw that there were some significant differences. The horn that formed the ridge over the eyes was more pronounced, and the fangs were larger, bulging behind the lips. Their talons were half again as long as those found on their kin outside the walls, glittering obsidian razors wrapped tightly around the hilts of their weapons. All those that he saw were huge males, taller than himself by a full head. Their bodies were thick and powerful, with heavy bones wrapped in powerful muscles. Their hair was braided, but in three braids, not the seven demanded by the Way. Their armor was angular, serpentine, and made of a more primitive metal than his own, but far thicker. While the added weight would be an impediment, he suspected that the physical strength of the warriors would more than make up for it.

He had seen images of his ancestors from the First Age, and they looked much like this. It was as if these warriors were from an earlier period in their evolutionary history, as if time had stood still in Ka'i-Nur while the rest of the Kreela beyond these walls had moved forward.

Perhaps, he considered, that was not far from the truth. And T'ier-Kunai had not been exaggerating when she had warned him of the potential threat from the warriors here. They were indeed formidable. He did not want to think of what a potential threat they could be if they had still possessed their Crystal of Souls, and the warriors standing before him had been priests.

A female in maroon robes stood halfway to the building that lay in the center of the courtyard. She was clearly a keeper, and was flanked by two massive warriors who made the others look like undernourished weaklings.

He began to walk toward her, moving slowly to make it plain that he offered no threat. He only used the senses of his body now, for to use anything else, even his second sight, could antagonize his hosts. T'ier-Kunai had warned him that the Ka'i-Nur harbored unabashed animosity toward their brothers and sisters in the other six orders, and would bristle at the slightest possible offense.

As he walked toward the waiting keeper, he could not banish the sense of oppression made upon him by the fortress itself. It was uniformly bleak, without a shred of color or embellishment. Everything was made of the same black stone, polished smooth. Even the cobbles over which he walked were ebony. Every surface was smooth as glass, like black mirrors. The air within the fortress walls was unbearably hot, between the direct sun burning down and what was reflected from the stone around him.

The rest must be below ground, he surmised. That would make a great deal of sense, considering the terrible conditions of heat and cold here at the surface. Underground, they could keep the temperature stable at a comfortable level.

Looking at the fierce, scarred faces of the warriors he passed, he doubted that comfort was high on the list of priorities for the dwellers of Ka'i-Nur.

He came to stand a few steps in front of the keeper and her escorts, who glared at him. The keeper, he could clearly see, was ancient, and he suspected hers was the voice that had spoken to him at the gate. Those of his race typically did not suffer atrophy with age, remaining in their prime until very near the end, when their bodies suddenly began to shut down. Of course, among the warrior caste, few ever lived to die of old age.

Among the non-warrior castes, there were some few whose bodies did begin to show signs of aging. By that time, they were very, very old, indeed.

Before he could say anything, she turned and shuffled slowly toward the entrance to the structure.

He followed her, remaining silent, and the two guardians fell into step beside him.

As they passed through the great arch that led into the mysterious structure, the desiccating heat fell away behind them. The air inside was cool and pleasantly humid, with the scent of a clear mountain spring. The walls around him, still of the same black stone, glowed to provide light in the same fashion that was found outside the walls of this unfathomable fortress.

The large atrium, which was guarded by six warriors, led to a spiral staircase in the center that was large enough to easily hold two tens of warriors standing shoulder to shoulder. In fact, the stairs appeared to be the sole reason for the building. While there were several alcoves evenly spaced around the perimeter of the building's interior, the rest of the space was devoted to the stairway that led below.

As they descended, he noted that the stairs were well-maintained. In so old a place as this, the steps should have been well-worn, the stone eroded away by countless footfalls over the ages. But these steps could have been from newly hewn stone.

They still have builders, then, he thought. While not surprising, the confirmation might prove useful. So very little was known about this place.

Ayan-Dar counted seventy-three levels past which they walked, spiraling down ever-deeper into the earth. He could gain no insight into what might have been on each level, for there were only closed metal doors beyond the circular landings. On some levels, he heard muffled voices. On others, sounds that could have been metal upon metal, or the hiss of strange machines.

The only sounds of which he could be certain were those made by the footfalls of himself and his escorts. The four of them were the only souls in the entire massive shaft through which the stairway descended. None of the other inhabitants of this underground city were to be seen.

At last, they reached the bottom level, where the stairway ended. Here, things were different. The black stone of the stairway gave way to beautiful red granite floor and walls that glittered with swirls of minerals, all of it polished to a high sheen. Sconces held torches that burned brightly, for the walls and ceiling here were bereft of the glow found on the other levels.

A single door faced the steps. It was ancient wood, twice as tall as Ayan-Dar and just as wide. On one side were four massive metal hinges that had clearly been forged by hammer and anvil long, long ago. On the opposite side was an iron ring, as large around as his head, hanging from a massive iron plate set into the door.

His two guards took up position on either side of the door. Then, to his amazement, the keeper, this ancient female, took hold of the massive ring on the door in one hand and gave a gentle tug. Without any evident machinery or pulleys to move it, the door, which Ayan-Dar could now see was as thick as the length of his arm, swung open smoothly.

Without a look back, the keeper entered, and Ayan-Dar followed.

But as he saw what lay beyond the door, he stopped and stared.

Before him lay a vast cavern, the far end of which was so distant that he could not see it. The entire city of Keel-A'ar could have easily fit inside, with much room to spare. The floor was level, made of the same granite as in the atrium behind him, covered with a maze of walls and pillars that rose twice the height of the walls surrounding the fortress, and yet only reached halfway to the mist-shrouded ceiling above. Every surface he could see, even the threshold where he now stood, was covered in writing, tiny script etched into the stone.

These, then, the words that had been so carefully preserved since the dawning age of their civilization, were the Books of Time that he sought.

He looked down at the script that covered the granite at his feet, but could not read it. It was in an ancient tongue that had probably died out in the fury of the upheavals of the First or Second Ages. That was the fate of many of the ancient tongues that had once been spoken. Yet, here they still lived, written and preserved for future ages.

Among the walls and columns moved a small army of keepers in maroon robes. While the ancient words were preserved in stone, the ability to both interpret them and index the information lay in the minds of the keepers. They were not only the scribes of the countless words here, but were also the living indexes of the vast repositories of information that made up the history of their race.

The ancient keeper who had been his guide had paused and was regarding him with a severe expression.

Reluctantly focusing his attention on her and the twisting stairway that led toward the main level below, he stepped toward her.

She turned around and began the long descent to the main floor.

When they arrived, a group of keepers was waiting. They stood in a semicircle, their hands clasped in the billowing sleeves of their robes. All eyes were fixed on Ayan-Dar.

The ancient keeper stopped, then turned to face him. "One question."

Ayan-Dar chose his words carefully. "What say the Books of Time of a female child, born in the shadow of a Great Eclipse, who has both white hair and talons of scarlet?"

The ancient keeper's eyes widened as she let out a slow breath. The others showed no reaction.

She knows something, Ayan-Dar thought, his expectation of disappointment turning to excitement.

After a long moment, the ancient keeper spoke. "The child of which you speak was foretold by the oracle Anuir-Ruhal'te before the Final Annihilation in the Second Age. Come."

She led him past the other keepers on a trek through the maze. The walls and columns he had seen from above had lacked any true sense of scale. Here, walking among them, they were titanic. And everywhere, on every flat or curved surface, was tiny writing in many tongues. Some of it was clearly rooted in the language in common use today. Others were only strange glyphs at whose meaning he could not even guess.

At last, she came to a stop before one of the great columns. Without a word, she levitated from the ground, taking him with her.

As they rose higher and higher, Ayan-Dar gawked at the immensity of the cavern and the wealth of information that must be stored here.

When they reached the top, the keeper stepped from the thin air upon which they were standing onto the solid granite surface of the column.

Ayan-Dar followed right behind.

Looking down, the keepers toiling below were no larger than tiny mites in his eyes, and the top of the column was so high that it was shrouded in the mist that concealed the ceiling of the gigantic chamber.

Kneeling on the hard, wet stone, the keeper ran her hands over the etchings until she found the one she sought.

Slowly, she read the words that were formed in an angular script that dated back nearly three hundred thousand cycles:

Long dormant seed shall great fruit bear,
Crimson talons, snow-white hair.

In sun's light, yet dark of heaven,
Not of one blood, but of seven.

Souls of crystal, shall she wield,
From Chaos born, our future's shield.

Ayan-Dar knelt beside the ancient keeper, his heart racing. He wanted to reach out and run his fingers over the ancient words, but knew that to do so was forbidden.

The keeper was looking at him closely. "You have seen the child of which Anuir-Ruhal'te spoke." It was not a question.

He did not want to admit the truth, but he was honor-bound to do so. "I have, mistress. In the city of Keel-A'ar."

"Thus, do you have the answer to your question, priest of the Desh-Ka. Now, it is time for you to leave this place." She stepped out into the open air that surrounded the column, and was held there as if she were standing on an invisible platform suspended high above the floor. She gestured for him to join her.

Ayan-Dar stepped out into space, where his foot found… nothing.

He was not caught entirely by surprise. All along, he had expected some form of treachery. As he fell forward, he tucked his chest in toward his legs and twisted to his right. This gave his left arm just enough extension that he was able to grasp the edge of the column, his talons digging into the polished stone as he uncoiled his body smoothly to face against the mountainous slab.

With a quiet grunt of effort, he lifted himself far enough that he could swing a leg over the top of the column before rolling his body to relative safety.

Calmly and gracefully regaining his feet, he turned to face the keeper, whose face betrayed disappointment. "I thought you were finished with your silly tests."

"This is no test, priest. The child of white hair and crimson talons shall not be allowed to live to fulfill the prophecy. One of our own is destined to rule over all. She shall restore the Ka'i-Nur to their rightful place, to be first among the seven bloodlines, as was the way in ancient times."

Glancing down, Ayan-Dar could see a brace of warriors rising along the face of the column. He had not used his powers to will himself away from this place, or simply to control his descent to the floor below when he had stepped off the column. He had not been willing to test himself in this accursed place unless he truly had to. It appeared that the time to do so would soon be upon him.

Baring her fangs, the ancient keeper said, "This shall be your tomb, priest of the Desh-Ka."

CHAPTER SIX

Syr-Nagath howled with bloodlust as her sword took the head from yet another enemy warrior. Around her, warriors hacked and clawed at one another along a battle line that ranged for leagues on either side of where she fought. The air was filled with the sounds of screams and snarls, of metal crashing upon metal, of flesh torn and bones crushed. She was intoxicated by the coppery smell of the blood that drenched the battlefield, and savored the taste of it on her lips where it had spattered from those she had slain.

The army facing hers was a coalition of the last kingdoms and independent cities in the eastern reaches of T'lar-Gol. The sea was only a few leagues distant, the blue-green water and frothing whitecaps visible from the tallest of the nearby hills. This army was now all that stood between her and the conquest of the entire continent.

But the enemy was not inclined to give up easily. More and more warriors were pouring forth into their lines, not only from the eastern kingdoms, but from those to the north and south. It was the largest force her army had ever faced, and was growing by the day.

She, in turn, was bringing forward more and more of her own warriors. While there had been times when her battle lines had been strained, she knew that in the end she would win. Millions of warriors were now beholden to her, and she knew the enemy could not match her strength. While the battle would rage on for some time, her victory was inevitable.

When the enemy finally surrendered and the warriors were bound to her by their honor, she would begin the next phase of her plan, the conquest of Urh-Gol, which lay beyond the Eastern Sea. That would be the open-handed move, the one that would be visible to all, and would captivate their attention.

With her closed hand, she would begin to weaken the Desh-Ka, using Ria-Ka'luhr as a pawn. He was the key to making them vulnerable. When she had completed her conquest of Urh-Gol, she would strike at the temple. By then, she would have a vast army and, just as important, the weapons she would need to destroy the Desh-Ka.

She knew that she had to deal with them first. While it was the smallest of the orders, it remained the most powerful. If she first destroyed either of the other two orders on the Homeworld, the Ana'il-Rukh or Nyur-A'il, the Desh-Ka would likely mount an attack that would prove devastating. But if she destroyed the Desh-Ka first, the other orders, which were far less powerful, could be dealt with in their turn.

And then she would reach toward the stars to take the Settlements.

She bared her fangs in ecstasy at the thought as she parried the strikes by a pair of enemy warriors before whirling inside the arcs of their blades. Driving her claws into the throat of one warrior, she jabbed the tip of her sword under the jaw of the other, the blade piercing the warrior's brain.

That was when she felt it. While she could sense nothing of the other six orders, her blood was closely bound to the Ka'i-Nur. She knew that something momentous had just happened, and she staggered with the intensity of the feelings that overwhelmed her.

Syr-Nagath knew the source all too well: the ancient mistress of the keepers. The Dark Queen saw a vision, a child with white hair and crimson talons, in a great walled city. And death. Her own, if the child did not die first.

"My queen!" Two of her warriors leaped into the gap as she staggered back from the line. More warriors ran forward from the reserve as the enemy, sensing weakness, surged forward in a roar of voices and clashing of steel.

To this and all else around her, Syr-Nagath was oblivious. She could focus only upon the images in her mind that were so intense they had blinded her. The child, unlike any she had ever seen. Her own death, a dark, cold shadow upon the future. And the walled city, which she knew well.

It was clear to her what must be done.

Whirling away, flinging blood from the tip of her sword into the roaring maelstrom behind her, she summoned her First and strode quickly from the field of battle.

***

Nil'a-Litan had been badly wounded in the day's battle and had been sent back to be treated by the healers. A young warrior just out of the *kazha*, she was part of Kunan-Lohr's retinue that served under Syr-Nagath. As with the other warriors, she had been proud to serve her master in the many battles that had raged across the lands of T'lar-Gol. But honor, not loyalty, bound her to the Dark Queen's service.

As she sat against a tree among the throngs of wounded, a mass of healing gel working its silent wonders on the deep wound in her left shoulder, she saw Syr-Nagath storm past, followed by her First and three of her senior war leaders. Nil'a-Litan recognized them, for they were the queen's favorites from among the retainers she had chosen after killing the old king. They were fierce warriors who did her bidding without question, and were greatly feared by their vassals, many of whom had found themselves shackled to the *Kal'ai-Il*. Or worse.

As the queen stalked by, her gaze swept the mass of wounded and lit upon Nil'a-Litan, who still clutched the banner of Keel-A'ar she had been given the honor to bear. In that fleeting moment, seeing the queen's expression change at the sight of the banner, Nil'a-Litan was sure that had she been closer the queen would have killed her. Never had she seen such an expression of unutterable hatred. Nil'a-Litan only gave thanks that she could not sense the queen's feelings. She could only wonder at what she had done to fall from grace in the queen's eyes.

Assuming the queen's ire had indeed been focused on her.

But she had looked first at the banner, she thought. *That is what had drawn her attention.*

Glancing around, she saw that there were no senior warriors of Keel-A'ar present. Struggling to her feet, she looked in the direction of the battle. She could see the banners of her master's warriors in the thick of the flashing swords and howling war cries, but there were no captains of her city's army anywhere close by.

Reluctantly setting down the banner beside one of her comrades, a ghastly wound in his abdomen just below the edge of his breastplate, she stood up and made her way slowly toward the pavilion. She did not need the many years of training and high knowledge of a priest to know that something was wrong, and she felt honor-bound to discover what it was. If she had made a transgression that had found ill-favor with the queen, she would redeem herself through whatever punishment Syr-Nagath chose to mete out. And if it had to do with the servants of Keel-A'ar or her master Kunan-Lohr, she would try to discover what it was so the senior warriors could address it before her lord returned.

She could not, of course, barge in on the queen, but it was within any warrior's purview to seek the counsel of the First.

Holding her wounded shoulder, hissing from the pain, Nil'a-Litan stood up straight and moved purposefully toward the entrance to the pavilion. Saluting the guards, she said, "I would speak with the queen's First."

With a nod, they let her pass, and she stepped into the entry vestibule of the palatial tent. She had been in here before with her master, but that had been during a planning session, and he had brought her along so she would gain experience in such matters.

Now, the vestibule and the rooms around it were empty.

Forcing down her misgivings, she moved toward the queen's chambers, which always faced toward the battlefield so Syr-Nagath could watch the progress of the fighting when she rested or planned.

Nil'a-Litan was just reaching out to draw back the cloth that formed a doorway to the queen's quarters, intending to peer inside to gain the attention of the First, when she heard Syr-Nagath say, "Ignore my command at your peril, Kanur-Han. Defy me now, and I will shave your hair and release you into the Great Wastelands."

A stab of fear lancing through Nil'a-Litan's heart and she froze. To have one's hair shaved was the worst of all punishments, worse even than death: it was a sentence to eternal darkness. She had no idea what horrible sin one could commit for Syr-Nagath to even consider such a punishment.

"I did not say I would not obey, my queen," she heard Kanur-Han say in a voice that betrayed no emotion whatsoever, not even fear. "I simply suggested that there was no need to take an entire legion. While we could spare the warriors easily from our campaign here, I believe it would make the task much more difficult. A single legion would not be able to take Keel-A'ar. I also know the captain of the guard there. He is no fool, and would not open the gates for trickery or bluster. Only the word of his lord and master, spoken from his very lips, would open those mighty gates for an approaching army."

"And one warrior, working alone, might be too easily stopped." Another voice, she was not sure which of the other two captains it was, spoke. But in this voice, there was indeed fear. "But perhaps three tens of warriors could move quickly, far faster than an entire legion. They could ride into Keel-A'ar under the guise of warriors returning home from the campaign, in need of food and rest on their journey. Such happens all the time, and the captain of the guard would see no reason not to allow them in."

"And once the gates were opened and our warriors let inside," Kanur-Han continued, "they could take and hold the gates while some of their number rode for the creche to kill the child before the warriors manning the walls could interfere."

"Then our warriors would simply ride out again," the other voice said. "The city's warriors could not pursue in force, for they have barely enough to defend the walls."

"But should the plan succeed, my queen, you will have a rebellion on your hands here," Kanur-Han warned. "Even after we kill Kunan-Lohr and his consort, the warriors here will sense something is wrong. And when word reaches them of what has happened in the creche…"

"It should be a simple enough matter to ambush Kunan-Lohr and Ulana-Tath on the road by which they must be returning even now." Syr-Nagath spoke slowly, thinking aloud. "That can be made to appear the work of a band of honorless ones. As for the creche…kill not only their child, but all the children. Only a band of honorless ones would ever consider such an act."

"My queen…" Kanur-Han's voice faded into silence. "Our warriors will not do this. I could gather enough to kill the child, for they could be made to see the reason for it, as the child is clearly a threat. But they will not massacre an entire creche."

"Send them to me." Syr-Nagath's voice was colder than the frigid winds that howled in the Kraken-Gol, the frozen wastes at the southern pole of the Homeworld. "But send me fifty, not the thirty you had planned."

"As you command, my queen."

Realizing that their discussion was over, Nil'a-Litan, moving as silently as she could, fled the pavilion, the pain of her mauled shoulder completely forgotten.

* * *

"Are you certain of this?"

Nil'a-Litan knelt before Eil'an-Kuhr, the senior captain of Keel-A'ar's forces fighting under the Dark Queen's banner. Drawing her dagger, Nil'a-Litan held it to her own throat, the blade drawing a thin line of blood. "With my blood and honor, all that I have told you is true, exactly as I heard it from the lips of the queen and the others. You have only to command me, and I will take my own life that you would believe my words."

"Put away your dagger, warrior." Eil'an-Kuhr spoke quietly now. They were in a small grove of trees on a rise that overlooked the raging battle in the valley below. It was a place of some privacy, but not much. The queen's army was spread out as far as the eye could see on this side of the valley, and there were warriors within a stone's throw of where they stood. But this would do. "I believe you. I confess I have difficulty believing what the queen said, for such an abomination is unthinkable to one of the Way. But I do not doubt that you have repeated faithfully what you heard."

Relieved that Eil'an-Kuhr believed her, Nil'a-Litan sheathed her dagger and stood beside the battle-hardened captain of warriors. "What are we to do?"

Eil'an-Kuhr's face reflected the bitterness in her blood. "We can do nothing until nightfall, when the end of the day's battle is called." Pointing to a long stretch of grappling, screaming warriors in the battle line, she said, "Save for the wounded, all our warriors are committed, and I cannot simply withdraw them. The line would collapse and the enemy would pour into the rear behind us. It would be nearly impossible to disengage without extremely heavy casualties." Letting her arm fall to her side, she inclined her head, drawing Nil'a-Litan's attention to more warriors, tens of thousands of them, encamped along the ridge line on either side of, and behind, the queen's pavilion. "Those who serve the captains you saw in the queen's pavilion have been held in reserve since the beginning, and would stand between our own warriors and the roads leading west, even if we could break free from the enemy and withdraw."

"The queen bleeds us!"

Eil'an-Kuhr gave her a dark look. "You see in one glance what we did not realize until the week after our lord departed for home. Yes, the Dark Queen now puts our swords on the line during the hardest fighting, and those of her favored warriors only enough to blood them and preserve the illusion of honor." She looked again at the battle line, where the banners of Keel-A'ar flew proudly. "Our numbers have been greatly diminished in the time since our lord departed. I fear there will be few enough of us left alive by the time he returns."

"So even if there was a rebellion..."

"It would be crushed all too quickly. Were it to begin at all, which it will not." At Nil'a-Litan's confused look, she went on, "None of us have the power to break the covenant of honor with Syr-Nagath, child. Kunan-Lohr pledged his honor to her, and through him, our own. Our lives are hers to spend as she wishes. Were she to order us to slit our own throats for no reason other than to serve her pleasure, we would be honor-bound to do so. If she wishes to bleed the legions of Keel-A'ar to the last warrior, that is her privilege. We live and die to serve those to whom our honor is bound. That is the Way."

Nil'a-Litan lowered her head, ashamed. "Yes, mistress. Please, forgive me." She felt very small at that moment, helpless.

She felt the elder warrior's hand on her uninjured shoulder, and looked up.

"While we cannot rise against the Dark Queen," Eil'an-Kuhr told her, giving her shoulder a reassuring squeeze, "we shall not let this wretched and dishonorable deed come to pass. I will assemble a group of warriors to ride home and warn our master."

"It may already be too late. Look!"

Eil'an-Kuhr turned, following the direction of Nil'a-Litan's gaze in time to see a group of warriors, fifty, by her estimate, file into the pavilion. A handful of others had split off and were heading toward the nearest grassy field where a herd of *magtheps*, some of them already saddled, grazed.

"Can the queen truly make them do this thing?" Even though Nil'a-Litan had heard the words herself, she still could not bring herself to believe that any of their kind would massacre an entire creche.

"We cannot afford to doubt it," Eil'an-Kuhr told her, "nor can we wait. If we are to warn our master, we must ride before they do. Otherwise, a rider or even a small group could be intercepted and stopped." She looked into Nil'a-Litan's eyes. "I cannot leave. It is up to you, young warrior." She withdrew a rod, half the length of her forearm, from a sheath on her right arm. "Take this. It is the *tla'a-anir*, the Sign of Authority, of our master. This entitles you to all privileges and honors that would be accorded him, but beware how you use it: Kunan-Lohr bears the burden of its use. With this you can get fresh mounts and food, whatever you need on your journey. You will have to ride now, this very moment, before the queen's assassins set out. I will send a party of warriors to trail them, but they may be ambushed, so do not depend on them to reach you." Eil'an-Kuhr gripped the younger warrior's arms in the way of parting, mindful of Nil'a-Litan's injured shoulder. "The greatest duty of your life now lies before you. You must warn our lord and master."

Nil'a-Litan bowed her head, unable to salute with her left arm. "I shall not fail, mistress."

"Go then, child, as fast as you can. And may thy Way be long and glorious."

* * *

The fifty warriors who knelt in Syr-Nagath's chambers within the pavilion stared at her with horrified expressions after she had told them what they must do.

As one, eight of them stood without a word and slashed their own throats with their talons. Each of those eight, who truly valued honor above their lives, stood until their eyes rolled up into their heads. One by one, they collapsed to the floor, which was now soaked in blood.

Syr-Nagath approached the nearest of the forty-two who remained. The warriors now had their eyes fixed on the rug. She knew that nothing she could offer in terms of rewards or riches would make them do the thing she demanded. Only fear would be sufficient motivation. She stood before the first one. "Will you do my bidding?"

The warrior silently shook her head.

The dark queen's sword sang from its sheath. In a glittering flash, the blade sliced through the first of the warrior's braids, the Covenant of the Afterlife. Screaming, the warrior fell to the floor, writhing in spiritual agony. Her soul had been isolated from the empathic and spiritual bond with the rest of her bloodline, and would be consigned to eternal darkness.

The Dark Queen gestured to a pair of warriors who stood behind her, and they quickly bound the still-screaming warrior in chains.

Syr-Nagath spoke to the remaining warriors, who did not lift their heads. "I will ensure that she lives a long life, waiting for the darkness to take her."

Then she stepped to the next warrior and repeated the same question. "Will you do my bidding?"

In the end, she had thirty-one warriors who pledged to commit infanticide, the most unholy of acts, in Syr-Nagath's name. The eleven who had refused were now bound by chains, their souls barred from the Afterlife. She ordered them hoisted on gibbets before the pavilion as examples of the price of disobedience.

For the eight who had committed ritual suicide, she commanded they be given the last rites and burned on funeral pyres as tradition demanded. Although they had defied her, they had done so with honor. While the Way she followed was not theirs, their self-sacrifice was one that she could respect.

After the last of the thirty-one warriors filed out to begin the long ride west to Keel-A'ar, Syr-Nagath summoned her First, who knelt before her and saluted.

"Yes, my queen?"

"Should any of those cowardly carrion-eaters survive," Syr-Nagath gestured in the direction the warriors had gone, "kill them upon their return and feed their bodies to the scavengers in the Eastern Sea after our victory here. I would not set eyes upon them again."

CHAPTER SEVEN

Ayan-Dar restrained the temptation to kill the keeper, who still hovered in the air a few paces from the top of the column, in easy reach of a *shrekka*. Killing a member of a non-warrior caste stood next to killing a child in terms of dishonor, although the old crone was hardly an innocent.

Below, six warriors, including the two massive guards that had accompanied the keeper, had reached the base of the column. They watched him with baleful stares, their swords held ready, as they quickly rose to meet him.

While they had the advantage of numbers, he held the high ground. He again restrained himself from trying to use his powers. If they worked when he truly needed them, they might save him. If they did not work now, the Ka'i-Nur would know for certain, and be emboldened in their attack. Even with his superior skills, their greater physical strength and numbers would eventually weigh against him.

Unlike a physical platform, whatever force was lifting the warriors did not allow them to spring up toward him. All of them tried as they neared the top, but there was nothing but air beneath their feet. They kicked out as if they were swimming in water, but without changing the steady pace of their climb. For just a moment, it confused them.

It was a small advantage offered in a very small window of time, but it was enough. With a series of lightning quick jabs and thrusts, Ayan-Dar killed five of them before they reached the top of the column. He derived some small sense of satisfaction when the ancient keeper was spattered with their blood, and she wailed like a frightened child.

Only the sixth warrior, one of the two massive brutes, survived, but not for long. He was a powerful and skilled warrior, but Ayan-Dar had faced far better. In a brutal but brief clash of steel, the warrior gasped as his left arm and half his chest fell away from a clean cut by Ayan-Dar's sword. Blood frothing from his mouth, the warrior fell backward off the column, to be borne slowly toward the floor.

Seeing his way out, Ayan-Dar jumped, straddling the warrior's body. As he did so, he lashed out with his sword at the keeper's feet, taking off all her toes. Screaming, she pressed shaking hands to the bloody stumps, as she, too, began to descend. His act was not out of cruelty. He had wanted to focus her attention on something other than signaling to whomever controlled this mysterious column of air (builders, he surmised) to let the body he was riding plummet to the hard floor below.

The keepers throughout the great cavern had been watching the spectacle, and now many of them began to panic. They fled toward the only exit, so far as Ayan-Dar could see, that led to the great stairway. He grinned as the mass of keepers, thousands of them, formed a solid blockage against the warriors outside who were trying to make their way into the chamber through the same doorway.

"May you be cursed by the ancient gods!" The keeper spat at him. She floated in the air as if she were sitting cross-legged on the floor, blood running through the fingers she had clasped around the stumps of her toes.

"Those gods perished at the end of the Second Age, mistress of the Books of Time. And I pray the honorless Ka'i-Nur will soon follow them into oblivion."

He was now close enough to the floor that he could safely land if he jumped. Deciding that now was a good time to test his powers, he slid off the body of the dead warrior and willed himself to float to the ground. He could not rise without some motive force, if only the power of his legs, but once airborne, he could sail through the air as he willed.

His cloak fluttering behind him, he flew across the floor to land in the exact spot he had chosen. Then he tossed his sword in the air to momentarily free his hand. Looking at his palm, he was rewarded with a fierce cyan glow, sparks of raw power that danced across his fingers.

Snatching his sword from the air, he headed toward the screaming mob that crowded the narrow stairs to reach the door and safety.

He ignored the wails of the ancient keeper behind him.

* * *

T'ier-Kunai stood on the dais in the center arena, watching the acolytes as they sparred with various weapons. While her eyes saw what was happening in the arenas, her mind was far away, focused on her second sight's view of the ancient fortress of Ka'i-Nur. She had watched Ayan-Dar disappear through the gate, beyond which she could not see, and now waited impatiently for him to reappear. It was unnatural for her to not feel the echo of his spirit in her blood, for it had been there since she had been a child, a youngling in the *kazha* of her city, where he had once been a master. She had grown to be his acolyte, and the day had come when he had shared his powers with her under the blinding, burning cyan flame of the Crystal of Souls here in the temple.

She had risen over the cycles through the ranks of the priesthood, at one point challenging and defeating her old mentor in the arena. That had been a day of tremendous honor for her, and she had knelt at his feet afterward, overcome with fondness for him. He had gently commanded her to rise, and gripped one of her forearms with his own.

Since then, many cycles had passed until she had finally risen to the position of high priestess. None had been less surprised than Ayan-Dar, whose obvious pride in his former acolyte had made her spirit sing.

You should not have let him go. There had been no choice, she told herself. She would not deny any of the priesthood, even an acolyte, a spiritual quest unless there was good reason. *The Ka'i-Nur are reason enough to have forbidden it. You know. You have been there in that wretched hive.*

She sighed. Too much time had passed since Ayan-Dar had been swallowed by the gate of the fortress after the pathetic attempts by the Ka'i-Nur to dissuade him. Even though she could not sense him, could not see into that evil place, she knew that something was wrong.

When she had told him that she was not prepared to risk war with the Ka'i-Nur, she had meant it. But she was not above paying a courtesy visit. Although the orders had all become so insular that it was rarely exercised, the right of visitation by the high priest or priestess of any order to any other was an ancient tradition, to which even the Ka'i-Nur had subscribed in ages past. Tradition demanded the most high be accompanied by no more than six of the priesthood, making seven in all, the number of all the ancient orders, including the Ka'i-Nur.

She did not know if seven would be enough to save Ayan-Dar, but such a number would hopefully be few enough to avoid open war with their sister order. While she had no doubt the Desh-Ka would prevail, there was no way to predict the repercussions. It was a dark path that was best avoided.

Her decision was made. "*Kazh!*"

The acolytes instantly stopped their sparring and knelt on the sands of the arena, facing her and saluting.

Returning their salute, T'ier-Kunai turned to her First. "Have the seven senior-most of the priesthood join me in my quarters immediately, and dismiss the acolytes from training." She paused, contemplating the worst of what could happen in the hours to come. "Once that is done, gather the priesthood and acolytes to the armory and prepare for battle."

* * *

When Ayan-Dar had reached the mass of panicked keepers trying to escape the great chamber, he had been content to find a defensible position in the corner of a pair of the titanic walls that rose high overhead. In that way, he could not be surprised from his flanks or behind. He was near enough to the front of the chamber that he had a clear view of the entrance, but was not so close that he was within easy range of an attack by *shrekkas* or other throwing weapons the Ka'i-Nur might use.

But his presence there, in clear view of the keepers, prompted a stampede. They trampled one another and tore at those in front of them, sinking their talons into the unarmored flesh of their peers to try and escape the priest of the Desh-Ka who stood, horrified, behind them.

"Stop! I mean you no harm, keepers of the Books of Time!" His bellowed words failed to calm them, and in fact had the opposite effect, throwing them into a frenzy.

What happened next brought him to the edge of being physically ill. From the doorway through which the keepers were trying to flee, he saw the glint of swords rising and falling. The blades were covered with blood, and cries of panic were joined by shrieks of pain and agony as the warriors coming for him began to hack their way through the keepers they were there to protect.

Dark streaks fell from Ayan-Dar's eyes, marks of mourning that turned the cobalt blue skin of his cheeks black as he watched the massacre. He bemoaned the fact that his people had forsaken the ancient gods, for he wished now that he had someone, something, to pray to, to relieve his soul of this dreadful burden.

"I did not wish this," he whispered. He knew, deep in his heart, that even had he known this would happen, he would still have come. The information he sought was too important. But this, even though he had not intended for any such thing to happen, was a blight upon his honor that he could never fully erase.

As he watched the warriors cut their way through the helpless keepers to reach the main floor, a fire kindled in his blood, a burning rage against these honorless fools who so callously were destroying a living treasure that belonged to their entire Kreelan race.

The warriors of Ka'i-Nur, covered in the blood of the keepers, surged toward him. While he had easily vanquished the few who had come for him at the top of the column, he had held all the advantages. Against this many...

If it is my time to die, then so be it. Drawing in a lungful of air, he roared a challenge as the brutes threw themselves at him in a raging fury, and his sword began its bloody work. He knew he would eventually need to draw on the powers within him that had long ago been granted by the Crystal of Souls, but he had decided to hold back as long as he dared in order to give the keepers more time to escape. Unleashing the full power of his own fury now would only result in more needless deaths.

Slashing, stabbing, and whirling, his spirit singing in the glory of battle, Ayan-Dar began to kill.

***

T'ier-Kunai stood before the seven priests and priestesses she had summoned to her quarters. Their expressions were grim.

"Remember," she told them, "our task is not to seek battle,

but to avoid it if possible. I do not know what fate has befallen Ayan-Dar, but I would not abandon him."

The others nodded solemnly. Not all of the priesthood took kindly to Ayan-Dar's eccentricities, but all had benefited from his wisdom, and none could argue his valor or honor as a warrior and priest of the Desh-Ka. They would not leave him, or any of the other members of the order, to the tender ministrations of the Ka'i-Nur.

She turned to the next senior-most priestess who would act in T'ier-Kunai's stead while they were away. "Are the others of the priesthood and the acolytes prepared?"

"Yes, priestess. All are fully armed and are standing watch along the temple perimeter, with a reserve held at the *Kal'ai-Il*. The children and the non-warrior castes, save the builders, have been gathered in the great dome for protection."

T'ier-Kunai nodded her approval. Should the temple be attacked, the warriors would mount an initial defense while the builders created a shield appropriate to the nature of the weapons used by the enemy. The builders beyond the temples were typically limited to structure of stone or wood. The abilities of those in the temples went far beyond such trifling constructs. In the last great war against the Settlements, they had erected a gigantic energy shield over the entire plateau that had withstood the assault of the enemy's antimatter weapons. And the great dome that now protected the other non-warriors was more than a simple structure of stone. Beyond the thick entry door was a labyrinth of space and time, created at the height of their civilization in the Third Age, that could not be destroyed. An enemy army passing through its doorway could search within for an eternity and never find what they sought, and would never find its way back out.

Those the priesthood held most dear would be safe. She realized that she was almost certainly overreacting, but the

Way of the Ka'i-Nur was alien to those beyond their walls. What the other six orders believed and held sacrosanct did not necessarily apply to the Ka'i-Nur. T'ier-Kunai would not underestimate the dark powers that might dwell in that ages-old relic in the Great Wastelands.

"Then let us go. I have been there before, and will lead you to the city gate. We must step through the barrier quickly to avoid any traps. I would take you straight inside, but our powers of teleportation will not work within the walls."

"Will our other powers work?" One of the priests wondered aloud.

"I do not know. When I was there, those many cycles ago, I had no reason or opportunity to try."

"So we may have to do battle — *if* we have to do battle — against the entire temple with only sword and claw?"

T'ier-Kunai nodded.

The other priests and priestesses bared their fangs, an expression of pleasure. It would be a most historic challenge, indeed, should it come to pass.

"Let us go." Clearing her mind, she focused on the old, dusty cobbles leading up to the horrid gate of Ka'i-Nur.

As one, T'ier-Kunai and six companions vanished.

* * *

Ayan-Dar had fought his way to the ninth level up from the great cavern when his strength finally began to wane. An endless stream of warriors had cast their lives away upon his sword, and the entrance to the Books of Time and the stairs below him was an abattoir, with blood cascading down the steps like a series of grisly waterfalls.

But the last warrior he killed had gotten lucky, his sword slicing into Ayan-Dar's right side where he had no arm to help defend his body. It had happened in a moment when Ayan-Dar had been too preoccupied with swordplay to allow the metal blade to pass right through him.

You are no longer young, my friend. The words echoed in his mind as he cut the legs from another warrior who charged him. *Well said. But the true strength of a Desh-Ka priest does not reside in the body, be it young or old.*

The keepers, at long last, were finally gone, the survivors having fled into chambers that led from the landings on the levels he had already passed, or higher up the great staircase.

It was time. As another group of warriors charged down the stairs, he flicked away the blood that coated the blade of his sword, then sheathed it in the scabbard at his side.

For the first time, the warriors showed more than just blind aggression and slowed for a moment, confused by his action.

"I would accept your surrender, warriors of the Ka'i-Nur," he told them. "Your kin have fought bravely, but there is no need for further bloodshed. You may live with honor."

The eyes of the lead warrior bulged in rage at his words, which he had spoken with all sincerity, for surrender after a battle well-fought was indeed honorable. Mindless slaughter was not part of the Way.

Except among the Ka'i-Nur, it seemed.

Bellowing in fury, they charged him as had the others before, but this time Ayan-Dar did not draw his sword.

Instead, he extended his open hand toward them, and cyan chain lightning exploded from his palm, burning them alive. The heat was so intense that it melted their armor.

The warriors fell in a screaming heap, their charred bodies filling the air with the nauseating stench of burning flesh. If healers tended to them right away, they might yet live, but that was beyond Ayan-Dar's concern.

As with his physical strength, the powers that lay within him were not without limit. If the Ka'i-Nur had so many warriors to sacrifice, it was unlikely he would ever again see the light of the sun before he was completely exhausted. Then they would quickly overwhelm him.

For a priest of the Desh-Ka, it would be a noble end worthy of an inscription in the Books of Time.

The thought made him smile.

Lightning snapping through the air before him, he rapidly advanced up the great stairway.

CHAPTER EIGHT

T'ier-Kunai and the others appeared in a swirl of cold air before the brooding metal gate of Ka'i-Nur. They immediately stepped forward, swords drawn, disappearing into the mass of the gate just as searing flames erupted from the walls to either side.

When they emerged on the far side, they were confronted by a century of warriors, grouped in tight ranks facing the gate.

The priests and priestesses who accompanied T'ier-Kunai were shocked at the appearance of their distant cousins, at the differences in body and armor, but said nothing.

Momentarily ignoring the warriors, who held no surprise for her, T'ier-Kunai focused on Ayan-Dar, trying to sense him...

There! He was indeed alive, his spirit singing the song of desperate battle. She could sense him within the walls.

They were not too late, then.

"I am T'ier-Kunai, high priestess of the Desh-Ka," she told the warriors who stood before her, "and I claim the right of visitation."

The warriors clutched their weapons, struck with indecision.

"Such a right to visit here has not been claimed by any of the orders for millennia." A female voice spoke from behind the tight ranks of warriors. "Why should we honor it now?"

The warriors parted to reveal a solitary figure, who T'ier-Kunai realized must be their high priestess. Unlike the other warriors, this one, a female, was modern in appearance, although her hair was bound in only three braids, not seven. Her armor, while serpentine and segmented like the others, was a brilliant crimson, with the rune of the Ka'i-Nur in the center of her breastplate. Unlike the Desh-Ka and the other five orders beyond these walls, she did not wear a Collar of Honor or a sigil of her order at her throat. That had passed with the disappearance of their order's Crystal of Souls ages ago.

She walked in measured strides to stand just beyond the reach of T'ier-Kunai's sword.

"You are not welcome here, priestess, and claiming the right of visitation means nothing." She glared at T'ier-Kunai, baring her fangs in anger. "Any such rights to which the Desh-Ka may have been entitled were lost when your priest began his massacre of the keepers in the chamber of the Books of Time."

T'ier-Kunai raised her hand to still the angry retorts about to spill from the lips of her companions. "If our priest, Ayan-Dar, drew his sword, it would not have been without good reason. We would take him with us now, and I give you my word of honor that I will do my best to make amends."

"You were here, among us." The crimson warrior stepped closer, eyeing T'ier-Kunai even as she ignored her words. "I remember you. The one who came to seek our aid when the great Desh-Ka were about to fall to the Settlements."

"Yet we prevailed. As we shall prevail now. Return our priest to us, alive, and we will go without further bloodshed."

To either side, the warriors began to back away from the crimson warrior, not in orderly ranks, but in barely restrained panic.

"We shall see, priestess of the Desh-Ka."

The world turned a brilliant white.

* * *

As Ayan-Dar cleared the fifty-second level, the warriors who had been hurling themselves upon him without cease disappeared. The stairway above and below him was empty, save for the dead and the dying. All he could hear were the moans and screams of the wounded he had left in his wake. The air was filled with the smoke of burned bodies and seared metal, and it was only with great difficulty, even with the incredible control he had over his body, to not cough and gag.

Exhausted, he sagged to his knees. Glancing back down the stairs, at least as far as he could see as the steps spiraled out of his view, he had difficulty imagining how many warriors he had brought down. How many could this underground city possibly support? And how many remained for him to fight?

The skin of his hand was a mass of ugly red blisters, not from the power of the bolts he unleashed, but from the heat radiated back at him from the armor of the warriors he had killed. Some of them had gotten so close that he had been forced to push them away, even as they burned. Some he had simply passed right through, as he had stepped through the metal of the gate, but he wasn't able to do that and unleash the cyan fire at the same time. Even priests of the Desh-Ka had some limitations.

But that was a trifle for a healer to mend. Assuming he survived.

While he was thankful for the respite he now enjoyed, he was troubled by the sudden disappearance of the Ka'i-Nur warriors. He would not allow himself to believe that he had slain them all, as comforting a thought as that was.

That was when he felt a deep change in his blood, a spark that rose in an instant to a brilliant flame. He grinned as he realized that it was T'ier-Kunai and six others of the priesthood. They were here, no doubt under the ancient right of visitation, in hopes of saving him.

"You may yet survive this, old priest." He spoke the words to himself as he knelt there, trying to recover his strength. He opened his heart to his priestess, that she would know he yet lived, before he got back on his feet to continue the journey to the surface.

He had only taken a handful steps when two things happened. He sensed T'ier-Kunai and the others as they were rocked by agonizing pain, and the great stairwell was filled with a bone-chilling roar that he remembered all too well from one of the quests of his youth.

The Ka'i-Nur had set loose a *genoth* somewhere along the great stairway.

* * *

T'ier-Kunai could smell her own flesh burning, but she shut the pain away as she leaped clear of the energy weapon the Ka'i-Nur priestess had unleashed.

The crimson armor the enemy priestess wore was more than the basic metal alloy that T'ier-Kunai and her companions were wearing. It was a biomechanical suit, not unlike those the warriors from the Settlements had worn in their previous bid to take the Homeworld. Just before the Ka'i-Nur priestess had triggered her weapon, a segmented helmet had extended over her head. Such weapons gave their wearers formidable capabilities, but could not compare to the powers imbued by the Crystal of Souls.

Blinded by the flash, T'ier-Kunai could not see with her eyes, but she did not need to. She could see better with her second sight. She had not been able to cast it through the walls of this place, but now that she was inside, she could see everything. The *genoth* that was now hunting Ayan-Dar deep in the earth. The masses of warriors that were charging up the great stairway to the surface. The ashen remains of the warriors who had been here a moment ago, killed by their own priestess.

T'ier-Kunai and her companions had scattered the instant before the weapon was triggered. All of them made it out of the blast zone save one, Sal'ah-Umir, whose left leg had been vaporized. He now lay on the glittering black stones, unconscious.

In rapid succession, her hand moving at blinding speed, T'ier-Kunai hurled her three *shrekkas* at the Ka'i-Nur priestess. She did not expect any of them to strike. She just needed a momentary diversion.

As the crimson priestess turned briefly to flick the three weapons away, she was struck in the side by a massive bolt of lightning from one of the Desh-Ka priests that sent her tumbling to the ground.

"Finish her!" T'ier-Kunai and three of the others sailed through the air to land in a circle around the Ka'i-Nur priestess, who was struggling to get back to her feet.

Holding out their hands toward one another, thick arcs of lightning exploded between the open palms of the Desh-Ka warriors, rapidly forming a globe of lightning that enveloped the enemy priestess. She looked up in time to realize her fate, but by then it was too late.

The crackling globe of pure cyan energy began to contract around her, intensifying as it grew smaller. The priestess triggered her energy weapon again, but that only aided in her undoing. None of the energy escaped the cyan globe that was rapidly collapsing around her. Her armor failed in a dozen places, exposing her frail flesh to the contained maelstrom.

Her shrieks of pain were mercifully cut off as the globe shrank, faster and faster, to consume her body. When it had collapsed to the size of T'ier-Kunai's fist, the globe flared and vanished.

There was nothing left of the Ka'i-Nur priestess, not even ash.

"Beware!"

The remaining priest who was tending to the injuries of their fallen comrade shouted a warning.

Blinking her eyes, T'ier-Kunai noticed with relief that her vision was slowly returning. At the blurry image that greeted her, she suddenly wished that she was still blind.

Hundreds of warriors were charging from the mouth of the atrium capping the great stairway. And all of them wore crimson armor and carried energy weapons.

* * *

Ayan-Dar leaped up the stairway, using his power to loft himself as far as he could, kicking off the walls as the stairway turned.

The *genoth* howled in rage and hunger, and he could hear the beast's diamond-hard claws scrabbling up the steps close behind him.

It had been one small measure of good fortune that the beast had been released below him, that it did not block his path to freedom.

Or so he had thought until his second sight revealed the mass of Ka'i-Nur warriors gathering above him. While he could only guess at their nature, he assumed these to be drawn from the same ranks as those T'ier-Kunai and the others now fought on the surface. If they were as formidable as the sensations from his companions indicated, his chances of survival were slim. He could probably kill the *genoth*, but there was no escape in the direction from which he had come. And above was the legion of warriors that was now pouring forth to engage T'ier-Kunai and the others, and which could easily overwhelm him as the *genoth* drove him toward the surface.

Some might have considered themselves trapped, but Ayan-Dar knew from long experience that was only a state of mind.

Sensing a group of warriors on the second level, just below the surface, who must have been waiting for him, he slowed his pace slightly, allowing the *genoth* to close the distance. It roared as it caught sight of him, the fury of its deep voice plain as a spoken word.

Ayan-Dar had not seen the full extent of the beast, only its snout and front claws as it tore up the stairs behind him, but he did not need his second sight to tell him that it was huge. The massive stairway shuddered at the beast's movement, and its roar was deafening.

Slowing just a bit, he was able to get a good look at the beast. The head, like the rest of the creature's body, was covered in thick scales that were as tough as armor. The head was enormous, and the jaws with their rows of needle-like teeth were large enough to swallow a *magthep* whole. The two horns at the top of the head were as long as Ayan-Dar stood tall, and the yellow eyes were fixed on him, its prey. He did not need to see the rest of its great body, with six powerful legs and feet boasting talons as long as his arm, or the whipping tail with its diamond-hard tip.

What shocked him was the thick metal band that he glimpsed around the beast's long, curving neck. It must have been raised here as a hatchling, for he could not conceive of an adult beast ever being captured alive by any means. And raising a *genoth* in captivity was nothing short of an act of madness.

It lunged for him, snapping its jaws a hands-breadth from his heel as he again kicked away from the outside railing of the stairway. Making sure he did not let himself get far from the beast's snapping teeth and fetid breath, he propelled himself upward.

The *genoth*, sensing it was gaining on its prey, sprinted toward him, opening its deadly jaws.

* * *

In the great courtyard, the priests and priestesses of the Desh-Ka stood in a line facing the oncoming crimson warriors of the Ka'i-Nur who poured from the entrance to the great stairway.

"Three hundred, do you think?" One of the priests speculated idly.

"Three hundred and thirty-eight, by my count." Sal'ah-Umir now stood with them, supported by one of the others, who had cauterized the stump of his leg with a controlled burst of energy. The healers could grow him a new one, assuming he survived.

"There are more within," T'ier-Kunai observed.

"They must be waiting for Ayan-Dar."

"Then we must deal quickly with these," T'ier-Kunai told them, "now that we have a better appreciation of what we face."

The enemy warriors had cleared the entrance and were organizing themselves into a series of cohorts, rather than simply swarming at the Desh-Ka.

That will make things somewhat simpler, T'ier-Kunai thought.

As if hearing her unspoken words, the Ka'i-Nur opened fire with their energy weapons in a massive barrage, the searing white light reflecting off the polished black stone of the inner walls and cobblestones.

All seven of the Desh-Ka raised their hands, and a curving shield of cyan lightning crackled into existence before them. The energy of the enemy's weapons thundered against it, and the very ground shook. The shield shimmered for a moment, as if weakened by the assault. Then it grew even brighter and began to expand.

The stone of the fortress walls nearest the battle began to glow from the enormous heat. The polished stone turned red, then white hot before oozing toward the ground like lava.

The wind began to howl as the clash of energy heated the air, and a superheated column rose swiftly, drawing cooler air behind it to fill the vacuum. In moments the entire fortress was swept by a gale that threatened to knock the combatants off their feet. Above the fortress, a huge cloud bloomed, quickly turning dark as water condensed from the surrounding air.

The Ka'i-Nur advanced, firing constantly. The warriors of the Desh-Ka reached deep within themselves, into their spirits, drawing out every last bit of energy to hurl against the enemy.

The cyan shield grew until it towered over the Ka'i-Nur. T'ier-Kunai's face contorted with concentration as she sought to control it, to bend the combined energy of herself and her companions to her will. The wall of energy they were projecting was no longer a shield, but a great hammer with which she would destroy their enemies.

Too late, the Ka'i-Nur realized what was going to happen. Many of them broke and ran, trying to escape as the gracefully curved wall of lightning rolled over upon them like a giant wave breaking upon a beach.

Watching with her mind as much as her eyes, T'ier-Kunai gave the great wall one final push, and it fell upon the enemy formation. Shattering like glass, it fragmented into a million bolts of lightning that incinerated everything in its path. The sound shook the very foundations of the ancient fortress.

When the last of the lightning had flickered out of existence, there was only white hot stone in the fortress square where the Ka'i-Nur warriors had stood.

* * *

Ayan-Dar sensed the destruction of the enemy warriors on the surface, but also sensed something else: the warriors who had been laying in wait for him were now charging down the stairway, fleeing from T'ier-Kunai and the others.

Better to be vaporized or eaten? The question was more than academic now as he again darted away from the *genoth's* snapping jaws.

In a way, the retreat of the warriors above him made things easier. Their panic might make them forget, if only for a moment, what was coming *up* the stairway.

Of course, there was always the pleasant possibility that the warriors might flee into one of the chambers above him, but he could not count on that.

Keeping the *genoth* as close behind him as he dared, he flew up the stairway toward the descending warriors. He could hear them now, their heavy footfalls on the stone audible above the mad scrabbling behind him.

The beast roared again, and Ayan-Dar heard and sensed the warriors above him come to a shuddering stop.

Despite the perils of his own situation, a fierce grin came to his lips as he imagined their predicament. To face the mad beast coming up from below, or die at the hands of the Desh-Ka who waited outside?

As he suspected, they chose to face the *genoth*. With the weapons they had, they could kill it, even if some of their number died in the process. For by now they knew the futility of facing the companions of his order.

All Ayan-Dar had to do was survive the coming encounter.

The warriors were suddenly *there*, and he did the *genoth* a small favor by blasting the first rank with a bolt of energy. He wasn't trying to kill them, just sow further confusion.

A handful of the crimson-clad warriors went down. Others, unable to stop in time in their headlong rush down the curving stairway, sprawled over the top of their fallen comrades.

Drawing his sword, Ayan-Dar leaped over the heads of those warriors still standing, slashing and stabbing to add a greater measure of confusion and mayhem.

Behind him, the *genoth* tore straight into the mass of warriors, trampling some and tearing others to bits in its massive jaws. The Ka'i-Nur fired their energy weapons at it, but in these close quarters the massive release of energy killed half their number while only wounding, and further angering, the *genoth*.

Ayan-Dar winced as some of the reflected energy seared his lower legs, but he ignored the pain. With a few more leaps, he reached the top level, where T'ier-Kunai and the others awaited him.

After he had sheathed his sword, they greeted as the long-acquainted warriors they were, clasping forearms.

T'ier-Kunai's expression on her badly burned face was grim as she spoke above the echoing roar of the beast below, still savaging its victims. "I hope you found the answer you sought, and that it was worth the price all have had to pay."

"I have, my priestess." He clasped her arm even tighter, a look of anguish on his face. "But I fear this is only a small glimpse of what is yet to come."

CHAPTER NINE

"I beg of you, summon the other orders. Call for a conclave." Ayan-Dar stood in the temple's central hall, which was now filled with the members of the Desh-Ka priesthood, while the acolytes went about their duties outside.

T'ier-Kunai, the burns on her body now gone after being tended by the healers, sat in the chair at the front of the great room, presiding over the assembly that Ayan-Dar had requested.

Two weeks had passed since the battle with the Ka'i-Nur. Two weeks that the Desh-Ka warriors had been prepared for an attack. But the dark fortress had remained silent as a tomb. T'ier-Kunai had posted two of the priesthood outside the fortress to provide warning should the Ka'i-Nur march out. While those sentinels remained, the unpleasant duty rotating among members of the priesthood, she had allowed the temple to resume its normal routine.

Once the imminent threat had passed, Ayan-Dar had begun begging her every day for an assembly to discuss the conclave, and she had finally given in.

"A conclave has not been called since before the other orders departed for the Settlements, thousands of cycles ago," one of the priestesses observed. "And that was for something that had never occurred before in our history, Ayan-Dar."

"As is this!" The old priest fought to restrain his frustration. He paced in front of his peers, trying to find the right words to convince them, and through them, T'ier-Kunai. "In fact, I believe the event of which we speak here is even more momentous. I believe this child is the key to the future of our race..."

One of the other priests interrupted. "Ayan-Dar, think of what you ask. All you have is a few lines of verse from a prophecy from the end of the Second Age, from a time when we cannot divine the difference between fact and legend." He gestured toward a male in maroon robes, the master of the temple's Books of Time. "Is this not true?"

"Such may be said," the keeper answered quietly. He was very old, although not so old, Ayan-Dar suspected, as the now-toeless old crone who fulfilled the same role at the temple of the Ka'i-Nur. "But it is also true that all that has ever been written in the Books of Time was originally based on fact, or something that was known or believed at the time to be such. Much of it we can repeat or recreate, but much has also been lost from those long-ago times before the Final Annihilation in the Second Age. Many of the ancient storehouses of knowledge were destroyed in the great devastation that swept our world in that terrible upheaval. Even the Books of Time held by the Ka'i-Nur are not complete. They contain far more information than is available elsewhere, but great gaps exist. In many cases, we have fragments of what once was, pieces of some larger puzzle, but we do not know how the completed puzzle was intended to appear to the beholder."

"But is it not also true," Ayan-Dar countered, "that every prophecy known to have been made by Anuir-Ruhal'te, the oracle who gave us the words that I believe speak of the child born in Keel-A'ar, came true?"

The keeper inclined his head. "Yes, that is so. Anuir-Ruhal'te was of the Ka'i-Nur, but her history is well-known among the keepers of all the orders. She predicted the Final Annihilation of her own age, and many things that came to pass long after. Only the Ka'i-Nur had complete records of her words, but of the other prophecies of which we know, all have indeed come to pass."

"But cannot a prophecy be interpreted many ways to fit an event, or an individual?" Another priestess, one of those who had gone on the expedition to Ka'i-Nur, asked.

The keeper slowly shook his head. "For many, such may be said, but not for those made by Anuir-Ruhal'te. While they did not contain dates or names, the words of her prophecies were so well-chosen that it was quite clear when they came to pass. Keepers in later ages recorded this fact, marveling at her singular vision." He looked over the gathered members of the Desh-Ka priesthood. "There have been many prophets and oracles throughout our history, who have said a great many things. Some of these things have come to pass, perhaps by sheer chance, and many have not. While I do not know how it could be, it is my belief that Anuir-Ruhal'te truly had visions of the future."

"And when was the last such fulfillment of her prophecies noted?" T'ier-Kunai asked.

"In the middle of the Third Age, nearly one hundred and fifty thousand cycles ago. It was a prediction of the great war that laid waste to the eastern half of T'lar-Gol and the famine that followed. She predicted the start of the war to the day based upon the timing of the moon cycles from the preceding Great Eclipse." He shook his head. "Such has been the accuracy of her visions, those of which we know."

As Ayan-Dar opened his mouth to speak, T'ier-Kunai raised her hand to silence him. "Are there any more such visions from this oracle?"

The keeper nodded, his expression turning grim. "There is no way for us to know if there are others still held by the Ka'i-Nur. But there is one other prophecy that we know, that clearly has not yet come to pass. It is believed to be Anuir-Ruhal'te's final vision before she died, for even the fragmentary records of the time not possessed by the Ka'i-Nur speak of her passing. She herself was a keeper, perhaps the greatest who has ever lived."

Closing his eyes, he reached deep within the storehouse of his mind, recalling the verse of the prophecy that was among the first elements of knowledge he had indexed as a young keeper:

> *Of muted spirit, soulless born,*
> *in suffering prideful made;*
> *mantled in the Way of Light,*
> *trusting but the blade.*
>
> *Should this one come in hate or love,*
> *it matters not in time;*
> *For he shall find another,*
> *and these two hearts they shall entwine.*
>
> *The Way of sorrows countless told,*
> *shall in love give life anew;*
> *The Curse once born of faith betray'd,*
> *shall forever be removed.*
>
> *Shall return Her love and grace,*
> *long lost in dark despair;*
> *Mercy shall She show the host,*
> *born of heathen hair.*
>
> *Glory shall it be to Her,*
> *in hist'ry's endless pages;*
> *Mother to your hearts and souls,*
> *Mistress of the Ages.*

The gathered warriors were silent for a time, trying to understand the meaning behind the words spoken by the keeper.

"Mistress of the Ages," Ayan-Dar said softly. "It is she."

"Please, Ayan-Dar." T'ier-Kunai's voice betrayed her frustration. "You leap to conclusions." Turning to the keeper, she asked, "How far apart in time were the two prophecies written?"

"I do not know." The keeper shook his head, then looked to Ayan-Dar.

"The keeper of the Ka'i-Nur did not say, and even had I thought to ask, she would not have told me." Ayan-Dar shrugged. "All I was permitted was a single question."

The keeper gave a low growl of disgust. "The Books of Time are for all the Kreela. Truly they have strayed from the Way."

"And paid the price." The others who had gone with T'ier-Kunai nodded grimly at her words. While the Ka'i-Nur lived on, it would be long before their wounds were healed.

And then, T'ier-Kunai feared, *they would have their revenge, if we are not vigilant.* "Keeper, are these prophecies related?"

He made an apologetic gesture with his hands. "As you know, priestess, our caste records and recites information of the past for the benefit of all, but we do not interpret it. To do so would violate the integrity of the Books of Time by injecting our own bias. It is up to you and the peers to make of it what you will. This is as it has always been, and so shall it always be."

"It is not mere coincidence." Ayan-Dar gestured toward the southeast. "The child that was born in Keel-A'ar to Kunan-Lohr and Ulana-Tath is an exact match of the child described in the prophecy related to me by the keeper of Ka'i-Nur. The child has hair white as the snow on the mountain peaks and talons the color of blood. She was born under the dark light of a Great Eclipse. A child with such traits has never been recorded in all our history."

The keeper nodded his agreement. "Based on our stored knowledge, and accepting that it is not complete beyond the end of the Second Age, this is so."

"*Not of one blood, but of seven,*" Ayan-Dar quoted from the verse he believe spoke of Keel-Tath. "She will unite the race, do you not see?"

"And then put a curse upon us?" One of the other priests, a giant among them, spoke in a deep voice that echoed across the chamber. "I would perhaps agree with you that the first prophecy speaks of this child, Ayan-Dar. But I must also say that I am deeply troubled by the words of the second vision. As you all know, I am not one who delves deeply into the way of words," that drew a chorus of grins and fangs bared in ironic humor, "but I would say that based on the second prophecy, which speaks of this curse and *The Way of sorrows countless told*, letting this child fulfill any destiny beyond being cloistered in a temple may be unwise."

To Ayan-Dar's dismay, many of his peers seemed to agree. "Every great age in our history has been preceded by darkness," he told them. "And the unification of our race would, I am sure, be no exception.

"But my brothers and sisters, think of it! What if all our kind stood united once more, as we know we once were at the dawn of history. When our race was united, we achieved things of which we cannot even dream now. What we could do, with the knowledge and powers that we have gained over the ages, would be limitless." He clenched his fist in frustration as he paced before them. "The Way now takes us on a path that is an infinite loop, a journey that leads us nowhere, and with no purpose other than to simply fight and die. We no longer even have the old gods to whom we can pray. Our souls are empty vessels that, perhaps, this child could help fill. She could give us purpose beyond maintaining an infernal equilibrium, and change our path to one that actually leads us to something greater."

"The Way is a circle because that is what keeps our race alive, Ayan-Dar." Yet another voice, one of the senior priestesses, spoke. "All is in balance here on the Homeworld, and even between the Homeworld and the Settlements after the last conclave decided to divide the orders and send three to the Settlements. The Way as we have followed it has allowed us to survive and not destroy ourselves as nearly happened in the Final Annihilation of the Second Age, which swept away the last remnants of the old ways." She held up her hands, showing her gleaming black talons. "We are not beings of peace. War and battle are in our very blood, it is part of what we are. There is nothing beyond the path we follow, because to do anything else would lead to our inevitable destruction. The Final Annihilation at the end of the Second Age was proof enough. *That* was the pinnacle of achievement of our forebears. Those few who survived that cataclysm lived in caves underground, as do the Ka'i-Nur still, for a thousand cycles before they could again venture out upon the surface. The Way as it is now was fashioned then, to save us from ourselves."

"And what purpose would the priesthoods serve?" Another spoke up. "We now have a clear reason for existence: to teach the Way to those who shall come after us, and to defend the Homeworld from the Settlements, just as the three orders that now live among the stars defend them from us." He looked around at the others. "What need is there for us if the race is united?"

That brought a strong murmur of agreement, and Ayan-Dar felt his blood begin to boil. He fought the urge to draw his sword and challenge them all to ritual combat. "That," he told them, his voice rising above theirs, "is what you are truly afraid of, is it not? You are not so concerned with the fate of our race, but with our own place in the world! We control the Way, we control the lives of those who live beyond the temples through the training we give them in the *kazhas*. And yet we abandon them by not involving ourselves with their affairs when those beyond our grounds are plagued with hardship and suffering, as many are now in this honorless time."

"That is enough, Ayan-Dar!" T'ier-Kunai's sharp words plunged the gathering into instant silence. "I called this gathering so you could voice your thoughts and discuss what has transpired, and what you believe, with the peers, and to help me decide if I should call for a conclave of the orders. But your last words take you on a path that will lead to the *Kal'ai-Il* if you do not curb your tongue."

For a moment, Ayan-Dar felt a bloody rage take him, the bloodlust that was the warrior's call to battle, the same bloodlust that had doomed his race to endless cycles of bloodshed.

And he was not the only one. The others of the priesthood were incensed with him, and he could feel their emotions echoing in his blood.

With a mighty effort of will he spoke, his voice far calmer than he felt. "Brothers and sisters, you know that I mean you no offense. But I believe these words, hard as they may be to hear, to be true." Before T'ier-Kunai could say anything, he quickly went on. "When I say that this is an honorless time, I mean that very literally. I speak of the Dark Queen, Syr-Nagath. May I remind you of the words the keeper of the Ka'i-Nur said to me after she had told me the words of the prophecy of the child. She said, 'One of our own, not of your six precious bloodlines, is destined to rule over all. She shall restore the Ka'i-Nur to their rightful place, as was the way in ancient times.' I believe she was referring to Syr-Nagath, who came from the Great Wastelands."

"That very well may be so, Ayan-Dar, but it changes nothing about the way the orders conduct their affairs, and our strict non-interference with the world beyond the temples and what is taught in the *kazhas*." T'ier-Kunai was furious with him, but he did not care.

"We may have to reconsider that, my priestess," he told her, "if, when she unites T'lar-Gol, she turns upon us."

"She would not dare." The reaction of the others of the priesthood ranged from outright guffaws to eye-rolling disbelief that one of their own would even consider such a possibility.

Ayan-Dar looked at the high priestess, whom he had known and cherished for a very long time. "If she is of the Ka'i-Nur, as I suspect, do you not think her gaze will fall upon this temple soon after she conquers the lands beyond the Eastern Sea and to the south? What would happen to your precious equilibrium if one of the orders, ours, was destroyed?" He looked at the others, who had grown thoughtful at his words. It was clear such a possibility had never occurred to any of them. "In this room are the most powerful warriors of our race, here on the Homeworld or among the Settlements. This is no mere boast, for we have proven it over the ages in every battle and war in which we have fought.

"But our numbers are few, far fewer than the other orders." He paused. "Were an army of millions, armed like the warriors we fought at Ka'i-Nur, to march upon this temple, could we prevail against them?"

Turning back to T'ier-Kunai, he knelt and rendered a salute. "I have spoken my heart and mind, high priestess of the Desh-Ka. I thank you for your indulgence."

Then he stood and calmly strode out of the chamber.

***

Leaning against the ancient stone rail that ran around the circumference of the massive dais of the *Kal'ai-Il*, Ayan-Dar looked to the southeast, in the direction of Keel-A'ar. Above, the great moon glowed, its light softly illuminating the buildings of the temple that sprawled across the plateau.

He glanced up at the shining orb, wondering at the beauty of something that had been so utterly savaged. The moon had been inhabited long ago, before the last great war that brought the Second Age to a close and very nearly destroyed their race. All who had lived upon the great moon had perished, victims of the terrible vengeance their enemies on the Homeworld had wrought after the moon dwellers had used enormous projectiles as kinetic weapons. In a final orgy of destruction, the armies of the Homeworld reduced the surface of the moon to little more than ash, and it had never been resettled in all the millennia that had since passed.

As he turned his eyes back to the world on which he stood, he had a clear view to a vast distance, and could see the lights of the cities and towns that dotted the landscape in the darkness. There dwelled those who toiled as porters of water, or seamstresses, armorers, builders, and the many other castes. But precious few warriors were there now to safeguard them and their offspring. Those who were born to the sword were now dying in droves in the current great war.

More troubling was that something was wrong, deeply wrong, in the east, beyond his growing concerns about the Dark Queen. He could sometimes sense a voice in his blood, a spiritual song that weakened day by day, that was nothing now but agony and desperate honor. And fear. Gut-wrenching, never-ending fear. The blood from which the song sprang was unfamiliar to him, and he very much would have liked to investigate.

He scraped his talons over the ancient stone in frustration, for he could not interfere in whatever was happening. He dared not even cast out his second sight to try and find the one whose song cried out, for he was already well beyond any reasonable measure of tolerance T'ier-Kunai need show toward him. Indeed, she was in danger of dishonoring herself by not punishing him, and that would have been a shame that he simply could not bear.

He sensed T'ier-Kunai approaching. "Should I shackle myself to the *Kal'ai-Il*, high priestess? If you punish me now, then perhaps I will earn myself the privilege of another foolish adventure."

"Do not speak such words to me." She came to stand beside him, folding an armored hand over his. "You know that would break my heart, you old fool."

"I do not mean to bring grief upon you, T'ier-Kunai. I trust you realize that."

"Of course I do. But you put me in a difficult position." She squeezed his hand. "I am at my limit, Ayan-Dar. I can tolerate no more of this, not before the peers."

"I know, my priestess. And I thank you for your tolerance." He glanced at her face. In his eyes, her beauty matched her powers and skills as a warrior. Had he been younger, much younger, he would have sought her as a consort. He pushed the thought aside. He was far too old for such things now. "I take it there will be no conclave."

"No, there will not. But I did command the keeper to consult with his peers in the other orders, even those among the Settlements, for any more insights into the prophecies of Anuir-Ruhal'te."

Ayan-Dar grinned, his fangs glittering in the moonlight. "So, you believe me at least that much."

"If I did not believe you, I never would have allowed you to even go to Keel-A'ar, let alone to the fortress of the Ka'i-Nur."

She turned to face him. "You must understand that it matters not whether I believe you, but that I am high priestess of this order. You are telling the peers that the very foundation upon which our civilization is built may crumble beneath their feet, all because of a child foretold in a prophecy by an oracle who passed from history ages ago." She shook her head. "You ask them — you ask me — to step out into an abyss, offering nothing but uncertainty and yet another prophecy that tells of ages-long suffering and doom."

"I wish I had more, my priestess. I would give my remaining arm and eye — my very life! — to have more to tell, more proof that I could offer the peers. But I fear that the proof, when it finally comes, will lead to our undoing if we are not prepared to deal with it."

"What would you have me do?"

Ayan-Dar growled, a sign of frustration and resignation, an evil brew of emotions in a warrior such as he. "I would have you request that Kunan-Lohr and Ulana-Tath let us raise the child in our creche, that we may ensure her safety, and see what comes to pass as she grows. And I would deal with the Dark Queen before the greatest of her designs, whatever foul things they may be, came to fruition."

"And I would take the eyestones from a *genoth* with nothing more than my teeth." They both chortled at such an absurdity. After a moment, her voice serious, she went on, "You know that I can grant neither of those things. And I forbid you to leave the temple for the next moon cycle. Neither your body nor your mind. Spend some time sharing your wisdom with the acolytes, as priests are supposed to do." She huffed with amusement. "Consider that as your punishment."

Ayan-Dar glanced at the looming shackles that hung from the arch of the *Kal'ai-Il* behind him. "I would rather be whipped and set free to do mischief, but I will do as you command, high priestess of the Desh-Ka."

CHAPTER TEN

Kunan-Lohr stood at the edge of the trees that ringed the camp where he had decided they would spend the night. He was weary of the long journey, and silently wished he possessed the powers of the Desh-Ka priesthood that allowed them to magically whisk themselves from one place to another. Or some of the technology that had long been known to his kind, but was thought dishonorable to use beyond things such as wheeled carts.

All I ask is a simple vehicle to convey me from one place to another without jarring loose my insides. He snorted in disgust, both at the strictures of the Way and his own mind in wishing for such creature comforts. It was not becoming of a warrior.

He looked to the east, and his thoughts turned grim. Against the emotional tumult of the Dark Queen's conquest, he could feel some nameless fear approaching closer with each passing day. Except for those closest to him in heart or blood, he did not have the clarity to sense a particular individual from the many millions of voices that sang among those born of the same bloodline. But he could not shake the sense that the one who approached did so with purpose, that he or she was seeking him out. It was a dark companion to the dread he had felt since he and Ulana-Tath had left their daughter behind in Keel-A'ar.

Then there was the tumult in the spiritual voices some days ago, when a handful of incredibly powerful spirits surged above even the emotional tides from the eastern war. Kunan-

Lohr and the others of his party had never before sensed such raw power, and he instinctively knew that priests of the Desh-Ka must have been involved. He was thankful he had not been any closer, for the intensity of rage and bloodlust had nearly incapacitated him and the others for a time.

It was an ill omen, as Ulana-Tath had whispered when they had all regained their wits.

"What beauty do you see in the night that takes you from your consort, great master of Keel-A'ar?"

Ulana-Tath had come to stand beside him, taking his arm in hers. Beyond the thoughts which troubled him, it was a beautiful night, with the stars shining bright and the great moon just rising above the horizon. Behind them, the fire of their camp blazed, and the rest of his party of fifteen warriors sat around it, eating and drinking ale. All save the four sentries, who stood watch at a distance where the fire, noise, and smoke would not hinder their ability to sense anyone approaching the camp.

"There is no beauty in the night or day that could long part me from you." He pulled her close, wrapping his arm around her shoulder. They had both removed their armor earlier, and now wore only their warm black undergarments. The warmth of her body against his felt good, helping to ward off the slight chill of the night. But even her presence beside him failed to dispel the sense of impending doom that gripped his heart.

"I feel it, too," Ulana-Tath whispered. "Something dark approaches. It is close now, very close."

Kunan-Lohr nodded. Ulana-Tath had a better perception of the emotional songs in her heart than did he.

She rested her head against his shoulder. "And I fear for Keel-Tath, my love."

"Anin-Khan will protect her." It was not an empty reassurance. Kunan-Lohr, too, was worried, but not for the immediate physical safety of his daughter. His concern reached ahead in the cycles to come, when Keel-Tath would have to make her way in the world, clearly standing out as unique among a race that was based on similarity and continuity. "Every warrior in the city and the non-warrior castes would stand to defend her, and the city is safe from anything but an assault by an army of legions." He paused. "I suspect the Desh-Ka priest may be keeping watch, as well."

"Even if he is, you know he cannot interfere. They have such powers, like the gods of old." She shook her head with sadness. "But they keep to themselves in their temple, immune and uncaring toward the fate of the world except when the Settlements come to call, or we carry war to the stars."

"Perhaps it is for the best." Kunan-Lohr held her closer and lowered his voice. "I do not wish to imagine the powers of the ancient orders in the hands of one such as the Dark Queen."

Before Ulana-Tath could respond, they heard a signal from the sentry posted to watch over the main road.

Someone was approaching.

* * *

Nil'a-Litan had lost count of how long she had traveled since leaving the queen's encampment on her mission to warn her master of the plot to kill his daughter. She had ridden day and night, stopping only long enough to acquire fresh animals and force herself to eat, using her master's Sign of Authority to get whatever she needed before moving on. The only sleep she had allowed herself had been in the saddle, binding her thighs to one of the cinch straps that ran under her mount's belly before she slumped over the *magthep's* shoulders. The beast always slowed to a leisurely walk when she passed out, but kept moving westward on the road. Toward Nil'a-Litan's master.

While healers had treated her injured shoulder, the healing gel they applied could not perform miracles while she was in motion, flexing the wound. The pain was agonizing, the ends of the severed bones grinding, and the slashed muscles were unable to mend. But she would accept nothing that would kill the pain, for that would dull her senses or force her to sleep. The last healer had simply looked at the wound and shaken her head, unwilling to apply more of the precious gel. That, more than any mere words, told Nil'a-Litan all she needed to know.

She was dying.

Death was something she would embrace with joy when the time came, but not before she warned her master. She could feel a spreading numbness in her legs, and beyond the fiery pain in her shoulder, the arm on that side was nothing more then a rod of useless and dying flesh. The skin had changed from its normal brilliant cobalt blue to black, the color of the mourning marks that now flowed down her cheeks from her eyes.

As fast as she was moving, it was barely fast enough. Three times had she caught sight of the riders the queen had sent, a rapidly moving column weaving through the ever-present traffic on the great road that was the main link between the eastern and western parts of T'lar-Gol. There were other roads, but this was the most direct path leading home to Keel-A'ar, and would be the road her master would be on, heading toward her. She could not let the queen's riders catch her, she could not let them pass. Otherwise her suffering would have been for nothing, and her master would be caught unaware.

She had focused on the melodies that ran through her blood, trying to filter out the millions of voices that held no interest for her, trying to find the only one that now mattered. It was not an act born of special training or gifts, but an act of desperate will. Her entire life, every moment that she had lived, everything she had learned, was now focused on finding Kunan-Lohr.

And she had. It was a thin filament to which she now clung, but it grew stronger with every passing hour as the *magthep* she rode ran westward. The more she focused on her master, on the song of his blood, the easier it became to hear. Its strength reassured her. Kunan-Lohr had been a noble master, and dying in his service would be a great honor.

But not before she spoke the words he so needed to hear.

It was night now, and she guided the *magthep* along the edge of the road. Her side was wet where blood seeped from the wound that the healing gel could not bind. All color had been sapped from her vision, and at night, as now, she was nearly blind. She knew she had little time left. She hoped it would be enough, for she knew that her master was very close.

Guided by the song of Kunan-Lohr's soul, she steered her mount away from the road in the direction of a small rise that she could just make out against the background of stars.

* * *

Kunan-Lohr did not have to summon his warriors to arms. In three breaths after the sentry's signal, all of them, weapons at the ready, had disappeared into the trees on the side of the encampment that faced the road. He and Ulana-Tath drew their swords as they watched several shapes approach in the darkness, quickly moving up the slope from the road.

"Riders from the east," Ulana-Tath said softly.

"No, only one. The others are spare mounts." Kunan-Lohr stepped forward as realization began to dawn that this was the bearer of the gnawing fear he had been feeling.

The other warriors gathered around him as the *magthep* bearing the mysterious rider came to a wheezing halt before him.

"My...lord." The warrior spoke only those words before she began to fall from the saddle.

Kunan-Lohr caught her in his arms, wincing at the sight of the ghastly wound in her shoulder, and the equally ghastly smell. He recognized her now as Nil'a-Litan, a very young warrior who had been serving under Eil'an-Kuhr in the east.

"To the fire, quickly!" Ulana-Tath led him to the center of the camp, and her consort carefully set the young warrior on his bed of hides near the fire.

While warriors were not healers, they were well acquainted with what could happen if wounds were not treated in time.

"We must get her to a healer," Kunan-Lohr said as he and Ulana-Tath carefully removed her armor. He winced at the sight of the infected and necrotic flesh of her shoulder, arm, and upper chest.

"She has already been." Ulana-Tath pointed to the unmistakable swirling mass of color that was a patch of healing gel, deep inside the wound. She took a bag of water and carefully drizzled some between the warrior's parched lips.

"My lord," Nil'a-Litan spoke again, pushing the water away as she reached for Kunan-Lohr with her good hand.

He took it, squeezing it gently. "I am here, Nil'a-Litan. Do not speak. Save your strength. We will find a healer from the road..."

Her grip, which was very weak, clamped down on his hand. In halting words, she told him, "No...time. The Dark Queen has sent riders, thirty of them, to Keel-A'ar. They are to kill your child and the others in the creche."

Kunan-Lohr and Ulana-Tath looked at one another, nearly identical expressions of disbelief on their faces.

"Child, you are very ill," Kunan-Lohr told her. "The Dark Queen is not without fault, perhaps, but she would never do such a thing."

"I overheard her very words, my lord!" Nil'a-Litan was suddenly overcome with a coughing fit, and a froth of blood streamed from her mouth. She let go of Kunan-Lohr's hand and reached down to pull something from her belt. "My captain, Eil'an-Kuhr, gave me your Sign of Authority to speed me on my way here."

"No." Ulana-Tath whispered the word that was echoing in Kunan-Lohr's brain. "Even Syr-Nagath would not contemplate such a terrible deed."

Kunan-Lohr tightened his grip around the metal rod that bore his name, inscribed in runes, along its length. He wished it was Syr-Nagath's neck. "I fear you are wrong, my love. Eil'an-Kuhr would never have surrendered this to anyone unless it was the most dire of circumstances." Turning back to Nil'a-Litan, he asked, "What of our warriors in the east?"

"The Dark Queen bleeds us, my lord. Eil'an-Kuhr said as much. Since you left us, our warriors have been used as fodder, nothing more. But Eil'an-Kuhr said she would not lead a rebellion while the honor of Keel-A'ar was pledged to the Dark Queen." She took his arm, the tips of her talons sinking into his flesh through the thin black undergarment. "My lord...you must ride home. Now. The queen's riders are perhaps only hours behind me, maybe less. Eil'an-Kuhr dispatched more to follow them...but they are too few to stop those who come to harm your child."

Another coughing fit took hold of her, but this time she could not stop. Bright arterial blood suddenly gushed from her nose and mouth.

In but a few seconds, it was over. Nil'a-Litan's body relaxed, and her hand fell away from his arm. Her sightless eyes now stared up at the stars.

"May thy Way be long and glorious, my child," Kunan-Lohr whispered as he gently closed her eyes with a brush of his fingers.

"What are we to do, my lord?" Ulana-Tath's words were spoken as his First and a senior warrior, not his consort. "Could we not set an ambush for the queen's riders?" Her eyes were ablaze with fear and rage.

The other warriors had formed a circle around them, kneeling in respect for Nil'a-Litan's passing as they waited for Kunan-Lohr's orders.

He stared at the dead warrior's face for a moment, trying to imagine the agony and suffering she had endured to bring him this warning. Then he thought of the Dark Queen, and his blood began to burn.

"If we had time, perhaps," he said. "But there is nothing but open road here, and so many groups of warriors travel upon the road that it might be difficult to make them out. We cannot take such a chance." Looking up at Ulana-Tath, he handed her the Sign of Authority. "You are to take ten warriors and return home to warn Anin-Khan and safeguard the creche. Go now and prepare, for you will leave at once."

Her expression hardening, she did not question him, but saluted and stood, choosing the warriors she would take with her.

From those who remained, Kunan-Lohr chose the two most junior warriors. "I would not leave Nil'a-Litan's body here to feed the beasts of the forest. She died with great honor, and deserves a warrior's funeral. When you have seen to her last rites, you shall ride as fast as you can for home."

"We shall build a pyre for her that will be seen from Keel-A'ar, my lord," the elder of the two said. They both saluted, then immediately disappeared into the darkness to gather wood for the pyre.

"As for you three," he turned to the warriors who remained, "you shall ride with me. We shall head east as fast as we can." He looked down at the Nil'a-Litan's body. "My captains there do not have the authority to break a covenant of honor with the Dark Queen." He bared his fangs in anger. "But I do."

* * *

"She will not let you live." Ulana-Tath's words cut through his soul, for he could not deny that they were true.

"I have no doubt that will be her plan once I announce my intentions," Kunan-Lohr told her as they both quickly donned their armor and weapons, "but I do not intend to succumb like a witless steppe-beast." He caught her eye. "Nor do I intend to face her in the arena." Both of them knew that to do so would be nothing less than suicide, although it was a path he would gladly take if it was the way of greatest honor for the people of his city. "An army is bound to me, and I would not have them beholden to that evil creature, even if we have to fight the other legions."

"But that is exactly what may happen." She could picture it in her mind, Kunan-Lohr and the other warriors under the banner of Keel-A'ar, encircled and crushed by the Dark Queen's hordes.

"Do not worry about me, my love," he told her. "Your concern is by far the greater one, the safety of our daughter."

"If there are only thirty riders, they cannot hope to get past the gates once Anin-Khan has been warned."

Kunan-Lohr frowned as he finished strapping on his chest armor. "Do not underestimate her, my love. As on the field of battle, she moves some pieces in the open for the enemy to see, and moves others they cannot. What she lacks in honor, she makes up in vicious guile. Do not forget that she wears the eyestones of a *genoth* that she killed with her own hand, a feat that few warriors beyond the priesthood may claim. There may be more to this plot than we know, or that Nil'a-Litan overheard." He took her by the shoulders. "Keep this in your mind: if something goes wrong, take Keel-Tath to the Desh-Ka."

"But they will not involve themselves with affairs beyond the temple!"

He nodded. "Exactly so. That is why I said for you to take her to them, to the temple, if you must. The Desh-Ka will be obligated to take her in, and I believe that Ayan-Dar would see to her safety."

Holding her close, he kissed her. "My heart is forever yours, my love."

"And mine, yours." She caressed his cheek, then pulled away. There was no more time.

"Ride now, my love," he told her, "as fast as you can. And do not look back."

CHAPTER ELEVEN

Ria-Ka'luhr, acolyte of the Desh-Ka and slave to Syr-Nagath, had been well on his way back to the temple when he found himself changing direction, heading back toward the great road that he had only recently left behind.

With every day that had passed since Syr-Nagath had taken him, he felt more like a helpless vessel that was being filled with the vile queen's poison, and perhaps that was not so far from the truth. He could see himself, as from afar, as his body and mind seemed to act on their own, according to her will.

His mind was flooded with the vision of a child, a mere infant, in a creche. But this child was different from any he, or any of his kind, had ever seen, for her hair was white and her talons were the color of crimson. The vision was so powerful that he wondered for a moment if he was not actually standing before her. It was the first pleasant sensation he had experienced since becoming Syr-Nagath's slave, and he seized upon it.

It was a beautiful moment, right up until he saw a dagger, held in his own hand, slit the child's tender young throat. He could feel the muscles of his arm going through the motion of the strike, feel the handle of the dagger in his hand, and the warm spray of blood on his face.

He wanted nothing more in the universe than to take that same dagger, the one now sheathed at his side, and plunge it through his heart. But he could no more do that than he could will his hands to keep the *magthep* heading for the temple, where there was some small chance the priesthood might be able to save him. Or at least stop him.

The part of his mind, his soul, that remained to him screamed in helpless rage as he cut loose the pack animals. Kicking his mount's sides, the *magthep* carried him at a full run back to the great road.

Toward Keel-A'ar.

* * *

Riding as fast as they could, Ulana-Tath and her ten escorts fled westward along the great road, desperate to keep ahead of the queen's riders. She was merciless on her warriors, the poor beasts they rode literally to death, and her own body. If the focus of Nil'a-Litan in her last days had been on finding Kunan-Lohr, Ulana-Tath was no less focused on reaching her daughter in time. None of them had slept and they had only had enough to eat and drink to survive when they changed mounts. Even for battle-hardened warriors, it was a grueling test of will, and Ulana-Tath marveled at the strength of young Nil'a-Litan, who had ridden so hard and long, injured and alone.

Your death shall not be in vain, my child, she told herself. *And you shall be remembered with the greatest honor in the Books of Time.*

As they stopped at cities and villages for fresh mounts, they sought to take as many as they could. She did this both to keep moving as quickly as possible, and to deny the queen's riders replacements for their own exhausted *magtheps*. She suspected the gambit may have been partly successful, because in a fleeting glimpse of their pursuers two days out from Keel-A'ar, Ulana-Tath saw that only twenty-five remained.

Her party had maintained their lead until the night before Ulana-Tath and her escorts were to reach Keel-A'ar, when the queen's riders had somehow closed the gap. She suspected they had taken a very dangerous shortcut through the deep forest east of the city, where they had lost another handful of riders.

Now, as the first rays of the sun broke above the trees, she saw that the enemy riders were right behind her.

Above the thundering of the *magtheps'* feet and their labored breathing, she heard the distinctive whirr of a *shrekka* through the air. One of her escorts cried out in pain, falling from her saddle to be trampled by their pursuers.

"My mistress!" Her First, an older warrior she had known for many cycles, cried out. "Ride on! We will hold them here!"

Before Ulana-Tath could say a word, he and her other protectors wheeled about, letting loose an ear-splitting war cry. The air was filled with *shrekkas* and the ring of sword against sword as the two groups of riders crashed together. The *magtheps*, normally docile and humble beasts, snarled and leaped at the commands of their riders. They tried to disembowel one another with their talons, and snapped at opposing riders and beasts alike with their flat grinding teeth.

Ulana-Tath could not help but pause a moment, just long enough to see the other warriors of Keel-A'ar who had been following the queen's riders thunder along the road to join the fray. She was nearly overcome with bloodlust, desperately wanting to charge into the mayhem, her sword singing through the air to bleed those who had come to kill her child.

Keel-Tath. Her child's name echoed in her mind, focusing her attention. She turned her *magthep* and kicked its sides, urging it to run for home.

While her First and the others had bought her a few precious moments, they were still badly outnumbered. Despite their heroic efforts, five of the queen's riders freed themselves from the vicious melee and followed after her.

* * *

With a final turn along the road, the *magthep* panting beneath her, Ulana-Tath saw Keel-A'ar, bathed in the glow of the morning sun against the magenta sky. She was so exhausted now, but the sight gave her a final breath of energy. Home, and safety for her child, was so close, now.

"Faster!" She smacked the beast's rump with the flat of her sword blade. Glancing behind her, she saw that the riders pursuing her were only a few lengths behind.

A glint caught her attention, and she jerked to one side as a *shrekka* whirred past her shoulder. Another passed over her head just before her *magthep* squealed in pain and stumbled, a *shrekka* having sliced through a tendon in one of its powerful legs.

The beast slammed to the ground and rolled. It would have crushed her, but warriors were trained for such things. Ulana-Tath leaped from the saddle, vaulting over the *magthep's* head as it went down. She rolled twice as she landed and came to her feet, one of her own *shrekkas* in hand. She hurled it at the nearest rider, the whirling blades slicing through his leg. With a cry of pain, he fell from his saddle to slam into the ground.

Another rider cast his *shrekka* at her, and she batted it aside with her sword.

"Anin-Khan," she prayed, "see me. Please, see me!" The sentries at the wall would be able to see that someone was out here, engaged in combat, but it was a long way for them to ride, even if they sortied now. She would have to hold off the enemy on her own.

One of the enemy warriors charged his *magthep* at her. She dodged out of the way as the beast leaped, trying to strike her with the talons on its feet. She slashed at the animal's side, and with a shriek of pain it staggered and fell to the ground. The rider dismounted, whirling to face her, before he could be pinned by the *magthep's* bulk.

The other three warriors dismounted, quickly surrounding her.

"You are lower than the honorless ones," she spat as they moved in. She took a *shrekka* in her free hand. "As outcasts, at least they have a reason for living like carrion eaters. Your souls will rot in eternal darkness!"

They did not answer in words, but she could feel their shame, their fear.

"Cowards!" She lunged with her sword toward the nearest warrior, making a feint. As he raised his sword to parry her strike, she whirled and threw a *shrekka* at the warrior behind her. The weapon tore through the armor of his shoulder, and he gasped from the pain. But it was not a killing blow.

Ulana-Tath had no hope now that she would survive. While she was a warrior of superior skill, the Dark Queen clearly had not sent neophytes to do her bidding. She could have taken one or two, but not all of them at once.

That the situation was hopeless did not mean she would surrender to have her throat cut along with that of her child. With a howling cry, she charged the queen's riders, her sword reflecting the rays of the morning sun as she attacked.

For a time, she drove them back with sheer ferocity. She drew blood from two of them before a third stabbed her in the back. The blade of his sword pierced the flesh of her hip and ground against the bone.

With a sharp cry, she gripped the blade in the talons of her free hand and turned, pulling free, just as one of the other warriors struck low, slicing deep into the muscle of her thigh. She realized they were not trying for a single killing stroke. They only sought to weaken her until she could no longer defend herself. Then she, and her daughter soon thereafter, would die.

"No!" Her cry was not one of physical pain, but of anguish at the knowledge that she had failed her daughter, her precious child.

She held her sword, raised in defiance, as the queen's riders moved in for the kill.

Such was her surprise when the head of one of them fell from his shoulders to land at his feet after a *shrekka* passed through his neck. A look of shock was frozen on his face as the body, blood pumping from the stump between the shoulders, collapsed on top of the severed head.

The other three warriors of the queen looked up in time to see an unknown warrior dashing toward them astride a *magthep*, a black cape billowing behind him. Two *shrekkas* flew from his hand in a blur. A warrior knocked one of the weapons from the air with his sword. The second *shrekka* slashed through another warrior's breastplate, opening up his chest as if he had been cleaved with an axe.

The two surviving warriors moved toward the newcomer, swords at the ready. They had dismissed Ulana-Tath as a threat, which proved unwise. As they stepped past her, she lashed out with her sword, amputating the leg of one, just below the knee. With a quick reverse, she stabbed her blade deep into the thigh of the other.

The screams of both warriors were quickly silenced by the newcomer, who made an impossible leap from the charging *magthep*, somersaulting in the air. Still airborne, he took the head from one warrior with a lightning swift stroke of his sword before stabbing the other through the heart, the tip of the blade's living metal easily penetrating the breastplate. Then his feet came to rest lightly upon the ground.

Ulana-Tath had never seen such a thing.

Pulling the blade free from the second warrior in a smooth motion, the newcomer stood for a moment before Ulana-Tath, blood dripping from the tip of his sword.

Looking at him, she could see the outline of the rune of the Desh-Ka against the black of his breastplate, and he wore a black metal collar with gold trim. He was obviously Desh-Ka, but the outlined rune and lack of a sigil on the collar at his throat told her he was an acolyte, and not yet a priest.

For a moment, he stared at her with an unreadable expression, his hand tight upon the handle of his sword, and she feared that he had come to finish what the queen's riders had begun.

He turned at the sound of approaching riders, and three warriors rounded the turn behind them, their *magtheps* at a full run.

The acolyte tensed before she shouted, "No, wait! They are with me!" It was her First and two of the others. They were all who had survived the brief but brutal encounter with the other warriors sent by the queen.

The acolyte blinked, as if snapping out of a trance, and his expression changed to one of deep concern. Flicking the blood from the blade, he sheathed his sword and knelt by her side as the three warriors rode toward them.

"I would thank you, acolyte of the Desh-Ka," Ulana-Tath said as she lowered her sword, "if I but knew your name." Unlike the priests, the acolytes did not have their names inscribed in pendants below their collars.

"I am Ria-Ka'luhr," he told her. A brief agonized expression passed over his face. Then it was gone. "And I would ask that you never thank me for this, mistress of Keel-A'ar."

* * *

After binding her wounds and tending to the three other warriors, Ria-Ka'luhr helped Ulana-Tath into the saddle of his mount, then nimbly sprang up to sit behind her.

"How did you come upon us?" She gratefully leaned back against him, overcome now with exhaustion and relief. In the distance, she could see the dark forms of warriors on the way from Keel-A'ar. Anin-Khan, captain of the guard, had wasted no time in sending a relief party.

Ria-Ka'luhr was silent for a moment. "I was not far from here, returning to the temple from a long quest, when I sensed that you were in peril." It was the truth, in part. What he did not tell her was that he had not only sensed her spiritual song, but had been overcome with another powerful vision, no doubt the will of the Dark Queen. The vision showed him plunging his sword into her chest. But it was not time. Not yet.

"I thought that members of the priesthood were not to become involved in affairs beyond the temple."

He bared in his fangs in humor. "I am not yet a priest, my mistress. No doubt the elders will look upon my act as one of foolish intransigence, but such can easily be overlooked when the idiocy of youth is taken into consideration." After a pause, he went on, "Those warriors were clearly not acting honorably, and I could not bring myself to stay my hand."

"My thanks to you, Ria-Ka'luhr. You will always be welcome in the city of Keel-A'ar."

The part of him that was still his silently cried, *You will not think that for much longer, my mistress.*

"Ulana-Tath!" Anin-Khan, leading two tens of warriors from the city, called to her as he reined his mount alongside her. The swords and *shrekkas* of his warriors were at the ready, and they looked at Ria-Ka'luhr with undisguised suspicion.

"Sheath your weapons," she commanded them, and they did so instantly. "I owe him my life."

Anin-Khan lowered his head, and she could sense the shame that filled his heart. "We rode as soon as we saw you, my mistress, but we could not..."

"Do not trouble your heart, captain of the guard." She reached over to grip his arm. "Never have I been so relieved as I was to see you riding toward me."

Anin-Khan grunted, casting an eye at the Desh-Ka acolyte. "I thank you, acolyte of the Desh-Ka, for protecting my mistress."

Ria-Ka'luhr only bowed his head in acknowledgement.

"If I may ask, mistress, why have you returned home? And where is our master, Kunan-Lohr?"

"The Dark Queen has betrayed us," she told Anin-Khan in a voice that trembled with rage. "She sent those riders to kill my daughter, to slaughter all the children of our creche."

"But why?" Anin-Khan could not hide his shock, and the other warriors that formed a protective ring around their mistress gaped in astonishment. "Why would anyone, let alone the queen, do such a thing?"

"We do not know. But we must protect our children. She will know those riders failed, and she will send more, legions, if she must." She thought of Kunan-Lohr, who must soon be reaching the queen's encampment in the east. She could sense him, feel his pride, his anger. His love. "Our master rides to break the covenant of honor with the queen. But she will not let him simply depart with our legions, or whatever may be left of them after she has bled them against the enemy."

The older warrior was silent for a moment, wondering at the fate that awaited his master. "I should die at his side."

"If you are to die, Anin-Khan, let it be defending our city and our children. Kunan-Lohr entrusted you with protecting that which we all hold most dear. You will honor him far more by protecting Keel-A'ar than falling at his side in a glorious but hopeless battle."

"As always, mistress, you speak the truth. Forgive me."

"There is nothing to forgive, my captain," she told him as they passed through the gate to the city, the sunlight glinting from the warriors arrayed on the battlements above. "Just keep our children safe."

Behind her, Ria-Ka'luhr said nothing.

CHAPTER TWELVE

Kunan-Lohr had always taken great risks in battle, for without great risk, there could be no great victory. Yet every battle he had fought, be it his blade against another's in ritual combat or leading his city's legions, had been well-considered, the risks weighed and balanced against what could be lost and what could be gained. Honor, of course, had always been the common and most important factor.

This time, he knew, things would be different. While breaking a covenant of honor was not unheard of, it was very rare. The reason was simple: few had been the times when one in authority had acted with such dishonor that his or her vassals were so aggrieved that they considered breaking the covenant that bound them. The sense of honor that drove them was trained into them from early childhood by the priests and priestesses of the *kazhas*. Those who acted with dishonor were ostracized from society at best, and, at worst, had their hair shaved, dooming them to eternal spiritual darkness.

That was the fate that he would have wished upon the Dark Queen for her outrageous plot against his child. Yet, he knew that would not come to pass, at least by his hand.

The three legions he had led from Keel-A'ar had been bled dearly, for he could sense many missing voices in the song that echoed in his blood. The challenge that lay before him was to extract the survivors from among the other legions that remained loyal to the queen. He hoped that eventually, when word of her deed came to light, they would turn upon her, but that would not help him now.

He had a plan that he hoped would work, but the first obstacle was getting word to Eil'an-Kuhr at the queen's encampment, telling her that he was breaking the covenant of honor with the queen. Even though he had given his Sign of Authority to Ulana-Tath, according to tradition, any object readily associated with its owner would do. He held his dagger, which had a wicked curved blade and had a handle made from a polished *genoth* bone. It had been handed down through his paternal side for over twenty generations. He had never known his father, for he had died shortly after Kunan-Lohr had been born. The heirloom had been left with the wardresses of his creche, who had given it to the priest of the *kazha* near the city. The priest there had presented it to Kunan-Lohr when he had survived his seventh and final Challenge.

"Take this." He held the dagger out to Dara-Kol, the eldest of the three young warriors who had come with him. Like her two companions, she was draped in the dark blue robes of the builder caste. They had no choice but to leave behind their armor, for its shape would have given away the disguise. They still carried their weapons, tied close to their bodies under the loose robes. "Eil'an-Kuhr will accept this as a Sign of Authority and act on the instructions I have given you."

Dara-Kol nodded in understanding as she accepted the dagger, bowing her head. "Yes, Lord."

Kunan-Lohr nodded, then sat back to consider their situation. They were in a small village near the front, hidden in the abandoned remains of an old storehouse. It had been no small feat to come this close to the front, near enough that they could hear the riot of battle in the distance. There were many warriors along the roads, but not all of them moving to or from the battle. Some were clearly posted as sentinels, screening the warriors who passed toward the battlefield.

No doubt, he thought, they were looking for him. He had to give Syr-Nagath credit: she was not one to take chances. In case her riders failed to kill him, she hoped to snare him as he returned to the front, ignorant of her treachery.

The sheer size of her army had worked in their favor. There were now half a million warriors stretched north and south from her encampment, with thousands more arriving every day. And this was only a fraction of the total strength bound to her. Millions more were spread across the face of T'lar-Gol, awaiting her call.

Finding one warrior among such a number, even one as distinguished as Kunan-Lohr, was not an easy task, particularly when such a warrior did not wish to be found.

But this village was as far as he dared go. For beyond this place would be enough warriors honor-bound to the queen who would recognize him no matter how he tried to disguise himself. He knew that some of them already sensed his presence, but their abilities were not so attuned that they could tell exactly where he was. If they had, his gambit would have already failed.

The three warriors with him were all young, and not likely to be recognized as coming from Keel-A'ar. But they could not simply march into the encampment and straight to Eil'an-Kuhr without risk of being caught. That, they could not afford. The stakes were far too high.

He had been stumped on how to get his messengers past the queen's guards until Dara-Kol had made a radical suggestion. "Could we not dress in robes as one of the non-warrior castes and simply walk in?"

Kunan-Lohr had looked at her with frustration. It was such a ridiculous idea. He was just opening his mouth to gently chide her when he realized that her suggestion was, in fact, an elegant solution. "I believe, child, that your suggestion has some merit." He smiled. "Should we survive this, you will be Anin-Khan's subaltern."

"Yes, my lord!" The young warrior bowed her head and saluted, and he could sense her bursting with pride.

He gave her a toothy grin. "Do not thank me. He is a fierce taskmaster, entirely unlike myself."

The three young warriors allowed themselves a brief moment of mirth before he went on. "Then let it be so. There are many stocks of clothing to be found in an encampment as large as this has become. Fetch what you require and return."

That had been last night, and the three had ventured out into a torrential storm. They had returned in the early morning with the dark blue robes of builders.

"Why did you choose the robes of builders?" Kunan-Lohr could not mask his concern as he fingered the fabric they had produced from a satchel, along with several thick cuts of meat and leather bags containing ale. He was worried because builders were almost never seen near a battle unless it was a city under siege, where they worked closely with the warriors to build and repair defensive works.

"My lord, the roads are filled with them!" Dara-Kol's exclamation was muffled by the meat that filled her mouth. It had been two days since any of them had eaten. They had pilfered the food from unobservant warriors, but would not eat any before they had served it to Kunan-Lohr. "We heard that many were already here, and hundreds more arrived this night alone. Hundreds, perhaps thousands more are coming."

Kunan-Lohr stared at them, unable to believe what he was hearing.

"We saw them, my lord." The middle of the three, a strong young male who favored the spear as his principle weapon, gestured emphatically. "We made no mistake." He glanced at Dara-Kol. "But the ones we saw were…"

"Different." Dara-Kol finished the sentence for him. "We saw some of them in the light of the fires where food was being prepared. Their faces were strange in a way I have never seen."

"None of us have seen such." The third warrior, another young male, shook his head. "It is difficult to describe, my lord. But I think they looked like the images of the ancient ones, before the end of the Second Age, that the keepers of the Books of Time from the Desh-Ka temple once showed us."

The others nodded in agreement as they cut strips of meat with their talons and hungrily shoved them in their mouths.

Kunan-Lohr sat back, the raw meat in his hand forgotten. "Are you sure?"

"That they were different, yes, my lord," Dara-Kol answered. "The other builders did not seem to wish to have anything to do with them. And the warriors seemed to be afraid of them."

"They were terrified," the spear carrier corrected. "The warriors watched these builders with fear in their eyes. It was plain to see. But why?"

"Because they are Ka'i-Nur." The name of the ancient order sent a chill down his spine. He had never had any dealings with them himself, but had heard stories from those who had. None of them were pleasant, and the stories were so fantastic that Kunan-Lohr had never truly believed them.

The three young ones looked at him with blank expressions.

"You know of the six ancient orders, among which are the Desh-Ka," he explained. "But there has always been a seventh, the Ka'i-Nur, which is not often mentioned. They have kept to themselves for millennia in a fortress deep in the Great Wastelands."

"But why do they come here?" Dara-Kol asked.

"That, child, I would like you to find out, if you can." He leaned forward. "You must, at all costs, deliver my commands to war captain Eil'an-Kuhr." The three nodded. "And if you can, find out what you might about these builders from Ka'i-Nur and why they are here. But do not stray from the first task. Do you understand?"

"Yes, my lord." The three answered as one.

"And under no circumstances try to mix into a group of the Ka'i-Nur builders. They will know instantly you are not one of their own."

"How, my lord?" The eldest asked. "Because we do not look like them?"

"And because you are not of their bloodline. Did you sense any of them?"

All three of the young warriors shook their heads.

"Nor would they sense you, which would immediately set them on their guard and give you away. So you must find a group of builders from one of the other six bloodlines, who look as we do, and among whom you can disguise yourselves."

"It shall be as you say, my lord."

Kunan-Lohr nodded, satisfied. The four of them ate in silence. When they finished, it was time.

"You must go now." Kunan-Lohr stood up and gripped each of the three warriors in turn by the forearms. "The rain still falls, which will make it easier for you to blend in with a passing group of builders." With great pride in his voice, he added, "May thy Way be long and glorious, warriors of Keel-A'ar."

They knelt and saluted him before once again heading out into the pouring rain. Above, a flash of lightning seared the sky.

* * *

Eil'an-Kuhr stood at the rear of the great battle line. The pelting rain dripped from the ridges over her eyes as she kept close watch on the segment of the line for which Keel-A'ar was responsible. The battlefield was a quagmire of rain and blood, and the warriors fought to keep their footing as much as they fought the enemy. The rain, an unwelcome nuisance, had run under her armor, giving her a chill as it flushed out the blood from the minor wounds she had suffered so far this day. She would eventually seek to be treated by a healer, but that could wait.

She had been fighting for hours throughout the morning since the day's battle had begun. She normally fought in the line, but the opposing warriors had redoubled their attacks against her sector. She had been forced to form a reserve, and led them to plug breaches in the line where the enemy threatened to break through. Above the incessant fall of the rain, she could hear the roar of hundreds of thousands of voices and the ring of steel upon steel. War cries and the screams of the injured and the dying.

To her and the others of her kind, the sound was like music. To fight was what she had been born to do.

The battle now stretched up and down much of the eastern seaboard of T'lar-Gol, with neither side able to gain an advantage that was decisive enough to force the other side to accept an honorable surrender. The opposing army had gained reinforcements from the northern and southern reaches of the continent, even as the Dark Queen poured more of her own warriors into the fray. It was a battle the likes of which had not been witnessed since the last attack on the Homeworld by the Settlements.

Eil'an-Kuhr would have been thrilled and honored to be a part of it, had she not known of the Dark Queen's treachery.

And yet, there was hope. She could sense her lord and master's anger and determination, so she knew he was still alive.

Come soon, my lord, she prayed as she saw another handful of her warriors go down under the swords of the enemy. Keel-A'ar had sent three full legions, over fifteen thousand warriors, to serve the queen. While the torn and bloodied banners of all three legions still could be seen in the seething mass of the battle line, Eil'an-Kuhr knew that for every warrior who remained alive, at least two had perished. To die in battle was the most honorable end a warrior could know, but to die under the banner of the Dark Queen had become a sacrilege in Eil'an-Kuhr's eyes.

From the corner of her eye she noticed three shapes in blue robes approaching, weaving their way through the rows of wounded and exhausted warriors who covered the slope of the hill behind the battle line. She had seen other figures in blue, builders, on unknowable errands on the battlefield in the last few days, but this was the first time that any had approached her. It was nearly unheard of to have any of the non-warrior castes this close to a battle outside of a siege defense, and the sight of builders had deeply disturbed Eil'an-Kuhr. She wondered what deviltry the queen was up to now.

She turned to the three as they came closer, their hooded robes easily shedding the rain. "What business have you with the warriors of Keel-A'ar?"

The three bowed and saluted. "We bring tidings from our lord and master, Kunan-Lohr," the leader said quietly in a voice that Eil'an-Kuhr recognized. It was Dara-Kol.

Eil'an-Kuhr closed her eyes, overcome with relief. She glanced around to make sure that no warriors other than her own were nearby. "Is he near?"

"Yes, mistress," the young warrior replied, her words nearly carried away by the rain. "And this is what he commands of you..."

* * *

As the sun set, the Dark Queen reluctantly had called for an end to the day's battle. While the warriors could easily fight at night, it was longstanding tradition, even among the Ka'i-Nur, to end a battle with the setting of the sun. It was difficult to tell when that was on a day such as this when the sky was a leaden gray from the storm clouds that swirled above. In an unusual fit of compassion, she had called a halt to the fighting early. As always, she had fought in the battle line, and had to confess to herself that combat in the rain and mud was an exhausting, grueling endeavor. She was not one given to pity, but she had concluded that it could do no harm to let her warriors have a few extra hours of rest. Of course, few would get any rest on a night of pouring rain like this, when the warriors could not even light fires to warm themselves.

But she knew that her army would not have to fight much longer. Not in this accursed mud pit, at least. Syr-Nagath had been confident of winning this battle quickly and taking the remaining lands that led to the Eastern Sea. The remaining cities and kingdoms facing her could have surrendered early on with honor, but had decided to fight. And fight. And fight. They had drawn reinforcements that Syr-Nagath had not expected, forcing her to commit even more of her own warriors.

She had finally decided that it was time to bring the battle to a close on her own terms. There were too many other things to attend to.

"We will be ready as soon as the storms leave us."

Syr-Nagath turned to the blue-robed builder who stood behind her. They were in Syr-Nagath's chambers in the pavilion. The Dark Queen had known this builder from childhood. She was the senior builder mistress of Ka'i-Nur, and had answered Syr-Nagath's summons.

"You have all that you require?" Syr-Nagath asked.

The elderly builder nodded, her strangely shaped face expressionless in the shadow of her hood. "We can create what we require from the blood-soaked ground, if need be." The old builder spoke with an odd accent that few outsiders would have recognized as having its roots in Ka'i-Nur. "And such is not far from the truth."

"The other builders have not questioned you?"

The builder shook her head. "No. They fear us, as they should. We will only require them for certain...non-critical things. The important elements of the weapons will be created and controlled by us. You will have what you desire."

Syr-Nagath made a quiet huff of amusement. She desired a very great deal, far more than the old builder could possibly imagine. "How soon will the storm pass?"

"The astrologers tell me that the sun will return to us by mid-morning tomorrow. We shall be ready then, and shall be prepared for your command."

"Very well." With a nod, she dismissed the builder, who saluted and left.

Turning to her First, Syr-Nagath asked, "There is yet no sign of him?"

The First, who knelt on the floor, shook her head. "No, my queen. I have not received a single report about Kunan-Lohr." She paused, willing herself to force out the words, fearing the queen's reaction. Syr-Nagath had been greatly displeased when the First had told her that she believed the riders had failed. That they had not killed Kunan-Lohr or the child. "He has disappeared."

"He is here, somewhere." Syr-Nagath struggled to control the rage that was building within her. She was confident that the Desh-Ka acolyte could kill the child and Ulana-Tath.

But Kunan-Lohr's escape had vexed her. He would not be dealt with so easily. She would have used the same ritual on one of Kunan-Lohr's senior warriors as she had on the acolyte to gain information, to control one who could sense him. But those who were closest to him in blood were all female, and the bond would only work on the opposite sex. Torture was an option, but she doubted that any of his warriors would succumb to such primitive methods before committing ritual suicide.

"Keel-A'ar has never been mastered by a fool, and he could cause a great deal of mischief unless we find him. And quickly." Syr-Nagath flicked a hand toward the entryway, dismissing her First. "Go now, and do not return to me until he has been found."

The First bowed and saluted before fleeing from the queen's chambers.

Gazing out into the rainy gloom, the Dark Queen slowly raked the talons of one hand along her opposite forearm, drawing stripes of blood that dripped to the floor.

* * *

Eil'an-Kuhr looked out over the encampment, giving thanks to the stars she could not see that they had been graced with a storm this night. The fires that normally burned in the encampments of both armies were absent, and the warriors huddled together in silent misery as the chill rain poured down.

The three warriors who had come disguised as builders to deliver Kunan-Lohr's commands were now in ill-fitting armor that had been taken from the dead. Any armorer would have instantly known something was amiss with one glance at them, but on this night no one could see far beyond an outstretched arm.

She did not worry over much about their emotions giving away their intentions to those around them who remained loyal to the queen. There was always an abundance of misery, fear, and trepidation, particularly among the warriors of Keel-A'ar after having been so ruthlessly used by the Dark Queen.

Even for warriors who lived for battle, to know that they meant nothing to the one to whom their honor had been pledged was a difficult burden to bear. For those from Keel-A'ar, who had been blessed with a long history of masters and mistresses who honored those who served them, the Dark Queen's indifference to their sacrifice was like hot ash upon their souls.

Surrounded by her lieutenants, Eil'an-Kuhr gave her final instructions. "Remember: try to prevent anyone from raising an alarm. If you are discovered or challenged, use what force you must to guard your passage and keep your warriors moving. But our goal is to leave unheard and unseen. The wounded will fill in for us, should anyone come to our encampment."

She had arranged for all but the most grievously wounded to move in small groups from the infirmary area near the queen's pavilion to their main encampment here. Those who were not able to fight had either committed ritual suicide or been given an honorable death by Eil'an-Kuhr's hand. She would not allow them to fall to the queen and suffer dishonor.

"These three," she gestured to the three young warriors sent by Kunan-Lohr, led by Dara-Kol, "will guide us to where our master awaits once we are beyond the main encampment."

"Why do we not simply fight now, tonight?" One of her lieutenants gestured in the direction of the queen's pavilion. "The queen will send her army for us in any case."

"Because that is not what our master commands. And yes, Syr-Nagath will come for us, but they will find us on ground of our master's choosing. And tonight we cannot fight as a legion. We would simply blunder around in the darkness." In clear weather, her race had excellent night vision. But in this rain, it was impossible to see anything.

The lieutenant nodded and saluted, offering her respect.

"Let it be done." Eil'an-Kuhr saluted them all, and they returned it before turning away. They disappeared into the rain to lead their warriors out of what was now enemy territory.

Eil'an-Kuhr paused, turning to a warrior who stood beside her. He was the most senior among the wounded. His leg bore a deep gash, and while he had been treated by the healers, it would be at least another full day before he could walk on it. She handed him Kunan-Lohr's dagger, which he took with great reverence. "You and those we leave behind shall be remembered with the greatest honor in the Books of Time." She clasped the other warrior's forearms, holding tight.

"May thy Way be long and glorious, Eil'an-Kuhr." The warrior, a male who stood half a head taller than did she, was filled with pride at the honor she was bestowing upon him, and sadness that his final hours had come. They had been lovers for a full cycle, and while he would find a glorious death, both their hearts were torn. The dark rain masked the mourning marks that flowed down their cheeks.

Without another word, she let go and turned to walk away, following the shadowy forms of the other warriors who were moving quietly through the rain toward what all of them knew would be a fleeting time of freedom.

CHAPTER THIRTEEN

"So much has she grown, even in the time I was away." Ulana-Tath marveled at her daughter, who lay asleep in the crib that held several other infants, all nestled together. She leaned forward and gently ran a hand through the child's white hair, careful that her talons didn't harm Keel-Tath's tender skin. The wound in Ulana-Tath's side caused her some small discomfort as she bent over the crib, but by morning it would be healed.

"She is very beautiful, mistress." Ria-Ka'luhr stood beside Ulana-Tath, but made no attempt to touch the child. Only the wardresses, and with their permission, the parents, were allowed that honor. "But she must not stay here. Syr-Nagath will know that her first attempt on Keel-Tath's life has failed. She will send more warriors — legions, if she must — for your child. She will not relent."

Anin-Khan, who stood on the other side of Ulana-Tath, growled, his gaze flicking to the warriors, the city's finest, who stood close watch around the creche, with four of them posted, swords drawn, right around Keel-Tath's crib. "The walls of Keel-A'ar have not been breached in over a thousand cycles. They will not be breached by any army of the Dark Queen."

"I would not stand in dispute over your words, for they are spoken with great pride and as truth. Yet what you do not realize is that she is building an army the likes of which has not been seen since the last war with the Settlements, perhaps longer. What she has now is nothing, compared to what she will eventually command. T'lar-Gol will soon be hers, and the lands beyond the Eastern Sea will fall not long thereafter." Ria-Ka'luhr shook his head. "Your warriors here will not face one legion, or ten. You could just as easily face a hundred, backed up by siege engines and weapons of war drawn from the darkest pages of the Books of Time."

"Impossible!" Anin-Khan threw the young acolyte a disbelieving look. "Even if she could amass an army of builders and concentrate their power, it would take cycles for them all to learn what they needed from the keepers to build such contraptions." He waved the thought away. "Syr-Nagath will break upon the shore of the Eastern Sea as so many others have before her. Many greater have tried, all but a few have failed. And even the few who breached that watery obstacle, even the handful in the past age who have reached the stars to confront the Settlements, eventually fell to dust."

Ria-Ka'luhr said nothing more, but bowed his head in respectful acquiescence.

"He is right, Anin-Khan." Ulana-Tath felt a chill run down her spine as she imagined a horde of warriors surrounding the city, and it made her think of Kunan-Lohr. He still lived, she knew, but how could he hope to make it home? *He does not intend to*, an unwelcome voice spoke in her mind. Blinking the thought away, she went on, "You have not seen her, as I have. There is good reason why she is called the Dark Queen. If she wants to kill Keel-Tath, she will if Keel-Tath remains here." She placed a hand on the elder warriors's shoulder as she sensed the fire rising in his blood. "This is not a dishonor for you to challenge or to bear. It is a fact. Even if Kunan-Lohr could return with what is left of our army, how long could we hold against tens of legions and unfathomable war machines?"

As Ria-Ka'luhr had done a moment before to him, Anin-Khan bowed his head in submission. "What do you command, mistress?"

"We must take her to the temple of the Desh-Ka. That is as our lord commanded me before we parted." She turned to Ria-Ka'luhr. "I know the priesthood is obligated to take her in, but..."

He shook his head, knowing what she wanted to ask. "Once she crosses the threshold of the temple, you will not see her again until she either becomes an acolyte or she leaves of her own free will." He paused. "If she does that, she can never return to the temple."

Looking at her daughter, Ulana-Tath felt an impending sense of loss. The thought of not seeing her again for many cycles, and perhaps never, drove a knife through Ulana-Tath's heart.

Yet, in the end, it was the only way her only daughter could survive.

"We will take her to the temple." The words were as ash upon her tongue. "Only the Desh-Ka have the power to save her."

"Then we should move her," Ria-Ka'luhr's suggested. "I could escort her and a wet nurse to the temple and be there quickly, before any more of the queen's forces can arrive here, and without diluting Keel-A'ar's defenses. We could be at the temple in a fortnight."

Ulana-Tath knew the young acolyte's words were no mere boast. She was a veteran warrior, but his skills, as she had seen when he had killed the last of the queen's riders, greatly outstripped her own. Besides, two travelers would draw far less attention than a group of warriors riding for the temple.

As for the city's defenses, Anin-Khan had few enough warriors now, and Ulana-Tath was contemplating stripping the guard to the bone to send reinforcements east to link up with Kunan-Lohr.

Before she could open her mouth to reply, Anin-Khan fell to his hands and knees before her.

"Mistress, I beg you, do not do this. I gave my solemn vow to our lord and master that I would defend your child. I would rather you take my head or shave my hair than not permit me to fulfill this duty." His talons scratched the stone of the floor as his hands clenched. "We both know it was his final command to me, and I would not take another breath knowing I could not honor it."

Anin-Khan was filled with many levels of misery as he awaited the answer of his mistress. But even in such a state, his senses were acutely aware of his surroundings. He noticed the subtle shift of Ria-Ka'luhr's weight on his feet, and out of the corner of his eye saw the acolyte's hand, casually resting on the hilt of his sword, tighten upon the weapon's handle.

More telling by far was the brief but intense flash Anin-Khan felt through the melody of the young warrior's blood that revealed only an impenetrable frozen darkness. Then it was gone.

His muscles reflexively tensing for battle, Anin-Khan sat back and put his hand on his sword as he looked up, catching the acolyte's gaze. On the floor, he was at a dreadful disadvantage, but...

Keel-Tath let out a sudden scream that shattered the stillness of the creche. One of the wardresses was instantly there, picking up the child. Ulana-Tath could feel her daughter's distress, and wanted nothing more than to hold the child in her arms. But that was not the Way.

Ria-Ka'luhr stepped away from the crib as if the scream was a physical blow.

Anin-Khan used the distraction to get to his feet, his hand tight on the handle of his sword as he stared at the acolyte, noting the unmistakable, if fleeting, expression of fear that flashed across his face.

Before he could say anything, Ulana-Tath, who appeared to be oblivious to the exchange, announced, "We will leave at once for the temple. Anin-Khan, I ask forgiveness for even considering going against Kunan-Lohr's command to you."

"I thank you, my mistress, for your wisdom." He saluted her, but never took his eyes from Ria-Ka'luhr.

"Then let us prepare."

* * *

"Something is amiss," Anin-Khan whispered as he watched one of the wet nurses prepare the infant child for travel. The nurse wrapped Keel-Tath in a soft, warm carrier that would hold her snug against the nurse's chest, even on the back of a galloping *magthep*. "Did you not feel it?"

Ulana-Tath stood close beside him in an alcove of the creche. Anin-Khan had dispatched the Desh-Ka acolyte with a pair of warriors to prepare *magtheps* for the trip. The command, for Anin-Khan did not pretend that it was a request, had clearly come as a surprise to the young warrior. "No, I did not. I sensed nothing unusual with Ria-Ka'luhr."

"I did not imagine it, mistress. He was about to strike." He looked more intently at the child. "I believe that she sensed it, too. Her scream was no coincidence, and was not the cry of a child in need of milk or in discomfort. She was terrified."

Ulana-Tath frowned. A fierce and accomplished warrior, Anin-Khan was also the sire of eight children. He had spent far more time in the creche than she. And yet she remained unconvinced. "You know that infants her age can sense almost nothing through their blood. It was coincidence, nothing more."

Shaking his head, Anin-Khan told her, "I will not argue, mistress, but I hold to my belief that she sensed the darkness in him at the same instant as did I. Ria-Ka'luhr is involved in some unknowable mischief. I do not trust him."

"Why would an acolyte of the Desh-Ka come to do us harm after one of their high priests vowed they would protect her?" She shook her head in frustration. "Why would Ria-Ka'luhr have bothered to save me? He could have killed me and none would have been the wiser."

"Had he come upon you earlier, perhaps. But we would have pursued him had he killed you out in the open where we found you. We knew who you were, and we saw his approach. He would not have escaped us had he caused you harm." He shook his head. "By saving you, he guaranteed his own entry to the city."

"Then why did he not kill us before Keel-Tath cried out?" Ulana-Tath was doing her best to restrain her anger at Anin-Khan's insinuations. He was a capable and cunning warrior, but she feared that in the shadow of the peril cast by the Dark Queen he was seeing wraiths among shadows, threats where there were none. "He could have killed us all and made good his escape in the confusion."

"I do not know, mistress, but I think that he fears her."

"An infant?" Ulana-Tath's incredulity was plain in her voice.

Anin-Khan clenched his armored fists. "Do not think me mad, mistress! I know what I felt, and what I saw. On his face in the instant your daughter screamed was an expression of fear, a fear sufficient to break his will."

"I do not wish to doubt you, but what would you have me do? Kill him? How many warriors would we lose if we tried? And how would we explain that to the Desh-Ka?"

Shaking his head, Anin-Khan said, "Of course not, mistress. We will go according to our plan. All I ask is for us to be vigilant. If we arrive at the temple safely and I am wrong, I will offer him my life to cleanse my honor." He glanced at Keel-Tath, who now rested comfortably in her cocoon against the nurse's breast. "It would be a small enough sacrifice to ensure that your daughter reaches safety."

* * *

Ria-Ka'luhr fought the nausea that swept through him as he helped the two warriors prepare the mounts for their upcoming journey to the Desh-Ka temple. Under any other circumstances, Anin-Khan's dismissal of him to such a menial task would have been an insult fit to spawn a challenge to ritual combat, but Ria-Ka'luhr was secretly relieved.

He had intended to kill Ulana-Tath and the child there, in the creche, and had been about to draw his sword when Keel-Tath screamed. It was not the sound that stayed his hand, but her spiritual voice in his blood. She had somehow seen into his soul in that brief moment, and he had felt his emotional defenses fall. The voice of her spiritual song had filled him with such mindless fear that his concentration had been completely shattered.

And Anin-Khan had known. Somehow, the savvy old warrior had known Ria-Ka'luhr was going to strike even before the girl-child screamed in terror.

By the time the elder warrior gained his feet, Ria-Ka'luhr knew he had lost his advantage. He was certain he could have bested the other warriors and Ulana-Tath, but Anin-Khan gave him pause. Kunan-Lohr would not have entrusted the safety of the city to anyone but the best of his warriors, and Anin-Khan had the trophy scars of many battles.

After the moment passed, and after he saw that Ulana-Tath's attitude toward him had not changed, Ria-Ka'luhr simply pretended as if nothing had happened.

Yet, *something* had happened, and Ria-Ka'luhr had to decide upon his next course of action. He could not simply leave and try to kill them again later, perhaps ambushing them along the road to the temple. That would make clear his malignant intent, and they would be prepared.

Or…he could continue to pretend nothing had happened, that he had merely been startled by the child's sudden cry, and that Anin-Khan had misread his reaction. Ria-Ka'luhr doubted that Ulana-Tath would openly confront him about any suspicions Anin-Khan might voice to her; to do so would be a deep insult to the Desh-Ka, and he would have clear right to challenge her to ritual combat.

No, he thought. They may be suspicious, but they would do no more than keep watch over him. His opportunity would come once they departed from Keel-A'ar. The road to the temple was a long and dangerous one.

CHAPTER FOURTEEN

The warriors bound to the Dark Queen were not the only ones who suffered the cold misery of the pouring rain. Builders, many hundreds of them, labored in the darkness to do her bidding.

Next to the healers, the builder caste was the smallest in number among their race. Few were born each cycle with the necessary genes, and fewer still were able to master the powers that resided in their bodies and minds. But those who survived their training could perform wonders. Whatever could be visualized, they could create, using whatever materials were at hand.

Their creative powers were limited only by the ability of a master or mistress to concentrate enough builders on a given task, and by the skill of the senior builder in guiding the others. He or she provided a mental image, a blueprint, from which the others could work. Most builders were well-acquainted with creating stone from other stone, for that was one of their most important tasks: building and maintaining the defensive works and other structures needed by a city.

The only structure not created by builders was the *Kal'ai-Il*, the place of atonement that was at the center of every temple and *kazha*. These were built by hand, from the labor of thousands of warriors directed by builders according to the old ways.

There was no theoretical limit to what the builders could do, so long as enough were focused on the task and the senior builder could guide them. But builders were so few and so precious that they were rarely given up to a rising leader such as Syr-Nagath. In the past, wars had been fought over one city-state refusing to relinquish its builders to kings or queens who demanded their service. This was one of the greatest obstacles for any monarch to overcome, and was the main limitation on the advancement of technology during each rise of civilization. The Books of Time held records of complex machines and weapons, but it took many builders and masters and mistresses skilled in focusing their powers.

Syr-Nagath had found both in the Ka'i-Nur. Unlike the descendants of the other orders, the builders of the Ka'i-Nur had long focused on things far more complex than glass and stone. While the Desh-Ka had not realized it during their recent visit to the great fortress in the wastelands, the weapons they had encountered there were not captured during the last great war with the Settlements, but had been created by the order's builders in the seventy cycles since. Creating each weapon had been a long, difficult process because they had so few builders. But they had become masters of focusing on complex mechanisms, and could easily lead other builders in the creation of simple machines such as those the Dark Queen had in mind for them now.

Led by the builder mistress of the Ka'i-Nur, the others of her order and the additional builders the queen had coaxed and threatened from her vassals marched from near the queen's pavilion along the mud-soaked paths that led to a natural depression in the ground nearly a league away.

It was perhaps fortunate that their arrival was in the pouring rain, for it helped to mask both the sight and stench of the place. For here was where the dead had been gathered. It was a mass grave, with tens of thousands of bodies. While warriors were generally sent off to the afterlife with a funeral pyre, wars such as this made it impossible. There were too many dead, and not enough wood for pyres. Normally the many bodies were burned in a collective pyre, but Syr-Nagath had decreed that the bodies would simply be dumped here. None had known why, nor had the porters charged with the grisly task asked or complained. The queen's word was law.

The builders could not see the mountain of corpses through the rain, but there was no mistaking the place as hands and feet, along with other unrecognizable body parts, became clear in their limited field of vision. At that distance, they could smell the bodies, as well, and many wrinkled their noses at the foul odor.

With a gesture of her hands, the mistress split the group of builders in two, with each now led by the senior Ka'i-Nur builders, who marched to the right and left around the great burial pit until they closed the circle at the far end. For every Ka'i-Nur builder in the line, there were several builders from among the other bloodlines. The Ka'i-Nur builders would amplify the visions of the senior mistress for the normals, to better focus their creative powers.

But before they could create, they had to destroy. The raw material for anything created by the builders had to be drawn from something; they could not create from nothingness. They normally used foundation material that was similar to what they sought to create. This was why much of what the builders did was based on stone or, in smaller cases, glass, for the transformation of the materials was more one of form than of substance. Creating something vastly different from the foundation material was possible, but took extraordinary skill and effort, and was terribly inefficient.

There was another way, however, that dated back to the Second Age, and had not been used outside Ka'i-Nur since those ancient times. The builder mistress, who was exceptionally gifted by the standards of any age of their history, had studied and practiced it on a small scale for many cycles. It is what she had used to create the weapons with which the order's warriors had fought the Desh-Ka.

She took a deep breath, forcing herself to achieve a state of complete calm. What she was about to do here, using the mass of bodies as a foundation, had not been done since the end of the Second Age.

Completely ignoring the rain and the crackle of lightning that lit the sky, the builder mistress closed her eyes and began to focus. It took her several moments, far longer than normal, for she had to seek out the spirits of the builders not of the Ka'i-Nur and bind them to her. It was like weaving a complex pattern in the dark, but this was a task she had been born to.

When it was done, she could sense the power at her command, and she trembled in the same ecstasy warriors felt in the heat of battle. Here, around this mountain of the dead, she had harnessed more builders than had been brought together in millennia.

She raised her arms, holding her palms forward, toward the dead. As if controlled by invisible strings, the other builders, hundreds upon hundreds of them, did the same, exactly mimicking her movements.

Then she focused on the dead, visualizing in her mind what she desired. The other builders saw her vision as if it was an extension of their own minds, and they focused their powers, as well.

Within the mass grave before them, the bodies began to soften. Melt. Skin began to disintegrate, sloughing away in a mass of black particles, like glittering ash. The muscle gave way, joining the mass of black particles that now looked like liquid, but was not. Then the bone. The black substance joined the putrefying slop at the bottom of the grave, which itself transformed into the same shimmering dark matter. The undergarments and metal of the armor that clung to the bodies, even the living steel blades of the weapons, all disintegrated.

As the builders labored in silence under the angry sky, the mountain of the dead began to slowly collapse in upon itself.

* * *

Kunan-Lohr stood alone in the meadow, surrounded by the darkness and hammering rain. His body, long accustomed to the deprivations of war, shook off the discomfort as he waited. He had chosen this spot because many of his warriors were familiar with it as a staging area they had used in the past when traveling to the eastern kingdoms before the war. It was close enough to the queen's encampment that there was little chance of them losing their way, but was also far enough from the main road that it was unlikely they would be seen, especially in this deluge.

Lightning tore the sky overhead, the glaring light shimmering from the raindrops as if from a million shards of glass. In that instant, he could just see to the surrounding line of trees and the dark shapes that moved toward him: his warriors, the survivors of Keel-A'ar's once-proud army.

"My lord!" Eil'an-Kuhr, his most senior war captain, bowed her head and saluted as she reached him. She had to shout to be heard above the rain.

"It is good to see you, Eil'an-Kuhr." He reached out and gripped her forearms in greeting. Then he leaned closer, speaking into her ear as more dark forms gathered around him, rendering their salutes. "Did you escape unchallenged?"

She shook her head. "No, my lord. I do not know what happened, but at least a full cohort was cut off from the rest of us. I fear they ran into the encampment of another of the legions. All I know is that our warriors turned and fought with great valor. I could hear their war cries clearly, even through the rain, and felt the joy in their hearts."

Kunan-Lohr nodded to himself. He had felt their spirits, as well, the song in their blood a raging fire that even now still flickered. It was unfortunate to have lost their swords, for he had great need of them, but they had been given the opportunity to die with great honor. "So shall it be noted in the Books of Time."

"What are your plans, my lord? Are we to return home?"

His other war captains had joined him, as had the more senior warriors, all of them clustering around him to hear his words as his diminished army formed ranks in the soaking meadow, awaiting his command. Other warriors, unseen to his eyes, lurked in the trees around them to provide warning should enemy forces approach.

"We would if only my wishes could bear us forth, but I fear that is not to be."

Eil'an-Kuhr and the others nodded their understanding. None of them had expected to return to Keel-A'ar alive. The thought brought no sadness, only acceptance. As long as death was attended by honor, the place and the time it found them were irrelevant.

"We will make for the pass at Dur-Anai," Kunan-Lohr told them. "I know the riders Syr-Nagath sent forth failed in their mission, for Ulana-Tath and my daughter yet live. The queen will next send legions to lay siege to the city to try and finish the task appointed to the riders." He paused. If the Dark Queen sent an army to Keel-A'ar, they would likely raze the city to the ground and kill every one of its inhabitants. It was the only possible way she might conceal her dishonor. "I do not know what Ulana-Tath will do, but we must buy her and Anin-Khan as much time as we can to prepare their defenses. At Dur-Anai we can hold off far more than our own number."

"How are we to get there, my lord?" One of the other captains asked. "It is nearly three days of hard riding along the main road from here. Even at a full run, we could not hope to catch a mounted force if the queen should send one forth to block the pass."

Nodding his agreement, Kunan-Lohr told him, "We will take the mountain trail to the north. It will be difficult this time of year, but will cut many leagues from the distance we must travel."

"Does not that trail cross a tributary of the Lo'ar River?" Eil'an-Kuhr's expression was hidden in the dark storm, but there was no masking the fear in her voice. To enter the rivers, especially at this time of year, was to invite death from the creatures that lurked there.

"It does, but there is a bridge."

Another warrior shook her head slowly. "I am sorry, my lord, but the bridge was washed away in a flood when you were home attending your daughter's birth. It has not been repaired."

Kunan-Lohr looked heavenward, closing his eyes against the rain as he fought to contain his despair and fear. There was no other way to reach Dur-Anai in time, and if he tried to make a stand anywhere else along the road before the pass, his warriors would be quickly massacred. "Then we must ford the river."

* * *

Syr-Nagath stood outside her pavilion in the downpour, quivering with rage. Around her she could hear the sounds of a pitched battle being fought, the howls of war cries and screams of agony as swords, axes, and other weapons did their bloody work.

Startled from a sound sleep by the sudden clash, her surprise was quickly overtaken by anger that the enemy had dared attack at night, which even Syr-Nagath recognized as a time of respite from combat.

Perhaps they know what shall become of them when the sun again shows itself after the storm, she thought. If they had divined her intentions, it was quite possible they would consider a preemptive attack, although it went directly against the fundaments of the Way.

"It is not the armies of the east!" That had been the report brought by her First. "The war captains nearest the line report all is quiet there. The fighting is within our army's encampment, to the west!"

Sword drawn, followed closely by her First, Syr-Nagath strode through the dark and pouring rain toward the closest sounds of combat.

Such was her shock to find how close the battle raged to her pavilion. *They were coming for me, the fools!*

Gaining the edge of the swirling mass of warriors, she was unable to tell friend from foe. With a howl of frustration, she made a few lightning-swift cuts at exposed legs, and her First dragged the now-screaming warriors from the fray for Syr-Nagath to examine.

"They are all ours!"

"Our warriors fight among themselves?" Her bellow carried above the rain, catching the attention of the nearby combatants. "What madness is this?"

"It is she!" One of the warriors gestured to some of the others with his sword. "The Dark Queen!"

The battle suddenly increased in pitch as many of the warriors roared and tried to fight their way toward Syr-Nagath. Hacking and slashing at their opponents with maniacal frenzy, several broke through, only to quickly perish at the Dark Queen's hand.

Quickly kneeling down to examine one of the slain warriors, blocking the rain with her body so she could see, she found that the skin of his neck bore the mark of Keel-A'ar.

"Kunan-Lohr," she said, "I will have your soul for this."

With her fangs bared, she waded into the mass of warriors that still surged in her direction, cutting down all who crossed her path.

* * *

In the end, it was a massacre, with every one of the traitorous warriors of Keel-A'ar slain. Some had been taken alive, but had swallowed their tongues or slashed their throats in ritual suicide. Kunan-Lohr's body had not yet been found, and probably would not before the storm cleared. It was nearly impossible to tell more than male from female without hauling the bodies into good light under a shelter to view them.

The outcome, many warriors dead in a confused battle, was just as well. She knew that Kunan-Lohr must have discovered her treachery, and passed the information on to his warriors. But the lips of the dead could not speak. Thus did her dishonor in sending warriors to kill children remain a secret beyond her First. The leaders of the warriors who had gone forth to carry out the terrible deed had all perished the same day the riders had departed, their blood streaking the blade of Syr-Nagath's First. And the First's lips were sealed by a covenant even more terrible than that which Syr-Nagath had used on the young Desh-Ka acolyte.

Yes, the mutiny had been put down, and Syr-Nagath had let the rumors run free that it had been an unfortunate case of confusion. Ritual combat, perhaps, that had gotten out of hand.

Her mind had largely put the matter to rest when her First ran into the pavilion, a sick look on her face. Dropping to one knee and saluting, she blurted, "They are gone!"

"What do you mean? Who is gone?"

"The legions of Keel-A'ar, my queen! They are gone!"

Syr-Nagath stared at her. "Has your brain become addled? They were killed in the battle during the night!"

The First shook her head. "No, my queen. We have learned that was merely a cohort, perhaps caught while escaping through the rain. We know now that there were not enough bodies, not nearly enough, to account for all of them. We went to their encampment to search...and found this."

A warrior, a tall, broad-shouldered male, limped into the queen's chambers, escorted by four others. His leg bore a terrible wound, and he carried a dagger in his hand that, with a sinking feeling, Syr-Nagath instantly recognized.

"Syr-Nagath." The warrior said her name with undisguised loathing, and did not bother to salute. He held forth the dagger, and she knew it was intended as a Sign of Authority. "I bring word from my lord and master, Kunan-Lohr, and speak on his behalf: For your dishonor in sending warriors to kill the children of my people and my own blood, our covenant is forever broken."

Before anyone could move or speak, the warrior slashed the blade of the dagger across his throat. He stood, a look of pride on his face, until the torrent of blood began to slacken. As his eyes fluttered closed, he collapsed to the crimson-soaked rug.

Syr-Nagath looked up from the body to meet the gaze of the four escorting warriors, who stared at her in shock at the dead warrior's words.

She felled three of them in the blink of an eye with her *shrekkas* before making a tremendous leap. Drawing her sword in mid-air, she took the head from the remaining warrior before his weapon was out of its scabbard.

Her First lowered her head, shivering with fear. "They left their wounded behind," she ventured quietly. "All were dead save this one, who awaited us."

Turning back to stare at the corpse of Kunan-Lohr's messenger, Syr-Nagath felt a cold tide of rage wash over her. She would find Kunan-Lohr and shave his hair, then reduce his precious city and all who dwelled there to ash. "Alert the provinces nearest Keel-A'ar. They are to send their legions to lay siege to the city. I want five legions from our reserve here to be on the march by dawn to hunt down Kunan-Lohr. Have them send their mounted warriors forward at best speed to block him at Dur-Anai. I don't want them delayed by the warriors who must travel by foot."

"What of the other path to Dur-Anai? The trail through the mountains?."

Syr-Nagath fixed her with a look of predatory glee. The First bowed lower, wishing she could burrow into the earth. "Let him try," the Dark Queen said softly. Then, after a moment, she added, "Send a legion up the trail. If he is there, have them drive him and his warriors into the river."

CHAPTER FIFTEEN

As five of the queen's legions prepared for the long march to Keel-A'ar, the builders completed the first stage of their labors. The mountain of dead warriors had been reduced to a small black lake. The surface was utterly still and flat like the black obsidian of the fortress of Ka'i-Nur. The rain made no impression upon it, for the drops simply disappeared as they touched it, absorbed into the sea of tiny particles that were not molecules, nor were they atoms. They were something else, something that had been discovered early in the First Age by the ancients, in the times when great machines were used to accomplish what was now done through body and spirit, through force of will. The particles were a matrix material that could be manipulated to create whatever was desired, on any scale, great or small. Creating it was extremely difficult, but using it was not.

On the side of the lake nearest the queen's pavilion, the builders had gathered in a wide, deep circle around the builder mistress of the Ka'i-Nur. She again raised her arms and focused on the mental image of what the queen wished her to create. It was an ancient machine that Syr-Nagath had once seen in the Books of Time that had taken her fancy. Although extremely primitive compared to many other weapons the Ka'i-Nur builders could create, especially with a reservoir of the matrix material, it had the virtue of simplicity. While the builders could create anything that had been recorded in the Books of Time, and anything else their imaginations could conceive, the warriors and other castes, as necessary, had to be taught how to use it. With the ancient engines of war the builders were to create now, little explanation would be necessary, and their effect on the enemy would be terrible, indeed.

Such simple machines could also be created easily and quickly, as the builder mistress was about to demonstrate.

While it was at first difficult to see except when lightning flashed overhead, wisps of the matrix material began to drift from the dark lake. It could have been mistaken for mist or smoke, except that it moved quickly, with a purpose.

In the open center of the circle where the builder mistress stood, something began to take shape. At first it was no more than a shadow, a vague angular outline of strange proportions, deeper black against the darkness. As the minutes crept by, the shadow became completely opaque and more details emerged. It was large, the length of ten *magtheps* nose to tail, and had eight wheels that were as big around as a warrior stood tall. But it was not a complex vehicle, for there was no propulsion system of any kind. It had been designed to be pulled by animals.

Atop the chassis was a wide platform that supported a strange device that none of the builders had ever before seen. As large as the platform on which it stood, supported on a pedestal mounting that could be traversed and elevated, it was rectangular in shape, but bent, curved, as if a huge pipe had been cleaved down the middle.

As the thing continued to take form, the curved device became brighter, finally revealing itself to be a huge mirror. Lightning flashed, and many of the builders cried out in shock and pain as they were temporarily blinded by the intense light the mirror cast in their direction.

A group of warriors stood by with *magtheps* wearing harnesses. When the builder mistress was finished, she lowered her arms and the warriors quickly strapped the beasts to yokes that attached to the weapon's chassis. A pair of warriors mounted the chassis and took their seats at the front. With a few cracks of a whip over the backs of the protesting beasts, they had it moving through the clinging mud.

After a few moments, the thing was swallowed by the rain and darkness.

"And now, children," the builder told her peers with the accent unique to those of Ka'i-Nur, "we shall build more. Many more."

* * *

The builders were arrayed in two lines, with one from Ka'i-Nur facing a builder from among the other vassals to the queen. After seeing, sensing, how the mistress builder created the first machine, all of them could replicate it. While it would be possible for a single builder to create a single machine, none of the other builders were nearly as powerful as the Ka'i-Nur mistress. But a pair of them could make short work of the task. A stream of the matrix material flowed from the great pit, a dark cloud that swirled between the two lines to congeal into hundreds of angular shapes that would become war machines for the queen.

Their labors did not go unnoticed.

"Tell me now that the Dark Queen's works are not our concern." Ayan-Dar stood next to T'ier-Kunai at the far end of the black lake. While their eyes could not see the builders and the fruits of their labor through the rain, their second sight could. The old priest had convinced one of the others of the priesthood to keep watch on the queen, and what the priest had seen the old Ka'i-Nur builder do this morning had prompted him to return to the temple and inform T'ier-Kunai. Grudgingly, she had given Ayan-Dar a temporary reprieve from his restriction to the temple in order to accompany her here, that they could see the work of the builders with their own eyes.

The high priestess of the Desh-Ka knelt down at the edge of the black pit, trying to peer with the senses of her body and mind into its depths. But it was as impenetrable to her efforts as it was to any form of light. Even when the lightning flashed overhead, the pit remained black as the space between the stars. The stillness of its surface was eerie. The storm poured rain from above, but the drops vanished as they came in contact with the dark pool.

"What is it?" T'ier-Kunai had never seen the like. She reached a hand toward the surface, and was surprised when Ayan-Dar quickly deflected her hand away.

"Do not," he warned. "Only the builders of Ka'i-Nur, perhaps, can tell you what it is. I have only read some of the ancient accounts of its use, and its dangers. Whatever touches it, becomes it, unless the builders determine otherwise."

"If that was the case, then what is here would consume the Homeworld."

He nodded. "That nearly happened in the Second Age. In fact, that is how the war that led to the Final Annihilation began." He nodded in the direction of the builders. "Even as they labor to create their machines, part of their consciousness is devoted to maintaining a barrier between the material in this pit and the earth beneath. But there is no need to shield the rain from harm. The raindrops, or anything else that should be thrown in, is absorbed and then transformed into this dark matter."

He drew a knife and knelt down, dipping the blade into the dark matrix. The blade, as with all edged weapons used by his kind, was of living steel, the most durable substance known.

After a few seconds he pulled the knife away. The blade was gone.

"And this...dark matter, it can be used to create anything?"

Ayan-Dar nodded. "Yes. Anything from the tiniest object imaginable to the greatest." He swept his arm around. "While it has never been done on such a scale, it could be used to create an entire world." He looked at her gravely. "Or destroy one."

"And this dark matter has not been used since the Second Age?"

"I requested that our keeper inquire among the other orders, to consult their Books of Time. Unless there are records at Ka'i-Nur that say otherwise, then no, this matrix material has not been used since then. The great machines and ships that have been built over the millennia since the Final Annihilation, during those times when great leaders have arisen, were created by builders, yes, but they did not use this material as a foundation." He nodded toward where the builders labored to create the queen's new arsenal of weapons. "It would have taken all those builders, working together, weeks to create one of those contraptions using traditional methods, and far longer to build a machine that could build other machines, which is how the starships the Settlements used during the last war were constructed." He paused. "It took them decades to build those ships, using thousands of builders working together."

"And when they were defeated," T'ier-Kunai said, "and the inevitable fall of their civilization began, all those machines were destroyed in the ensuing chaos."

"Yes, just as happens here with each fall. The knowledge of each generation's accomplishments is preserved in the Books of Time, but the ability of the builders to recreate what once was, or to create something new, is limited because making complex machines is inherently difficult. The ancients who first gave us the precepts of the Way understood this, I believe. It is that, as much as anything else, that binds us to following a simple life, cherishing simple things. In such a system, achieving an advanced level of technology that we could use to destroy ourselves is a rare thing."

"But even then," T'ier-Kunai said, "the true power has always been with us, with the martial orders."

"Since the end of the Second Age, yes." His mouth compressed into a hard, grim line. "But the equation has now changed. Weapons that would take time and great effort to create, or were even impossible to make since the end of the Second Age, the Dark Queen can now build in minutes or days. I believe the eastern armies of T'lar-Gol will fall this day, and it will not be long before Syr-Nagath rules the entire Homeworld." He turned to face his priestess. "She will no longer need the Desh-Ka and the other orders to maintain the balance with the Settlements, or preserve the Way. She will seek to destroy us all."

* * *

Syr-Nagath stood at the head of her army as the clouds receded. Both sides had used the respite of the rain, miserable as it had been, to bring forward more reinforcements. She knew from the reports provided by her First that the coalition of the eastern armies had committed their full reserves, concentrating them here, opposite where she stood. It was a truly formidable force, and would actually have given her pause for concern if she had not already determined the fate of her enemies. She regretted the coming waste of so many warriors that she could have added to her own strength, but there was no other way. The fighting here had gone on far too long, and her enemies had refused to yield with honor.

Now that the builders had provided what she needed, the war for T'lar-Gol would shortly come to an end.

Her warriors were arrayed on the slope of the ridge overlooking the main battlefield where they had been fighting for weeks. None had advanced to the main killing ground, where the enemy ranks now stood, waiting. Tens of thousands of them stood before her in ranks a hundred deep, with hundreds of thousands more arrayed to the north and south. At the head of each army group stood the king or queen, waiting impatiently for Syr-Nagath's army to engage them.

Along the top of the ridge behind her, the strange machines created by the builders formed a line that stretched the length of the battlefield. Even now, more machines were being built and quickly moved into positions along the distant wings.

Syr-Nagath turned to the builder mistress of the Ka'i-Nur, who stood beside her. "The warriors understand how to use these devices?"

"Yes, my queen. It is very simple, actually. One warrior looks through an aiming device to align the weapon while the others turn cranks to align the mirror to the point of aim. The mirror itself is...intelligent, and able to change shape as needed to focus the maximum amount of energy on the target. You will not be disappointed."

Frowning, Syr-Nagath only nodded. She was not accustomed to hearing words like "target" or "aiming device" in the context of a battle. But those words and many more would become part of her vocabulary soon.

The opposing warriors began to shout encouragement to her army to come forth and give battle. They did not jeer or mock, for that was not part of the Way. They simply wanted to fight. That was what warriors did.

But not today.

"Soon," the builder said. The clouds were thinning now, and the sky began to brighten, revealing a beautiful magenta hue where there had only been oppressive dark and gray.

The sun suddenly emerged. It was not on the horizon, but was midway toward noon, rising in the eastern sky above the enemy positions.

"Perfectly positioned," the builder mistress said quietly. "When you are ready, my queen."

"Let us finish this." Syr-Nagath turned to her First. "Activate the weapons."

* * *

Ayan-Dar and T'ier-Kunai had moved, changing their vantage point to an unoccupied knoll behind the lines of the queen's army. They masked themselves using an ancient technique that made it nearly impossible for anyone to see them. It was not the same as being completely invisible, but only someone looking directly at them, who knew they were there, could see them.

They had an excellent view of the battlefield and, more important, of the war machines that were aligned along the ridge behind the queen's battle line. From here, they could see beyond the enemy lines all the way to the foam-flecked shores of the Eastern Sea.

As the sun broke from the clouds, the landscape came alive. Even trampled as it was, the battlefield and the ridges to either side exploded into the deep green of the steppe-grasses and ferns. Where the conditions suited it, yellow and orange lichen blazed. A freshening breeze whipped in from the ocean, the air clean and crisp after the rain had washed the stench of the living and the dead from the air.

"A beautiful day." T'ier-Kunai breathed in the salt air from the ocean, enjoying the scent after having momentarily set aside the reason she was here. "A good day for battle."

"I fear not." Ayan-Dar pointed at the nearest of the war machines. Like the hundreds of others arrayed along the ridge line, the great mirror mounted on the pedestal was tilting. All of them had been pointing straight up, but in synchrony they were now all tilting and turning toward the sun. It was a sinuous motion that reminded him of the carnivorous *zhel'aye* plant, just before it struck its unwary victim. "Not for the armies of the east."

There were cries and shouts of surprise and anger from the opposing armies as their warriors were dazzled by the massive mirrors. Ayan-Dar and T'ier-Kunai could see the rectangles of light overlaying the lead ranks of opposing warriors along their entire line.

The curved surfaces of the mirrors began to slowly flex, focusing the full energy of the sun on their targets, and the cries and shouts of the enemy warriors suddenly turned to screams of agony. The kings and queens were reduced to smoldering piles of burned meat, and the warriors in the lead ranks, those most senior in each of the armies, went down, their bodies charred and smoking. Their leatherite armor burst into flame, and the breastplates melted into their flesh.

By the thousands did they die.

The warriors operating the queen's weapons swept the blazing focal points of the mirrors over the packed masses of warriors with methodical thoroughness. With their leaders and senior warriors gone, and never having seen such weaponry before, many of the warriors simply stood rooted to the ground in shock and disbelief.

"It is a massacre."

Ayan-Dar did not need his emotional bond with the high priestess to sense her revulsion. He could hear it in her voice. "This, my priestess, is but a glimpse into what is yet to come."

* * *

From her vantage point, Syr-Nagath watched the carnage with clinical detachment. Her nose wrinkled at the stench of burning flesh and seared metal carried by the smoke that began to pour from the dying and the dead.

"Once the smoke becomes too thick," the old builder warned, "the mirrors will no longer work as well."

"There will be more than time enough." Syr-Nagath gestured toward one of the massive phalanxes of warriors opposite them. Fully half had been reduced to crumpled heaps of burned meat, or were flailing on the ground in agony. The remaining warriors were kneeling and saluting. The Dark Queen turned to her First. "Lift the fire from those who wish to surrender. Send runners to them to bring their senior warriors here, that I may bind their honor to me."

After saluting, the First turned to a group of other warriors, relaying the queen's instructions. Runners immediately dashed forth down the slope toward the first group of enemy warriors who had surrendered.

One by one, the other groups of warriors, entire armies, began to surrender. Others, despite the loss of their leaders and senior warriors, charged forward. Those were met by the queen's warriors and quickly overwhelmed.

Long before the sun had reached its zenith, the battle, and the war for mastery of the continent, was over. Syr-Nagath was now the undisputed ruler of all T'lar-Gol.

CHAPTER SIXTEEN

The mountain trail to the pass at Dur-Anai led Kunan-Lohr and his warriors along the edge of vertical cliffs that, at their height, dropped nearly half a league to the river below. The trail had been cut into the mountain very early in the First Age, even before the great east-west road had first been laid. It was a narrow, twisting path that was perilous under the best of times. The rock was brittle, and often fell from the mountain face above without warning or crumbled along the edge. The trail had been widened many times, so much so that in some sections it was more like a tunnel dug into the mountain, save that one side was open to the cliff.

He had lost more than a few warriors to the perils of falling stone, and some had plunged to their doom when part of the trail gave way, or slipped and fell on the water-slicked rock. This was a path that was usually only taken by a few hardy souls at a time, traveling with great care and in good weather, not by several thousand warriors moving at desperate speed through a storm.

And speed, above all, was of the essence. Kunan-Lohr drove himself and his warriors without mercy. They ran through the morning until exhaustion overwhelmed them. He gave them a time of rest when the sun finally emerged, driving away the rains. Then they staggered and shuffled until nightfall when even their acute night vision could no longer make out the weakened areas of the path. Only then did he let them rest against the cold stone.

They could build no fires for warmth, nor had they food, and precious little water. Where the trail rose high enough to touch the snow line, the parched warriors grabbed handfuls to melt in their mouths. It was all they had, and so they made do.

The warriors of his rear guard, trailing the main group by half a league, were watching an entire legion that had been sent in pursuit. The enemy warriors were still at a distance, but were closing the gap quickly. Unlike the warriors of Keel-A'ar, who had been forced to flee with nothing more than their weapons and armor, the legion sent by the queen were provisioned with food and water, and were not suffering from acute exhaustion.

When Kunan-Lohr called for a stop to rest each night, he and Eil'an-Kuhr, who now acted as his First, had made their way along the line of warriors, offering encouragement. A few words and a bit of humor from their lord and master helped to keep the warriors in good spirits.

But this day had been different. While Kunan-Lohr and his First had made their way along the line as they had the morning before, but their mood now was somber. For today they would have to cross the much-feared tributary of the Lo'ar River.

The trail descended rapidly from their previous night's stop. Kunan-Lohr, who was always at the head of the column, heard the rush of water long before he saw the river. He was relieved that the torrential rains that had swamped the battlefield to the east had already passed through, leaving the water in the river at a normal level.

"At least we need not face a raging current," he said grimly as he stepped to the edge of the path at the river's edge.

Eil'an-Kuhr looked at him with a carefully controlled expression. She had never shown fear on the battlefield, but he could sense it in her now. Fear had wrapped its icy fingers around the hearts of his warriors, and himself. But he would not let it rule him, or his army.

The trail on this side of the river ended on a flat shelf that was as far across as five warriors with their arms spread wide. There was nothing left of the simple suspension bridge, which had been rebuilt countless times over the ages after being washed out by torrential rains. On either side of the river, the sheer face of the cliffs rose above them, disappearing into wispy clouds that moved rapidly across the sky, blocking what little sun made it into the great crevasse.

Flocks of flyers circled above, periodically darting toward the surface of the water, where their clawed feet snatched out wriggling fish.

But the fliers did not have full sway. As Kunan-Lohr and the others watched, one of the fliers, with a wing span as great as a warrior stood tall, swooped to the surface of the water, intent on snatching its prey. A much larger fish burst from the water, snapping its jaws shut on the flier's lower half. With a shriek of pain, the flier disappeared into the water, dragged down by the fish. A long smear of crimson on the water's surface drifted by the watching warriors.

Kunan-Lohr stared at the river, acid welling in his stomach. The river was small, tiny in comparison to the downstream segment that ran through Keel-A'ar. His strongest warrior could throw a stone to the far bank, and with the water running as it was now, the deepest part here would only reach the waist. The water was swift, but not so much that it would carry a warrior away too far downstream.

No. The water itself would not have given him the slightest pause were it not for the things that lived in it. He saw flashes of silver just below the rippling surface. Some seemed to hang in place, while others darted in and out of sight. Some, he could tell, were small, glints that were no longer than a finger. Others, like the one that took the flier, were much larger, as big as a warrior's arm or leg. And all of them, even the small ones, had formidable teeth.

He turned to his senior warriors, whose eyes were locked on the water and the horror it contained. "We will not have much time before the queen's warriors arrive, so we must hurry." His expression hardened. "I will need some warriors who can swim."

* * *

Dara-Kol stood next to three other warriors along the edge of the river. Like those standing beside her, she had the great misfortune of knowing how to swim. The dark water swept by a mere hands-breadth from their toes. She and the others were nude, and the four of them shivered, but not from the chill air. They had removed their armor, weapons, and black undergarments, for their weight and drag would slow them down in the water. And every moment in the water was a moment spent with Death.

Around their waists were tied lengths of rope, the ends of which were held loosely in the hands of warriors behind them. The job of these first four warriors was to reach the far side of the river, then pull the rope across. The first rope would be used to pull others, and in a short time they would have a functional, if very primitive, rope suspension bridge.

That assumed, of course, that any of the four survived. There were more warriors waiting to take their place, but not many. Few who lived on this continent ever learned to swim, for rare was the body of water that did not have fish willing and able to kill them. And wading across would be nothing more than suicide.

More warriors stood in two lines on either side of the swimmers, stretching back to the entrance to the trail. Each of them held two rocks, about the size of a fist. At the rear of the two lines, more warriors hurriedly piled up even more such rocks. Each warrior had sliced open one of their palms with a talon, drizzling a few drops of blood onto each rock.

Dara-Kol felt her master's hand grip her shoulder, and she fought to suppress the tremors that wracked her body.

"Force your fears aside, warriors," Kunan-Lohr told them. "This is a battle, with the creatures in the water as our enemy. As battles we have fought before, we will win by fighting together, as one. Not all of us will survive, but those who die, shall die with great honor."

"Yes, my lord." Dara-Kol and the others saluted and bowed their heads, and Kunan-Lohr returned the honor.

"May thy Way be long and glorious," he told them. He reached down to take a pair of rocks, smeared with his own blood, that he had set aside. "Let us begin!" He flung one rock as far as he could upstream, the other as far as he could downstream.

The warriors in the two lines beside the swimmers did the same. After the front rank of warriors had thrown their rocks, they turned and ran to the back of the line to pick up more. The next pair of warriors quickly stepped forward to throw theirs before they, too, ran back to the end of the line. It was the same technique they often used in battle when facing an organized opponent, with each rank rotating to the rear after a short time fighting the enemy. In this way, they could fight for hours without becoming exhausted.

Plumes of water shot up where the blood-stained rocks landed in the river. In mere moments, the surface of the river up- and downstream from where the swimmers waited was churned into a froth as the predatory fish went into a feeding frenzy, drawn by the scent of blood.

"*Go!*"

At Kunan-Lohr's shouted command, the four swimmers, arms outstretched before them, leaped into the water, the ropes trailing out behind them. A third line of warriors rushed forward with yet more rocks to add to the confusion of the ravenous fish.

Dara-Kol swam for her life. Her heart hammered in her chest as she kicked her legs and drove her arms into the water as she had been taught at her *kazha* when she was a child. She had not grown up in Keel-A'ar itself, but in a small village in the mountains of Kui'mar-Gol that owed its allegiance to the master of the city. Near her home was a lake that the priest had told her had once been a crater made by an ancient weapon, that over time had filled with rain water. It was inhabited by small aquatic creatures, but none of them were dangerous, let alone deadly. She had spent much of her youth in and near that lake, but knew that after this terror, she would never again willingly take to water.

Breathe, she admonished herself. She had been holding her breath in fear, but realized that her muscles needed as much oxygen as her lungs could provide. Turning her face to the side, she blew out, then sucked in a great lungful of air before turning her face back into the water as the priest had once taught her.

She could see in glimpses to the side that the other three warriors were falling behind her. She did not know if that was bad or good. She was tempted to slow down, as she felt terribly exposed swimming alone. Swimming together, perhaps the fish would not be so bold.

The warrior who was farthest upstream from her let loose a piercing cry of pain. He floundered for a moment, then went down. A few seconds later his head broke the surface, and Dara-Kol caught sight of a glittering shape the length of her forearm firmly attached to his throat, blood spurting from the wound. In the instant just before she forced her face back under the water with the next stroke, even more glittering shapes swarmed over the warrior. The water around him heaved and turned crimson.

No safety in numbers, then. She drove herself forward, kicking even harder, pulling with all her might with every stroke of her arms.

She felt something brush one of her legs. Then she swept her hand across what felt like a set of prickly spines. It took all her will not to scream in the water. She forced herself to breath, to kick, to stroke.

Something else, much larger than the other things, thudded into her side and bounced off. She moaned, fighting off the panic. She had no idea how far she was from the shore, and was too terrified to look.

There was another scream behind her, but she was not sure who it was. It no longer mattered. Each time her face broke the surface for a breath, she saw a snapshot of horror. Screams and shouts. A torn and bloodied hand rising from boiling, bloody water. A silvery horror leaping from the water, a hunk of flesh clutched in its mouth.

Kick. Stroke. Breathe. That was her existence in a time that dragged on forever. Her arms and legs, already on the ragged edge of exhaustion from the journey along the mountain trail, were burning like fire. She gritted her teeth as she willed her body onward. *Do...not...stop.*

Something nipped at her leg and she screamed. Before she could stop herself, she inhaled some water and began to gag.

More silver flashes appeared in the water around her. The sleek fish sliced through the water, their wide mouths open to reveal rows of teeth as sharp as her dagger. They were so close that she could see their soulless black eyes.

The fish streamed past her, drawn by the sound and scent of the feast that lay behind her, the sacrifice of the other warriors giving her one final chance.

Holding her breath, fighting against her gag reflex, she shot forward. If she did not reach the opposite side of the river in the next few seconds, it would not matter, because...

There! Her leading arm slammed down on something hard and unyielding. Rocks. Clawing at them with her talons, she dragged herself forward as she fought to get her feet under her. Choking and coughing, she heaved herself out of the water just as a silver arrow rippled across the surface in her direction. With a cry, she yanked her feet clear and rolled away from the water's edge. The spiny dorsal fin of the fish twitched as it turned away, disappointed.

Dara-Kol vomited, but only a little water came forth. She lay there for what to her seemed a long time, shivering with cold and fear.

She at last became aware of a sound that she finally understood were cheers from the warriors across the river. Getting to her knees, barely able to control the shaking of her body, she turned to face them.

Kunan-Lohr stood next to the water, an unmistakable look of pride on his face. To her amazement, he knelt and saluted her. The other warriors instantly did likewise, their cheers falling into reverent silence.

She returned the salute, her master's honor warming her. Then, with trembling hands, she began to pull the rope toward her.

Such was the surprise of all when after only a few pulls the tattered end emerged from the water. Dara-Kol felt a spear of ice through her heart.

The fish had bitten the rope clean in two.

* * *

"No." Eil'an-Kuhr had spoken in a whisper, but her voice carried far into the tightly packed ranks of warriors behind her. She stared at the bit of rope Dara-Kol held up, a sick look on her face. The warrior who had been holding the other end of the rope quickly reeled it in, then held the tattered end in her hand.

"Stand fast, Dara-Kol!" Kunan-Lohr called across the river, which was still seething with fish snapping at the last scraps of the other three warriors. Turning to Eil'an-Kuhr, he spoke so that all could hear. "The rope's parting is an inconvenience. Getting a warrior to the far side was the most important task. I need a warrior who can cast a spear to the far side!"

While most warriors preferred swords, some used spears or even exotic weapons, such as the *grakh'ta* whip. A brace of warriors carrying spears moved forward, the others parting to allow them to pass.

But as they saluted Kunan-Lohr, another warrior came forth. He was smaller than the others, but the other spear carriers immediately stepped to the side.

"My spear can easily reach the far side, my lord." His companions nodded emphatically.

Kunan-Lohr recognized him as one of the young warriors who had gone with Dara-Kol disguised as a builder. "Even with a rope attached?" Kunan-Lohr gestured for the warrior holding the end of the rope to come forward.

"I can only try, my lord." The warrior took the rope and carefully knotted it around the shaft of his spear. He hefted the weapon, then moved the knot farther forward to improve the balance.

A cry of warning went up from the rear of the column, which was still trapped on the narrow confines of the mountain trail behind them.

"The queen's warriors will soon be upon us." Kunan-Lohr nodded to the young warrior, then stepped out of the way. "We must hurry."

The warrior stood still for a moment, looking across the water. Dara-Kol was on her feet, standing ready to seize the rope. The far side was nothing but rock, with no surface into which the tip of the spear could sink.

The warrior stepped back several paces. Then, after taking a deep breath, he bolted toward the water, one arm held out before him, his spear arm held cocked by his head. A few paces before the water's edge, he cast the spear forward with all his might, releasing it as momentum carried his body forward. He rolled on the rock and would have gone straight into the river had Kunan-Lohr and Eil'an-Kuhr not grabbed him.

The spear, with the rope trailing behind it, sailed up and over the water. On the far side, Dara-Kol stood as if she expected to capture it by letting it pierce her body.

With a metallic clang, the spear hit the rock on the far side a hands-breadth from Dara-Kol's foot. She snatched it and pulled the rope taut to keep it out of the deadly water.

Again the warriors cheered, but their revelry was short-lived as the unmistakable sound of battle broke out at the rear of the column.

They had run out of time.

* * *

Dara-Kol slid free the rope that had been knotted around the spear and quickly tied it off in a large metal eye that had been sunk into a stone pillar that had long been used to support this end of the bridge. She would use this rope to pull across the others, but did not want to risk letting it slip back into the water.

One of the warriors on the far side gestured that the other ropes were ready, secured to the end of the first, and she began to haul them over. Her arms were a blur as she pulled hand over hand, hoping that the dreaded fish would ignore the ropes. They were heavy, and she could not keep them dipping into the river.

While the surface of the water twitched and sets of spiny fins emerged, the beasts left the ropes alone.

"Tie the thick one off at the bottom!"

She nodded understanding at the warrior's shouted words and did as he commanded. Taking the thick rope, which was actually two that had quickly been twisted together to form the foot rope, she secured it to a metal eye near the base of the pillar.

On the opposite side, the warrior tested the knot for strength. Then a ten of warriors pulled on the foot rope, taking out the slack before the warrior tied a complex knot to hold it.

"Now the upper rope!"

Dara-Kol took the end of the remaining rope she had hauled over and secured it to another metal eye set at chest height and offset to the left. This rope would help the warriors keep their balance. Normally there would be a third rope on the right side, lattice strands from the foot rope to the hand ropes, and the foot rope would be far thicker, but there was no time now for finesse.

The warrior on the far side threaded the upper rope through the matching eye on that side, and the warriors behind him again pulled it tight before he tied it off.

The rope bridge would be treacherous to use, she knew, but at least it was strong. Made of a material similar to the black undergarments they all wore, a strand as big around as her smallest finger could support a ten of warriors easily over this distance. The rope they were using now was twice as thick, and the double-stranded foot rope was as big around as her wrist.

No, the rope would not break, and would hold as much weight as they chose to put on it.

The greatest danger they faced would be the simple, terrible fate of slipping and falling into the river.

**

Kunan-Lohr wasted no time. As soon as the final knot was tied off, he ordered, "Move across!"

The warrior who had thrown the spear and tied the knots was the first in line. He carried with him, bound in a satchel on his back, Dara-Kol's armor and weapons. It was a perilous load to bear across the flimsy bridge as it bounced and swayed, but he kept his balance and made it across without incident.

As the warrior handed a grateful Dara-Kol her things, more warriors began following him across at a close interval. The rope bowed dangerously close to the water, and in the middle of the river actually dipped below the surface when one of the warriors lost his footing and nearly fell.

"Keep going." Kunan-Lohr moved the warriors along as the sound of battle behind them grew louder. "Quickly! Quickly!"

One of the warriors on the bridge screamed as she lost her footing and fell. She managed to grab onto the foot rope, but the lower half of her body was in the water. The fish wasted no time in attacking, and the warrior shrieked as the ferocious creatures tore into her.

"Cut her loose!" Kunan-Lohr bellowed to the warriors now standing, paralyzed with fear, on either side of her on the bridge. His greatest fear now was not the fish, but that a hapless warrior such as this one would accidentally cut the foot or hand ropes with her talons.

Without hesitation, two warriors drew their swords and slashed at their fallen comrade's forearms, severing them before flicking the amputated hands from the rope. The warrior disappeared into the churning, bloody water with a sickening gurgle.

Hardening his heart, Kunan-Lohr turned to the warriors who stood around him on the shore, transfixed by the horrid spectacle. "Keep moving."

* * *

At the rear of the column, still on the winding, deadly trail, Eil'an-Kuhr led the warriors of Keel-A'ar in a ferocious battle with the forces the queen had sent in pursuit. At first she had thought it had been only a cohort of warriors. Then she had caught sight of the dense column of warriors flowing in their direction, much farther back on the trail.

"Inform our master that an entire legion is behind us," she told a young warrior, who saluted before turning to run as fast as he could past his fellow warriors to reach Kunan-Lohr.

Eil'an-Kuhr hoped the warrior did not fall in his haste.

Moving forward, she took her place at the tail of the column where the fighting was. A pair of enemy warriors attacked her, thrusting their swords at her chest, as she took the place of one of her own who had fallen. She parried their attacks, driving both blades downward to allow the warriors on either side of her to slash at her opponents.

They had room enough for four warriors abreast on this section of the trail. She tried to rotate them as best they could, much as Kunan-Lohr had done with the warriors chosen to throw rocks to distract the fish in the river. It was perilous to do so, for there was very little room for those on the short fighting line to step back and allow fresh warriors to move to the front. Several had already slipped or been pushed over the edge and had fallen to their doom.

The same was happening to the queen's warriors, and worse. The warriors at the front were being forced into Eil'an-Kuhr's warriors by mounting pressure from the warriors behind. The enemy was so tightly packed at the head of their column now that the warriors barely had room to draw back their elbows to thrust with their swords. More and more of them were being squeezed off the trail by their companions as the entire legion pressed forward along the open-sided trail. The screams of those who fell echoed from the sheer walls of the great chasm.

The enemy warriors also had to contend with the growing pile of bodies in their path, while Eil'an-Kuhr's warriors simply backed away, closer to the river. The enemy had to step or leap over the bodies of the dead and dying, and Eil'an-Kuhr and the others took every opportunity to knock their opponents from the trail as they did so.

Her greatest enemy was exhaustion. The queen's warriors were tired from the exertions of running to catch up with Kunan-Lohr's army, but they had eaten and had water and ale to revive their strength.

By contrast, every muscle in Eil'an-Kuhr's body was on fire, and her breath came in heaving gasps. In the brief moments she gave herself to rest, backing a few paces out of the line while another warrior took her place, her body trembled as if she had been stricken with a palsy.

Most of her warriors were even weaker, and their fatigue had begun to take its toll. Some came to the front line barely able to lift their swords. Some were struck down, adding to the pile of bodies in the enemy's path. Others grappled with enemy warriors, using the last of their strength to hurl the enemy, and themselves, into the abyss.

At long last, a glance to the rear told her that they had arrived at the river. She saw Kunan-Lohr wade toward her through the group of warriors set to defend this end of the bridge.

* * *

Kunan-Lohr's heart swelled with pride as he watched his warriors fight off the queen's legion. He had suffered heavy losses, but the queen would be lucky to have more than an over-strength cohort left. A constant stream of bodies was falling from the trail as the bulk of the legion continued to crush forward, driving the lead warriors into the swords of his warriors or into the abyss.

Such waste, he thought. He held no ill will toward those who fought against him. They were following the Way, and simply did not know that the queen for whom they sacrificed their lives was a beast, without honor.

Most of his own army had crossed by now. Many warriors had volunteered to remain behind and hold this end of the bridge for the remaining warriors still fighting on the trail.

He caught sight of Eil'an-Kuhr and pushed his way through to her. With a desperate lunge, she speared an enemy warrior on the end of her blade, then tossed his body off the trail before stepping back. Another warrior leaped into her position, slashing and hacking at the endless stream of enemy warriors.

"My lord." She was panting like a *magthep* that had been forced to run from dawn to dusk. Her face and armor was covered in blood, and he counted no fewer than nine wounds upon her body.

She stumbled, and he caught her. Lifting one of her arms over his shoulder and wrapping his other arm around her waist, he guided her to the landing.

"Can you make it across the bridge?" He propped her against the pillar that held the ropes as the last exhausted warriors made the crossing. The others, the volunteers, now fought a pitched battle that would not last long. Their lives would be spent buying just a few moments more for Kunan-Lohr and the last warriors to cross.

"My lord," she said as she wiped a stream of blood from her lips, "my Way ends here, today. Long have I served you, and I hope well. But our paths must part. You cannot stay here. You will be needed at Dur-Anai, and in the defense of Keel-A'ar." Setting down her sword, she reached out with both arms and took him by the forearms. "May thy Way be long and glorious, Kunan-Lohr, honored master."

Kunan-Lohr held her forearms tightly. "I will see you in the Afterlife, Eil'an-Kuhr."

With a heavy heart, he stepped out upon the rope bridge, the last warrior of Keel-A'ar to cross.

Eil'an-Kuhr waited until he was safe on the far side, and she offered him her last salute.

Then she picked up her sword and cut the ropes.

Alone, Kunan-Lohr watched from the far bank as Eil'an-Kuhr and the rear guard, terribly outnumbered, fought bravely and died.

CHAPTER SEVENTEEN

Ulana-Tath rode next to the nurse who carried her child. Keel-Tath seemed to enjoy the bobbing motion of the *magthep* that carried her at a steady trot, and she periodically let loose a squeal of pleasure.

"She is born to it, my mistress," the nurse had remarked more than once. It was nearly unheard of for a child this young to be removed from the safety of the creche, and Ulana-Tath was relieved that her daughter found delight in traveling. Keel-Tath's tiny face peered out of the bundle on the nurse's chest, her bright eyes drinking in the sights and sounds of the world. Her spiritual song was clear and unafraid, a stark contrast to the fear Ulana-Tath felt herself.

She knew that Kunan-Lohr yet lived. Of that much, she was certain. Ulana-Tath could sense his song in her blood, an anxious mingling of fear and anger, expectation and acceptance. And above all, love. Love for his city and its people. Love for his daughter. Love for Ulana-Tath. The marks of mourning cascaded down her cheeks and neck as she thought of him. More of her skin darkened with each passing day, for she knew in her soul that her consort, her love, had no intention of ever returning. She had no way of knowing what he planned, but she had come to know him well. Even if he could have somehow extracted Keel-A'ar's legions from the clutches of the Dark Queen, he would never have simply marched home, nor would the queen have allowed it.

No. He would do all he could to buy his people time to prepare for what must come on the heels of the failure of the queen's riders in their mission to kill Keel-Tath. Even had the riders succeeded, the queen would seek to destroy Kunan-Lohr and all who followed him after breaking the covenant of honor with her. She would pursue him to the ends of the world. His only hope would be to kill her in battle or by right of challenge. The prospects for victory in either case were slim, for he could neither defeat the queen's legions with the city's army, nor had he a realistic hope of defeating her in the arena. Ulana-Tath suspected he would challenge the queen in the end, but it would make no difference. She knew of no warrior who stood a chance against Syr-Nagath, save one from among the priesthood.

Before leaving Keel-A'ar, Anin-Khan had done what he could to prepare the city for the siege that must come, in the event that he and Ulana-Tath could not return before the queen's army arrived. The garrison there should be able to defend the walls for some time, with the help of the builders who were adept at repairing the ancient stone. The city had an ample stock of food and water, which could easily support the inhabitants for a full cycle or more. Ulana-Tath knew the city's history, and that it had fared well in most sieges of the past. But against the Dark Queen, she could not be so sure. There was a cancer within Ulana-Tath, a gnawing uncertainty about the future that she had never before known. She was afraid not just for her child, but for her city. Even for her race.

What will be, will be. She had no gods to pray to, no one and nothing to whom she could appeal or ask deliverance. Her people had once worshipped gods, but they had proven themselves false in the collapse of civilization at the end of the Second Age, in the Final Annihilation. The civilizations that had eventually arisen from the ashes in the Third Age, clawing out of the depths of the cataclysm, had lost faith in the old gods and had left them behind without pity or remorse. Faith was something to be placed on oneself and on those to whom one was bound by honor, not in deities that had no substance, that did not exist.

But that philosophy had left an immeasurable void in the Kreelan soul. Ulana-Tath wondered how many of her people wished the gods had been real, had been faithful. One god or many, it did not matter. She simply wished to have something or someone greater than herself, than the kings and queens that rose and fall, in whom she could believe. Someone to turn to in the darkest of hours. Someone to ask for redemption.

But there was no one. While all believed in the Afterlife, for proof of its existence was incontrovertible from the senses of the spirit, the gods themselves were no more than bitter, empty memories.

The only surviving relic of that long ago age were the martial orders such as the Desh-Ka and their priests and priestesses. Long ago, they had led the people in worship of the gods. Then, as now, they were a guiding force in the world. After the Final Annihilation, the very name of which spoke as much to the destruction of the old faiths as to the devastation of their race, the priesthoods changed. They continued to form the foundation of Kreelan life through the training of the young in the kazhas and through their own godlike powers. But the spiritual heart of the people no longer pulsed. They lived now not to serve anything higher than the master or mistress to whom they were bound by honor. They lived and they died, but, as Ulana-Tath reflected now, there was little point to it all. She and her kind were not so far removed from the small creatures who lived in colonies beneath the ground, living out their lives in fulfillment of a function before they died.

Only love separated them from such tiny things that she could crush beneath her sandal. She shivered as she recalled the sensation of the first time Kunan-Lohr had kissed her. Closing her eyes, she seized upon the memory, willing it to stay with her forever. The warmth of his body holding hers, the tender, almost fearful way in which he had brought his lips to hers. It had been his first, as he had confessed afterward. A great warrior with a tender heart, so much as a smoldering glance from him made her feel like a goddess.

The thought that she would probably never see him again was nearly too much to bear.

"My mistress."

She glanced over at Anin-Khan, who rode on the opposite side of the nurse's *magthep*, and was looking at Ulana-Tath with sympathetic eyes.

"If it were in my power, I would gladly change places with him," he told her.

"You know he would never allow it."

Anin-Khan offered a rueful smile. "I would not offer him a choice."

Ulana-Tath bowed her head in respect, and Anin-Khan returned his attention to keeping his mistress and her child safe. His sword hand never left the handle of his weapon. His face once again wore its perpetual fierce scowl of concentration as his eyes darted back and forth, watching, just as his ears were always attuned for any sign of danger.

Ten of the city's finest warriors surrounded them as they moved along the road that would lead them to the Desh-Ka temple, their senses alert to any potential threats. Two more riders were up ahead, just out of sight, to warn of any ambushes or parties moving along the road toward them. Two more rode behind, to warn of anyone following.

Ria-Ka'luhr rode at the head of the main group, which in any other circumstance would have been a place of honor. In this case, Anin-Khan had placed him there so he could both keep an eye on him and keep him as far as possible from Ulana-Tath and her child without being too obvious about it. Anin-Khan knew that Ria-Ka'luhr must soon reveal his treachery. Most of the journey was behind them now, and only three days separated them from their destination. Once the child crossed the threshold of the temple, Keel-Tath would be safe from the acolyte, or as safe as she could be anywhere.

But three days was ample time for misfortune to befall her.

Assuming they made it to the temple, Anin-Khan had decided that he would seek out the old priest, Ayan-Dar, and inform him of his suspicions of Ria-Ka'luhr. Even if it was perceived as an insult and Anin-Khan died in a ritual challenge, the seed of doubt would have been planted. Someone at the temple had to know, and by doing the deed himself, he would protect Ulana-Tath and her daughter from any possible dishonor.

He snorted to himself as he thought of the old priest, Ayan-Dar. Anin-Khan had not the slightest doubt the priest could defeat him as easily as he could crush a dry leaf, but he also doubted that his warning about Ria-Ka'luhr would give rise to mortal offense. Or so he hoped.

"What are your thoughts, captain of the guard?"

Again looking over at Ulana-Tath, he said, "I was considering the odds of one of the Desh-Ka priests returning me home with their magic, rather than having to ride these beasts." His scowl broke into a momentary grin and he raised his voice slightly for the benefit of the warriors around them. "Defending the city, rather than riding into battle each day, my hindquarters have grown soft and unused to such abuse."

The other warriors grinned at his humor. Few of them had ridden any long distance in some time, and all were feeling the pounding that was characteristic of the *magthep's* trot.

Ria-Ka'luhr glanced around, a grin on his face, too, but he said nothing.

Anin-Khan stared at him, meeting his gaze with a stony expression, until the acolyte finally turned away.

* * *

The tiny, tortured soul that had once been Ria-Ka'luhr did not understand how the others could not sense the evil that now controlled him. Whatever dark magic Syr-Nagath had worked upon him had masked his true emotions completely. He no longer had a sense of the feelings he was projecting to those of his bloodline, but he could still sense theirs. The nurse gave no clue that she knew anything of his true nature. She was in awe of him, even though he was only an acolyte. Ulana-Tath still looked upon him with deep respect, indeed reverence. Her feelings were tinged with a sense of disbelief, no doubt from the words of warning he suspected Anin-Khan must have spoken to her.

Only Anin-Khan and through his word, no doubt, the escorting warriors, were suspicious. Their fear peaked when they watched Ria-Ka'luhr, and there were at least two sets of eyes on him constantly. During their infrequent stops, half of the warriors kept a wary eye upon him, although they did it without being obvious.

He wished he could gain control of his body for just a few seconds. He would not waste them on shouting a warning, but would have simply slashed his own throat in ritual suicide. They would not have known exactly why, but it would have allowed him to die with honor.

Instead, he would have the blood of a child on his hands, as well as her mother and the others around him. He knew in his heart that he could, and would, kill them, even without the full powers of a priest. Even if he could not, the child would be killed easily enough with a *shrekka*, and had to die first, for that was the queen's priority.

Yet the queen clearly had other plans for him, because he had a very clear sense that, while she would sacrifice him if need be in order to kill the child, she wanted him to survive. That is why the part of his mind that she controlled had decided to take the chance of waiting to strike until they were at the base of the plateau on which the temple stood. Here, along the main road, Anin-Khan and the others had enough room to maneuver, and might be able to overwhelm him. Once they started up the side of the plateau, the road would narrow to allow only two riders abreast. That would greatly limit Anin-Khan's options for battle.

The only major risk was that someone else along the road might witness the deed. If it were a priest or priestess, Ria-Ka'luhr would die. If not, he would kill them, and concoct a story that might or might not be accepted by the high priestess.

He simply had to wait for the best opportunity to take action, and let events unfold as they would. The only thing of which he was certain was that he would kill Keel-Tath.

As his soul writhed in agony at the thought, his body, playing the role of puppet under control of the Dark Queen's desires, turned to grin at Anin-Khan's jest.

* * *

Far to the east, Syr-Nagath rode at the head of one of the legions that was marching toward the city of Keel-A'ar. Somewhere ahead, the mounted cohorts drawn from all five legions, totalling nearly a thousand swords, were racing to cut off Kunan-Lohr before he could reach the pass at Dur-Anai. Her First had informed her that she suspected he had somehow forded the river in the mountains, for there had been a great wave of anger and a surge of fear from the warriors of the legion that had been sent in pursuit.

Syr-Nagath was neither surprised nor disappointed. Kunan-Lohr would not be stopped easily, but he would be stopped. And she planned to be there when it happened. She had given her warriors very explicit instructions that her warriors were to slay all under his command, but he was to be taken alive at all costs.

Where the battle had been won against the eastern armies, the warriors who had surrendered were busy gathering up the dead and dumping them into the ever-expanding pool of matrix material. The mirror weapons, too, were cast in. Syr-Nagath had no more use for them now. They had been perfectly suited for that battle, but would be useless in the conquest of Keel-A'ar. For that, the Ka'i-Nur builder mistress had other ideas for war machines. Building them here and moving them along the road would be impractical. Instead, Syr-Nagath had ordered the builder mistress to take as many builders as she required and ride fast with a heavy escort along the southern road to a province to the south of Keel-A'ar. There, they were to build the necessary war machines and move them into place, escorted by more legions Syr-Nagath had ordered to surround the city.

All that would take some time, but Syr-Nagath could afford to wait. Once her legions brushed past Kunan-Lohr, they and the others that would join them from nearer Keel-A'ar would lay siege to the city. No one would be able to escape the example Syr-Nagath intended to set. It went counter to the principles of the Way as those outside the walls of Ka'i-Nur understood it, but that did not trouble Syr-Nagath. The Way, as taught in Ka'i-Nur, had been as it was before the Final Annihilation of the Second Age. Reducing a city to rubble and exterminating its inhabitants, including non-warriors and children, would not violate her own sense of honor.

After the builders had finished making what she needed to reduce Keel-A'ar to ash, they would begin work on what would be required for her armies to conquer Urh-Gol, the continent that lay beyond the Eastern Sea. That would take quite some time, for the scope of what the builders would have to create was far greater in size, number, and complexity, and the warriors would have to be trained in the use of the vessels and weapons.

She planned to use the time wisely by stripping as many more builders as she could from her vassals, while her legions hunted down the honorless ones that roamed the land. While she had used them as a tool to capture one of the Desh-Ka acolytes, they were of no further use to her, and she would not allow their cancer to grow in the heart of her domain. The campaign to exterminate them had already begun, for she had given the order the day she had turned the acolyte, Ria-Ka'luhr. Those warriors pledged to her who had not been engaged in the fighting in the east or manning the garrisons of their cities or villages had been scouring the countryside since then, killing the honorless ones without mercy. Some, she knew, attempted to pledge themselves to her cause, but she would never take them. Even though she despised the Way as taught beyond the walls of Ka'i-Nur, at least those who followed it were noble in their own fashion. Those who had turned away from the path taught by the priesthoods were nothing more to Syr-Nagath than dangerous beasts.

"My queen." The First, who rode next to her, interrupted Syr-Nagath's thoughts.

"What is it?"

"I believe our mounted warriors have found Kunan-Lohr."

* * *

Standing on a rock outcropping that overlooked the great east-west road, Ayan-Dar watched as Syr-Nagath rode by. The air was filled with the footsteps of the twenty-five thousand warriors of the five legions that accompanied her. Some of the warriors glanced up at the rocks where he stood, perhaps out of idle curiosity during the boredom of a long march, or because they sensed his emotions, he could not tell. None of them saw him, of course, for he had masked himself from their sight.

After witnessing the dark matter created by the builders, T'ier-Kunai had modified the terms of Ayan-Dar's punishment. Rather than being cloistered, he was free to watch the Dark Queen's army as he would, reporting his observations to T'ier-Kunai.

"You may observe her actions, Ayan-Dar, but you may not interfere." Her words echoed in his mind. "And you will restrict yourself, even your second sight, to following the queen's movements. If you range beyond that, you will be cloistered in your room."

He had bowed his head and saluted. Disappointed that he could not do as he chose, he was also thankful that she had seen the potential danger Syr-Nagath posed, and was willing to give him some degree of freedom to at least remain apprised of her actions.

Now, as his eyes followed the Dark Queen, he wondered what thoughts ran through her head. But he could no more discern those than he could her emotions, for he could not sense the song of her blood. So far as he knew, no one could.

He worried about Ulana-Tath and her child. None of the priesthood had been willing to look in on their progress, for they did not see the need. Ayan-Dar suspected they must be on their way to the temple, but he was blind beyond the sense of their emotions. He had asked T'ier-Kunai if he could observe the child periodically, but the high priestess had only glared at him.

While it could be considered a loose interpretation of his orders, Ayan-Dar had also observed Kunan-Lohr on the grounds that he was being pursued by the queen's forces. Ayan-Dar had watched Kunan-Lohr's warriors ford the river as they fought off an entire legion of pursuers, and had been touched by his pride in and sorrow for those who had perished. Kunan-Lohr was a warrior of great honor, and it sickened Ayan-Dar that his life would be spent upon the queen's blade.

"I will see to your child, Kunan-Lohr." He whispered the promise upon the wind as the queen's warriors filed past. He pulled off his armored gauntlet with his teeth, then sliced his palm with the edge of one of the blades of a *shrekka* that clung to his shoulder. Blood dripped from the wound as he slid his hand back into the gauntlet, proof of his blood oath. No one would ever know about it but him, but that was enough. It would have to be. "She must cross the temple's threshold, yes. But once she does, no harm shall ever come to her, even at the price of my honor and my life. That is my vow to you, master of Keel-A'ar."

He looked to the west, toward the blue shadow of the escarpment that defined the edge of the great plateau that spanned most of this part of T'lar-Gol. The road would lead the queen there, where even now Kunan-Lohr was making his final stand at the pass of Dur-Anai.

CHAPTER EIGHTEEN

The pass at Dur-Anai was a marvel that was frightening in its majesty. A relic of one of the great civilizations that had risen before the Final Annihilation of the Second Age, the pass had been cut through the great escarpment that divided the continent of T'lar-Gol into east and west.

Not content to build a tunnel, the ancient engineers had cut into the cliff of the escarpment as if with a sword. The great east-west road made only the most gradual of inclines as it entered the face of the escarpment, and it continued straight as a ray of light through to the far side, hundreds of leagues away.

Standing here, at the entrance to the pass, Kunan-Lohr stared up at the sheer rock walls that rose straight above him nearly two leagues to the top of the escarpment. The rock was so smooth that it gleamed like glass, the fused surface revealing the geologic history of the place in breath-stealing beauty and splendor.

The road inside the pass had changed little in the long millennia since its creation. It was as wide as fifty warriors, laid head to toe, over twice the width of most of the rest of the ancient road. For beyond the pass, the endless wars had devastated the entire length of the great highway, and it had never been repaired to its original glory. The original surface, which still remained intact here, was stone, and yet not stone. It was hard and resilient, looking now as new as the day it had been created. While smooth, it gripped well, even when wet.

It will allow us to keep our footing when the blood spills from our enemies, Kunan-Lohr thought. He looked up as the pass began to sing, the wind howling through the cut in the land like the air through a whistling child's teeth. This day, at least, the wind in the pass favored them, and was at their backs.

They would need every advantage they could get in the battle that would soon begin.

Beside him stood young Dara-Kol. He had chosen her as his new First to replace the fallen Eil'an-Kuhr. It was a purely honorary role, for there would be little for the proud young warrior to do but fight and die with the rest of his warriors. But she had earned the honor with her bravery in crossing the river and her exploits in aiding in the escape of Keel-A'ar's army.

Glancing at her, he could see that she was exhausted and worn. Her lips were cracked from dehydration, her cheeks sunken. There had been little time to forage for food, and they had found precious little water in the two days since they had left the river. Her face and armor were caked with dirt and mud from the journey, and the braids of her hair were frayed. The other three thousand warriors who had made it this far, the last survivors of the fifteen thousand he had pledged to the Dark Queen a lifetime ago, looked much the same.

"We are truly a fearsome-looking lot now, are we not, Dara-Kol?" He smiled, an expression of ironic mirth.

She returned his smile, bowing her head. "All the better, my lord. The queen's warriors will tremble in fear at the sight of us."

That brought a hearty laugh from Kunan-Lohr and the nearby warriors who heard her words.

"Indeed, they shall, fierce warrior," he told her, smiling again as she puffed out her chest with pride. "Indeed, they shall."

Despite their hunger and thirst, the discomfort of armor that chafed against their starving bodies, their lack of sleep and chronic exhaustion, his warriors were in good spirits. Every one of them knew that few armies could have accomplished what they had done, escaping from under the nose of the Dark Queen, covering such a great distance so quickly and without preparation, and with an enemy legion snapping at their heels until Kunan-Lohr's warriors had crossed the river. The queen's warriors had not been able to pursue them beyond the river, for Kunan-Lohr had left a small party of warriors to prevent any swimmers from reaching this side of the river. He had drawn no small entertainment from the emotional frenzy of anger and frustration shown by the pursuing legion, now held at bay by a mere handful of young warriors.

He and Dara-Kol stood at the head of the defensive line facing east, the direction from which the queen's forces must come. Half of his warriors were arrayed in a semicircle, fifteen warriors deep, around the entrance to the pass. The other half, he had split into several groups. Some had been tasked with scouring the neighboring villages for water and food. Some had been sent to hunt in the nearby forests. Others were gathering wood for fires and to use as makeshift pikes and spears.

The largest group had been sent farther into the pass to warn travelers along the road of the coming battle. Or to fight them if they forced a challenge, protecting Kunan-Lohr's back. While there were still some cities and distant provinces that had not given their honor to Syr-Nagath, she was now the effective ruler of T'lar-Gol. Beyond the walls of Keel-A'ar, any warriors Kunan-Lohr's forces encountered now would technically be enemies. It was simply a question of whether they were aware of that fact or not.

"My lord!" Dara-Kol pointed to a hill that lay to the east along a bend in the road. "The signal!"

A bright flash shone from among the trees near the top of the hill. Then more. Kunan-Lohr watched as the party of warriors he had sent there to watch for approaching forces told him with signals from a mirror what was heading toward him.

"A thousand mounted warriors," Dara-Kol murmured as she interpreted the flashes aloud, "riding fast."

Kunan-Lohr turned to face his warriors. "The Dark Queen sends a thousand mounted warriors to us." He shook his head theatrically, as if completely appalled. "A thousand!"

"I may spare some for your pleasure, my lord." It was the young male warrior who had thrown the spear and gotten the rope across to Dara-Kol at the river. "But I fear that I may need a longer spear."

The battle line erupted in laughter, and Kunan-Lohr could feel their spirits rising, their bloodlust turning from a flicker to a flame. He knew that the riders now approaching were only to fix him in place and prevent him from escaping through the pass. As if he would have even tried.

A cloud of grief washed over him for a moment as he thought of Ulana-Tath and his daughter, Keel-Tath. He had known when he had parted from his consort that he would probably never see her again. They had shared much in this life, and his parting gift to her would be a chance at living, and a chance for their daughter to do the same. He could only hope that she had fled the city to escape the path of the queen's vengeance, for he knew Syr-Nagath would never rest until their daughter and all who sheltered her were put to the sword. Or worse.

He could sense her song in his blood, her fear, her anticipation. He instinctively knew that she must be on the move, and had taken his words to heart about bearing Keel-

Tath to the safety of the Desh-Ka temple. With all of T'lar-Gol now falling to the Dark Queen, their daughter would not find safe harbor anywhere else. And there would come a day, he knew, when she would be a fugitive from the entire Homeworld.

"Run, my love," he whispered as the mounted cohort of the queen's army came into view, the feet of the charging *magtheps'* talons sparking on the cobbles of the road. "Run as fast as you can." He took in a deep breath before whispering aloud, "And know that my heart is forever yours."

* * *

Dara-Kol clenched her fists to help ward off the fear she felt take hold of her as the mounted cohort drew near. While *magtheps* were normally placid, docile animals, they were large and powerful, and in the hands of a trained rider could be extremely deadly. And in a massed charge such as this...

"Perhaps it is time we prepare a welcome for our guests, do you think?"

She turned to Kunan-Lohr. "Yes, my lord. Should I send runners to recall the warriors who are foraging?"

He shook his head. "No. They are all veterans. They will know what to do." Leaning closer, he told her, "And having some of our swords out of sight along the enemy's flank and rear is never a bad thing."

"Yes, my lord." She bobbed her head in understanding. Then she turned to the ranks of warriors behind them. "Pikes to the front!"

Over two-hundred warriors stepped forward. Each held a pike made from nearby trees that grew straight as an arrow and were hard as steel. Roughly as big around as a warrior's forearm and as long as three warriors stood tall, they had been cut down and sharpened with swords and axes. The warriors who carried them were among the largest and strongest in the army, and could handle the ungainly weapons easily. They set the pikes down on the ground, facing the approaching enemy, for theirs would not be the first weapons to strike.

"Bales!" Dara-Kol's bellow summoned another group of warriors, who rolled thick bales of dry steppe grass about thirty paces forward. The bales had been soaked in pitch, and warriors along the front rank held torches, waiting for the signal to light the barrier.

"It will not stop them," Kunan-Lohr had explained earlier to Dara-Kol, "but it will add an element of confusion in their attack, and will prevent them from bringing to bear more than a few tens of warriors at any one time." He had given her a wicked smile. "*Magtheps* do *not* like fire."

Kunan-Lohr drew his sword, and the warriors behind him did the same. The sound of the glittering metal blades singing from their scabbards echoed from the sheer walls of the pass.

The charging group of mounted warriors changed formation from the mass column more suited to the road to a line that was roughly the same breadth as Kunan-Lohr's. The sound of the beasts' feet striking the ground and the war cries that erupted from the throats of the warriors filled the air, just as did the cloud of dust that rose in the wake of their thundering passage.

Dara-Kol felt the fire in her veins ignite, a passionate bloodlust that swept aside her fears. She could sense the same emotion in the charging warriors, and she threw back her head in a howl of challenge.

All along the defensive line, the warriors did the same. Kunan-Lohr added his own deep roar. The sound was magnified by the rock walls around them, and Kunan-Lohr could sense a momentary spike of fear in the hearts of the attacking warriors.

Just before the *magtheps* reached the barrier of pitch-soaked steppe grass, Kunan-Lohr nodded at Dara-Kol.

"*Fire!*" While she was young, she had mastered the art of the command voice, and the word boomed above the tumult.

Torches arced away from the defensive line to land in the bales just as the first riders leaped over the obstacle, their *magtheps* braying in protest.

The bales exploded into flame. *Magtheps* and riders were caught in the maelstrom, and the war cries of both sides were drowned out by the screams of flaming beasts and warriors.

In addition to the bales themselves, the road on either side of the barrier had been liberally coated with pitch, and was now burning with lethal fury. It stuck to the *magtheps'* feet, and the beasts went berserk trying to escape the searing pain. Riders were thrown to the ground, where they, too, were shrouded in flame as they were trampled.

But, as Kunan-Lohr had predicted, the queen's warriors did not stop. More came pouring across the wall of fire, and some began to make it far enough to reach the defensive line.

"*Pikes!*" At Kunan-Lohr's command, the warriors armed with pikes knelt down and lifted the long, sharp points of the weapons toward the onrushing enemy warriors. They kept the tail end of the pike on the ground, and more warriors braced the end with their feet, as the surface of the road offered nowhere to plant them.

The *magtheps* brayed and screeched as they ran forward, urged on as much by their desperation to escape the flames as the frenzied kicks their riders delivered to their ribs.

Holding the pikes were all veterans of many campaigns who were not in the least intimidated by the charge. Each one carefully aimed his or her weapon, hands clenching the hard wooden poles, at the approaching *magtheps*.

The riders slammed into Kunan-Lohr's line. *Magtheps* squealed in agony as the pikes speared them through the chest or belly. Most of the riders were thrown forward, but few lived long enough to even hit the ground before their bodies were hacked to pieces by the swords of the defenders.

But the opening of the battle was hardly one-sided. Riders with more experience in this type of attack deftly sidestepped the pikes, or dropped the pikemen with well-placed *shrekkas* before stampeding into the mass of Kunan-Lohr's warriors. Holding the reins with one hand and their swords in the other, they guided the *magtheps* through leaps and twirls as they slashed at their opponents on the ground. The talons on the animals' feet were longer than a warrior's extended palm and fingers, and could tear through or puncture armor, as well as flesh. While the *magthep* was a herbivore, when frightened or enraged their mouths could be deadly, the flat grinding teeth quite capable of crunching bone.

Dara-Kol guarded Kunan-Lohr's left side, for he was a right-handed swordsman. A riderless *magthep*, its hide aflame, ran toward them from the maelstrom. While it had thrown its warrior, it was still deadly.

Stepping to the side, Kunan-Lohr opened its throat with a quick cut of his blade. The beast charged on a few more steps before it collapsed.

Two more beasts, with riders this time, charged forward. One of them leaped in the air, bringing up its feet and talons to strike.

Dara-Kol darted out of the way of the deadly talons, which were coated with burning pitch, before jabbing the tip of her sword into the beast's side, just behind the madly waving forelegs.

As she pulled the blade free, she dodged the slashing sword strike of the warrior on the beast's back.

Turning to attack the rider, she was knocked to the ground by a massive impact. Rolling onto her back, she looked up to see the second *magthep* was in the air, its feet poised to tear her to ribbons.

A glittering blade flashed twice, so quickly that she could barely see it. The beast was liberated of its feet and crashed to the ground beside her, bellowing in agony.

Kunan-Lohr was there beside her, as if by magic. His sword flashed a third time, taking the head of the rider who was pinned under the hapless beast. Two paces away lay the other *magthep* and rider, the one she had stabbed, dead.

"More of a challenge than ritual combat in the arena, is it not?" Kunan-Lohr gave her a fierce grin. His entire body appeared to have been painted in blood. Even his teeth were stained with it. He reached out his free hand to help her to her feet. "Come, child, there are more waiting to be killed!"

* * *

The battle went on for hours, until the sun had passed onward to the west and the struggling warriors and beasts were cast in the cool shadow of the great escarpment.

The fiery barrier had long since burned out. Once the flames had finally guttered and died, the queen's warriors mounted proper charges against Kunan-Lohr's line. Masses of them, hundreds of riders at a time, smashed against his warriors over and over. Most of the pikes had been broken or were hopelessly stuck in their victims, and his warriors had to absorb the mounted charges with their swords and bodies.

It was a desperate, bloody affair. While Kunan-Lohr believed from the outset that he would win this first engagement, he also realized the mounted warriors were merely to keep him entertained until the queen arrived with the main body of her forces.

But his victory had not been easily won. More than once the riders had driven deep wedges into his line, killing many of his own warriors before the riders were brought down. Once, a group had actually broken all the way through, and for a time his warriors had to fight back to back, as it were. That was when the groups of warriors who had been foraging broke from cover and attacked the enemy from the flanks and rear, inflicting severe casualties and forcing the riders to retreat and regroup.

Finally, after one last charge by fewer than a hundred enemy warriors and one last orgy of killing, the battle was over. The road was awash with blood, the entrance to the pass a gruesome abattoir. The stench of blood and offal and flesh filled the air, as did the cries of wounded warriors and the pitiful mewling of dying *magtheps*.

Kunan-Lohr and a handful of other senior warriors moved with slow deliberation among those who suffered. Those with minor injuries were bound up with strips of the black undergarment taken from the dead. As for the rest, those from whom life was slipping away, Kunan-Lohr himself administered the last rites. Then he consigned the soul of the warrior, his own and enemy alike, to the afterlife with a dagger through the heart. Most would have survived had there been healers to tend them. But the healers in the nearby villages refused to come, for they knew that Kunan-Lohr was an enemy of their queen and to give them succor was forbidden.

Dara-Kol led a group that was slaughtering the injured beasts to put them out of their misery. If nothing else, Kunan-Lohr thought darkly, his warriors would eat well for a time. *Magtheps* were not typically used as meat animals, but none of his warriors would quibble over such trivialities. Other warriors corralled the surviving *magtheps* in a rope enclosure off to the side of the road where they could feed and be close at hand in case they were needed.

The rest of his warriors had the unpleasant task of dealing with the dead. Kunan-Lohr had ordered the bodies stacked across the mouth of the pass. "Build a mountain of the dead over which the queen's warriors must climb to reach us." It was a grueling, unpleasant task, but body by body the wall grew. It would not affect the final outcome, he knew, but would buy them more time.

After the last wounded *magthep* had been dispatched, Dara-Kol collapsed on its still-warm body, utterly exhausted. She barely noticed as Kunan-Lohr sat down beside her.

"You fought well today, child." He put a bloodstained hand on her shoulder.

"Thank you, my lord." Her voice was hoarse from shouting and screaming. She could barely hear herself speak, for her ears still rang from the din of battle.

"I have one more task for you, which I fear will be most unpleasant for you to bear."

"My life and honor are yours, my lord." She bowed her head and saluted, wondering at how she had become so covered in blood. As with all warriors, she had fought many times in the arena, and had also fought in some of the smaller battles of this war. But it had never been like this. She had never seen the gloss black of her armor so thoroughly covered in crimson.

Kunan-Lohr was silent for a moment. Then he undid the scabbard of his sword from the belt around his waist. He slid the weapon a hand's breadth out of its scabbard to admire the glittering blade. While it had been nicked and torn from the savage use to which he had put it this day, the living metal had already mended itself. He could take a strand of hair and let it fall upon the edge, and the hair would part in two.

With a sigh, he slid the blade back into the scabbard before handing the weapon to Dara-Kol. "You are to take two warriors with you, whomever you should choose. I would give you more, but a larger party will only draw more attention in a land where we are now the enemies of all. Take as many *magtheps* and provisions as you need and ride south. The queen has not yet taken all the lands there, and there are other roads that will lead you west toward home. I wish you to find Ulana-Tath, and give her this sword. I intend it for my daughter, when she comes of age." A wistful smile crossed his face. "Perhaps as a priestess, if that should come to pass, for I hope you will find my consort and daughter at the temple of the Desh-Ka."

He shook his head as Dara-Kol opened her mouth to speak. He could sense the disbelief, the anger, the hurt in her heart. "This is a hard thing to ask of a proud young warrior, I know. But this is my last wish before the queen's blade falls, and I know that you are resourceful enough to see that it is done." He looked at the devastation around them. "It is a far greater honor than dying at my side."

"Yes, my lord." She took the sword as black mourning marks began to make their way down her cheeks from her eyes. "I shall not fail you."

"I know, child." He stood, and she followed suit. "That is why I chose you. Tell Ulana-Tath...tell her that I shall await her in the Afterlife." Extending his arms, he gripped hers. "May thy Way be long and glorious, Dara-Kol."

CHAPTER NINETEEN

"He will strike today."

Anin-Khan had whispered those words to the other warriors in the dark of early morning before they began the final leg of the journey to the Desh-Ka temple. After hours of riding, the great plateau now rose above them, and he could clearly see the zigzag trail that led up its face in the bright golden glow of the late morning sun.

The party rode in the same formation as they had before, with scouts out ahead and behind, and the young acolyte at the head of the main group.

As before, Anin-Khan rode beside the nurse bearing Keel-Tath, with Ulana-Tath on her other side. His senses were tingling with alarm. What worried him was that it was not just his suspicions about the acolyte, that he would choose this day to unveil his true intentions. There was something else, as well.

"You feel it, too?"

He glanced over at Ulana-Tath, whose face betrayed the tension within her. The nurse also looked worried, and she had no inkling of the threat posed by the acolyte.

"Yes, I am, mistress. I believe we should..."

His words were stolen by a sharp cry from the warriors riding ahead. The road here was straight enough that they were within his sight. The two scouts had whirled around on their *magtheps* and were racing toward him when one was caught by a *shrekka* that sailed out of the thick woods along the road. She fell from her saddle, dead. Another *shrekka* flashed out toward the surviving scout, who batted it away with his sword. A cloud of *shrekkas* erupted from the trees, and he and his mount were cut to ribbons.

"Honorless ones!" Anin-Khan bellowed his warning, although he need not have done so. The other warriors in the escort had already discerned the nature of the threat. They pulled up in a defensive circle around Ulana-Tath and the nurse as over twenty riders emerged from the brush and trees around them, swords drawn.

He heard Ulana-Tath hiss in anger, and could feel her rage and that of the other warriors in his blood.

Only Ria-Ka'luhr's emotions remained calm, which worried him more than anything else.

"We ride with the consort of Keel-A'ar's master," Anin-Khan announced, "and are bound for the Desh-Ka temple. By what right do you bar our passage?"

The leader of the group, an older female warrior, bared her fangs in challenge. One of them, Anin-Khan could clearly see, had been snapped off at the root. She was dirty and unkempt, her exposed skin discolored and twisted with scar tissue from terrible burns. Her breastplate was in deplorable condition, the many dents hammered out by hand, probably with a rock. It was so old and in such poor condition that the metal had begun to oxidize, transforming the gloss black of the metal into a scabrous patchwork of rust. The leatherite armor that covered the rest of her body was old, abraded, and poorly fitting. Even her *magthep* was in poor condition, the undernourished animal's ribs showing through its dull fur, and a stream of yellow mucus dripped from its nostrils

The others in her party were little better. Some had newer armor and weapons that they had no doubt taken from their previous victims. In all they were a sorry lot, pitiable in Anin-Khan's eyes.

Only the fact that they outnumbered his warriors by two to one gave him any pause at all. Otherwise he would have simply brushed them aside or, failing their willingness to yield, slaughtered them.

"Leave us now," he told the elder warrior, "and you shall not come to harm. We have no quarrel with you."

"Spare me your compassion, captain of the guard of Keel-A'ar." The leader of the honorless ones spoke in a rasp. Her throat bore a scar from a long-ago battle that had damaged her vocal cords.

Anin-Khan grunted in surprise.

"Yes, I know who you are." She pointed her sword at Ulana-Tath. "And we recognize you, too, mistress." With a twisted grin, she told them, "But you need not worry for your lives. Dismount from your animals, and we will spare you." Then she turned to Ria-Ka'luhr. "Such will not be the case for you."

"You would dare threaten an acolyte of the Desh-Ka?" Ulana-Tath exclaimed, shocked. "If you had even the sense of a *magthep*, you would flee for your lives."

Ria-Ka'luhr, Anin-Khan noticed, said nothing, nor did his emotions betray anything other than placid calm.

The leader of the honorless ones shook her head. "The Dark Queen long ago offered a great bounty for any who captured an acolyte and delivered him to her alive. We captured three who did not survive." She gave Ria-Ka'luhr an appraising look. "Perhaps this one shall be different."

Anin-Khan watched as another two tens of honorless ones, on foot this time, stepped from the woods. They all carried swords and spears, which would be effective weapons against the *magtheps*.

In the short time he took to reflect upon it in the moments that would follow, Anin-Khan realized that, had he not been staring right at the leader of the honorless ones, his life and honor would doubtless have come to naught. He would have failed in the greatest responsibility with which he had ever been entrusted.

The leader of the honorless ones was staring at Ria-Ka'luhr, and in a single instant, Anin-Khan saw her eyes widen and her body tense. Her emotions betrayed not fear or anticipation, as might have been the case had she been the focus of an attack, but surprise and shock.

Reacting purely by instinct, Anin-Khan flicked his sword to his right, bringing up the flat of the blade as a shield in front of Keel-Tath, who was snuggled tightly in the bundle bound to her nurse's chest. The child cried out, and he could sense a spike of fear and anger in her that he had never felt before from an infant.

Whipping his head around toward the child, he saw a *shrekka* glance off his blade. It missed Keel-Tath by no more than a hair's breadth before the whirring blades sliced into the nurse's upper chest. With a wet gurgle, blood spewing from both the wound and her mouth, the nurse slid from her mount.

"Ria-Ka'luhr!" It was all he had time to say before chaos exploded around him.

* * *

As the dying nurse fell toward the ground, Ulana-Tath dove from her own mount, her hands reaching for her helpless child. Taking hold of the bindings that held Keel-Tath to the dead nurse, Ulana-Tath's talons sliced through the tough material. She pulled Keel-Tath to her armored breast just before Ulana-Tath slammed into the ground on her left side. A painful crunch told her that something, some ribs, perhaps, had broken, but she forced the pain aside. Fighting against the helpless, panicked feeling of having had the wind knocked from her lungs and the sudden agony of taking a breath, she struggled to her knees, cradling her daughter.

Standing before her was one of the honorless ones who was on foot, his spear held at Ulana-Tath's throat.

"Mercy!" She would never have begged for her own life, but she would for that of her child. She had dropped her sword, and the warrior facing her would have killed her before she could draw her dagger. "I bear a child! You may have strayed from the Way, but even you would not let a child come to harm! I beg you!"

The warrior's expression softened in the moment before a charging *magthep* crushed him to the ground, the beast's talons tearing into the his vitals as it stomped him.

"Mistress!" The warrior, one of her own, who rode the beast slid quickly to the ground and reached for the child. In the heat of the moment, Ulana-Tath had forgotten the warrior's name. "Take my mount and flee with your daughter!"

She did not argue. Handing Keel-Tath to the warrior, Ulana-Tath leaped into the saddle. The warrior carefully handed her the bundle containing her precious daughter, whose mouth was open in a ceaseless scream. Then he handed her his sword.

"Go!" He brutally slapped the *magthep's* rump, sending it into a full gallop just before a spear emerged from his chest, driven by one of the honorless ones. He crumpled to the ground, his hands wrapped around the spear's bloody shaft.

Ulana-Tath snapped her attention to the desperate battle that had engulfed her companions. She saw that Ria-Ka'luhr was surrounded by Anin-Khan and several other warriors, of Keel-A'ar and the honorless ones alike, their blades flashing in the sun like the deadly silver fish that inhabited the Lo'ar River as they fought the acolyte and one another. It was clear that the Desh-Ka acolyte was trying to fight his way toward her to finish the task of killing her daughter. Ulana-Tath felt boundless shame that she had not heeded Anin-Khan's warnings.

For a brief moment, their eyes met, and he nodded.

"Protect our mistress! Protect the child!" Anin-Khan's shouted orders carried over the furious sounds of clashing steel and raging warriors who fought in a snarling melee that swept outward from where Anin-Khan fought to block Ria-Ka'luhr's advance.

Ironically, for just that moment, none of the warriors, hers or the honorless ones, had their attention focused on her. While she wanted to fight to help kill the treacherous Ria-Ka'luhr, she did the only thing she could.

Savagely kicking the big *magthep* in the ribs, Ulana-Tath clung tightly to her daughter and fled. The *magthep* knocked down a pair of grappling warriors as she passed beyond the boundary of the swirling battle, just before another *shrekka* hurled by Ria-Ka'luhr found its mark in her back.

* * *

Anin-Khan fought as he had never fought before in his life. The Desh-Ka acolyte was a demon with his sword, holding his own against as many as six or eight other warriors trying to take him down.

The acolyte's only weakness, Anin-Khan had discovered, was that his skills at handling a *magthep* in combat were weak. Despite the acrobatics he had used when he had saved Ulana-Tath from the queen's riders, he clearly had no experience in mounted combat.

Having served as a mounted warrior for many campaigns in his younger years, Anin-Khan could make any trained *magthep* move in a coordinated display of lethal grace. Now, he constantly drove his *magthep* against that of Ria-Ka'luhr, shoving it off-balance before Anin-Khan whirled his own beast around to slap the acolyte's mount again with the tail. Were not so many other warriors crowded in against the acolyte, inhibiting Anin-Khan's own movements, he might have been able to kill Ria-Ka'luhr with his *magthep*.

But there was no point in wishful thinking. There were too many others pressing in around them, and it was just as likely that Ria-Ka'luhr's superior swordsmanship would have decided the issue in any case.

Anin-Khan took a precious moment to glance back at where he heard Keel-Tath's high-pitched cry. He saw Ulana-Tath mounting one of his warrior's *magtheps*, just before the warrior was stricken by the spear of one of the honorless ones.

He saw her gaze meet his own, and he nodded his obeisance to her, unable to make a formal salute of parting.

Turning back to the warriors struggling to keep Ria-Ka'luhr at bay, he bellowed, "Protect our mistress! Protect the child!" Then he again drove his *magthep* into the fray, his sword seeking the young acolyte's neck.

But he was too late. With a cry of horror, he saw Ria-Ka'luhr pull a *shrekka* from the shoulder of an honorless one he had just killed. With only a brief glance in Ulana-Tath's direction, the acolyte hurled the weapon in a smooth blur of motion.

The weapon caught Ulana-Tath in the back, near the bottom edge of her backplate. Had it hit the leatherite that was her only protection where the backplate ended, she would have been killed instantly. As it was, the weapon raked a deep, bloody furrow through the flesh and bone across the back of her ribs, missing her spine by a finger's breadth.

Anin-Khan did not hear her cry out, but felt her pain in his blood and watched as she slumped forward, clinging to the saddle with one hand as she cradled Keel-Tath with the other.

With a roar of fiery rage, the captain of the guard of the great city of Keel-A'ar redoubled his attack against his enemy.

* * *

Using all the skills he had been taught in a lifetime spent at the temple of the Desh-Ka, Ria-Ka'luhr fought off his attackers. The part of his mind that remained his own would have laughed aloud at the irony of the honorless ones wanting to take him. He was the product of what the queen had wanted the honorless ones to accomplish, and she had also ordered them to be killed. The word had simply not spread this far yet. But it would, soon enough.

He cried out in solitary anguish as, one after another, the warriors of Keel-A'ar were stricken by his sword or claws. He even felt pity and remorse for the honorless ones, who were only being hastened to their inevitable demise by his flashing blade.

Despite the chamber of madness in which he found himself, his joy had been absolute when he had thrown the *shrekka* that had been destined for the infant child and it had been deflected by Anin-Khan's blade. The duality of his existence was destroying what little was left of his own rational mind, for he knew what his body was going to do, as if he could see into the mind of his other self. He could sense the thought process, the desired outcome, the risks, and all the other factors that went into making any decision or taking any action.

And he was powerless to change any of it.

More warriors went down around him. Only Anin-Khan seemed to be immune. Anin-Khan was more skilled, and also knew how to use his *magthep* as a weapon. Ria-Ka'luhr silently cheered him on, hoping Anin-Khan would send his mount into a leap to slash Ria-Ka'luhr with its talons and end this insufferable torment.

But it was impossible. There were too many pressed in against Anin-Khan for him to maneuver.

Out of the corner of his eye, he caught sight of Ulana-Tath riding away, the child clutched in her arms.

He screamed in silence as he felt his free hand reach for a *shrekka* on the armor of an honorless one he had just killed.

Mercifully, his eyes turned away from her as he threw it, and he did not have to see it strike home. For he knew it would. He never missed.

Please, Anin-Khan, he begged in silence. *Kill me...*

* * *

Ignoring the blood that he coughed up from his pierced left lung, Anin-Khan fought on. Only he and two other warriors remained alive. The rest, his own warriors and the band of honorless ones, lay dead in the trampled and blood-soaked earth around him.

They now fought Ria-Ka'luhr on foot. Several of the honorless ones had finally brought down the acolyte's *magthep*, thinking that he would be more vulnerable on the ground.

They had been quite wrong. The move had eliminated his only real weakness, and they had paid the price in blood for their mistake.

Anin-Khan knew that he and the other two warriors would not be able to hold him much longer. While they had wounded Ria-Ka'luhr several times, his stamina and strength had barely diminished. If this was the power of a mere acolyte, Anin-Khan could not imagine how powerful a priest or priestess must truly be.

All the more reason to see that this beast never joins the priesthood. Ignoring the agony burning in his chest, he lunged forward, timing his attack to coincide with the other two warriors.

As he had before, Ria-Ka'luhr parried them with a series of deft strokes of his sword. This time, he exploited the failing strength of one of the other warriors. After deflecting the warrior's sword downward, the acolyte landed a killing blow to the warrior's throat with the outstretched talons of his free hand.

Seizing the opportunity, both Anin-Khan and the remaining warrior attacked.

But they had both been duped. Ria-Ka'luhr, with his talons still buried in his latest victim's throat, smoothly pivoted, putting the warrior's body between himself and Anin-Khan.

Unable to stop his own momentum, Anin-Khan's blade pierced the warrior's back armor, finishing what Ria-Ka'luhr had begun. The thrust also momentarily immobilized Anin-Khan's sword, leaving him completely open to attack.

He instantly let go of his weapon and rolled to the ground just as the acolyte's sword scythed through the air where his neck would have been.

The remaining warrior made an overhand cut against the acolyte, who blocked it with the body he still held impaled on his talons. The blade was pinned by flesh and bone, and in that instant Ria-Ka'luhr took the warrior's head with a ferocious slash with his sword.

Anin-Khan snatched one of the many swords that lay strewn upon the ground as Ria-Ka'luhr yanked his talons free and turned to face him. The agony that filled the left side of Anin-Khan's chest had become overwhelming, and he knew that his time had come.

"May your wretched soul rot in the darkness of eternity!" Summoning his remaining strength, he lunged at Ria-Ka'luhr, thrusting his blade at the acolyte's chest.

Anin-Khan was surprised at the momentary look of sorrow he saw on Ria-Ka'luhr's face before the younger warrior's sword pierced his heart.

* * *

Ulana-Tath knew only pain and desperation as she rode the *magthep* up the steep switchbacks that led up the face of the plateau toward the Desh-Ka temple. She could not see it, but she knew that the wound in her back was a savage one. Ribs grated together where they had been sawn through, nearly blinding her with pain, and a rivulet of blood poured down her right thigh from a severed blood vessel. She coughed now and again, leaving a fine coating of blood on the *magthep's* neck. Her vision was turning gray, the color leaching out of the world as the life drained from her. The armor she wore had saved her from instant death, but death was yet stalking her, close behind.

She had let go of the *magthep's* reins, for guiding the animal was hardly necessary along the narrow path. Instead, she used both hands to hold Keel-Tath, who had stopped screaming. With numb legs, Ulana-Tath urged the exhausted *magthep* onward with periodic kicks to its ribs.

Keel-Tath's tiny face peered out from the cloth cocoon, her beautiful silver-flecked eyes staring up at her mother.

Glancing back, Ulana-Tath saw another *magthep* starting up the ancient trail. It was no more than a dark form slipping in and out of sight among the emerald trees. She did not need a priest's powers of second sight to know who it was. She had sensed Anin-Khan's final moments, and could only hope that the keepers of the Books of Time would record his valor as the fallen captain of the guard deserved.

She thought, too, of her consort, the warrior who owned her heart. Kunan-Lohr. He still lived, still fought, but she knew through the senses of her blood that his time would soon be upon him. The Dark Queen would crush his body, but could not do so with his spirit. He had lived and would die with great honor, yet she wished that he could have been with her, that they could have shared the end of their Way, just as they had shared in living it.

Knowing that Kunan-Lohr could only feel her emotions and not her thoughts, Ulana-Tath focused on her love for him, that he would know how much he meant to her now, near the end.

May thy Way be long and glorious, my beloved. As the ancient words of parting ran through her head, she could feel her heart breaking.

Turning her eyes away from the evil that pursued her, she looked up. She was more than halfway up the face of the plateau now, and could make out the shape of the low wall that stood along the edge of the temple, and the gate that led inside. That was her goal, the objective that consumed her conscious mind. For that gate meant safety for Keel-Tath. If she could just get the child over the threshold, the worn stone over which all must pass to enter the temple, her daughter would be safe.

As she stared at the gate, willing the *magthep* forward, she saw the glint of sunlight on polished armor.

A solitary figure stood just beyond the threshold, watching her.

* * *

Ayan-Dar clenched his fist in frustration as he watched the *magthep* that carried Ulana-Tath make its way up the trail. He wanted to help her, but could not interfere. It was maddening.

He had been watching Kunan-Lohr's battle with the queen's forces until a short time ago, when he had sensed Keel-Tath's distress. The child's spiritual voice in his blood was preternaturally clear to him now. Risking T'ier-Kunai's wrath, he had whisked himself to the edge of the confused battle that had erupted between the warriors escorting the child and a host of honorless ones.

A bare breath had passed after he had appeared when T'ier-Kunai materialized at his side in the wake of a chill wind. Her eyes bored into his, and he could feel her sharply focused anger.

"I already have one of our fold who must be disciplined for breaking our covenants." She nodded her head toward Ria-Ka'luhr, who was completely surrounded by enemy warriors. "Do not shame yourself, as well."

"He is alive!" Ayan-Dar stood for a moment, transfixed at the sight of his long-lost acolyte. He had not heard, or had not recognized, his spiritual song for months, and had thought him dead.

And yet fate had delivered him here, fighting to save the child, just as he would have himself if he had been able.

T'ier-Kunai said nothing. Seeing that Ayan-Dar was rooted to the ground with shock at seeing Ria-Ka'luhr, she took his arm and whisked them both back to the temple.

"He is alive," Ayan-Dar said again. He looked down toward the forest.

"So he is." She, too, was shocked. But an explanation could wait until Ria-Ka'luhr's return, assuming he survived the battle.

But her shock had not overridden her anger at the priest, and friend, who stood beside her. "Ayan-Dar, you cannot continue to live on the edge of our Way. I understand the importance of all you have shown me, Ayan-Dar. I am not blind. But our lives are governed by forces that even I cannot readily change." She sighed. "As it is, Ria-Ka'luhr will find himself shackled to the *Kal'ai-Il* upon his return. If he returns."

Ayan-Dar gaped at her. "For helping to save the child's life?"

"No, you fool! For becoming involved at all!" T'ier-Kunai's voice betrayed her growing fury. "To do what he has done was forbidden, just as I forbade you. I do not do this on a whim, Ayan-Dar. It is one of the principles that guides us. You know this every bit as well as I. Whatever happened to Ria-Ka'luhr in the course of his final quest, one place he should not be is where he is right now." Seeing the older priest's expression of disgust, she told him, her voice sharp, "Do not dare hold me in contempt."

Turning away, Ayan-Dar said, "Of course, my priestess."

His voice held no sarcasm, but she knew that was an illusion. She stood there for a moment, deeply stung. "You wound me deeply with those words, old friend."

Then she walked away.

Ayan-Dar turned, intending to call after her, to beg forgiveness for his thoughtlessness. But whether from pride or cowardice, the words never slipped from his tongue.

Miserable and feeling great shame, he had stood there, alone for some time.

At last, deciding that his disgrace in T'ier-Kunai's eyes could only be made worse by small degree, he cast his second sight back to where the battle was being fought in the forest. Drawn to the terrified child's spiritual song, he focused on her as her mother, whom he sensed must be badly wounded, raced toward the temple.

* * *

Ria-Ka'luhr whipped his *magthep* mercilessly, driving it up the trail in pursuit of Ulana-Tath. He was gaining rapidly, as her own beast had slowed considerably. He could tell that she was wounded, for she left a clear trail of blood on the trail. Looking up above to where her *magthep* plodded along on the next switchback, he could see that she was slumped forward in her saddle, no longer urging her mount forward. All of her remaining strength and will must be focused on simply holding onto her daughter, preventing the infant from falling to the ground.

However the Dark Queen was doing it, his emotions now matched what those who knew him might expect. He was radiating intense compassion and fear, not for himself, but for the welfare of the mistress of Keel-A'ar and her child.

The sliver of his soul that survived railed at this travesty, but could do nothing about it. Instead, he continued to bless Anin-Khan and the others for their noble sacrifice, and urged Ulana-Tath to ride faster. She was so close to safety now, but his evil alter ego would catch her if she did not quicken her pace.

Beware, mistress! Death comes behind you...

* * *

The world was nearly dark now. Ulana-Tath was breathing rapidly, panting as her heart and lungs sought to get enough oxygen to her brain and extremities to survive. The flow of blood from the vein cut by Ria-Ka'luhr's *shrekka* had slowed to a trickle now, for her body had little blood left to give.

She sensed a warm, squirming bundle in her arms. Keel-Tath. The thought of her child sent a brief wave of warmth through her body, which now felt cold. So cold. She sensed Keel-Tath's spirit, so very strong for such a tiny child.

Ulana-Tath's body had fallen forward the last time she had passed out, but her chest had put enough pressure on her arms against the saddle to hold Keel-Tath in place. Otherwise, Ulana-Tath would have dropped the child without even knowing it. She dwelled on the horrible thought, an imaginary horror of the child falling to the hard ground replaying over and over in her mind.

She heard the hurried footfalls of a *magthep*. It took her a moment to realize that she feared the sound. After another precious moment, she remembered why.

With a moan, she lifted her head and looked behind her. It was Ria-Ka'luhr, making the last turn in the switchback just below her.

"No." Blood trickled in a thick stream from her lips as she looked forward. The threshold to the temple was there, and she could see the old priest, Ayan-Dar, waiting, and sense the urgency and fear of his spirit.

She tried to kick the *magthep*, to make it go faster. But she only managed to pull her feet from the stirrups, and with a sickening sensation she slid from the saddle. There was a brief fall before she slammed into the ground.

Screaming, Keel-Tath rolled from her grip, coming to rest just beyond the reach of Ulana-Tath's fingers.

The sound of the *magthep's* footsteps behind her were as loud as peals of thunder in her ears, overshadowing the pounding of her own heart and the screams of her terrified daughter.

The old priest stood but a few paces away. He was shouting something, but not at her. He was calling to the evil thing who came to kill her daughter. The priest did not know what lurked in the acolyte's heart. She could only hope that in the priest's care, Keel-Tath might be safe.

With the last of her strength, her heart about to burst in her chest as it tried to pump a last trickle of blood through her body, Ulana-Tath reached forward with her hands. Sinking her talons into the packed earth of the trail, she hauled herself to Keel-Tath. Forcing herself to her knees, Ulana-Tath gathered the child to her chest in one arm and crawled toward the priest. She could barely see him now through the darkness that was coming to claim her.

On your feet. It was the last command she would give her body, and her mind insisted that it be obeyed. Unsteadily she rose, taking one faltering step. Then another. One more, and she held out her child toward the priest as darkness claimed her.

***

Never even considering the consequences of his action, Ayan-Dar lunged forward just in time to catch the child as Ulana-Tath fell forward. The mistress of Keel-A'ar collapsed to the ground, dead.

Holding Keel-Tath with the utmost care in his great hand, Ayan-Dar stood. As he did so, the child passed over the threshold into the temple.

Ria-Ka'luhr suddenly reined his charging *magthep* to a stop, just short of Ulana-Tath's body. His face registered confusion for a moment, as if he could not quite decide what expression would be appropriate.

Ayan-Dar did not notice. He knelt beside the fallen warrior, whose eyes were open, staring at him.

"On my life and honor, I shall care for and protect her." He did not know if she could hear him in the seconds that separated life and death, but he spoke on the chance that he could ease her soul as it crossed into the afterlife.

He looked up then to Ria-Ka'luhr, who had dismounted beside him. "Close her eyes." Ayan-Dar would have done it, but he could not let go of Keel-Tath.

Nodding, a solemn look on his face now, Ria-Ka'luhr knelt beside Ulana-Tath and gently closed her eyes with a brush of his fingers.

"The child crossed the threshold," Ayan-Dar told him. "She is with us, now. As are you again, my long-lost friend."

Ria-Ka'luhr nodded. "I will tell you of my adventures later," he said. Nodding at Keel-Tath, he said, "You will care for her?"

"Yes. I made a vow, and it is one I intend to never break."

"I wish all your vows would be so honored. Now I must punish you both."

Ayan-Dar stood and turned to find T'ier-Kunai, who regarded him with a frigid glare.

It took Ayan-Dar only a moment to understand. He knew, of course, why Ria-Ka'luhr was to be punished. As for himself...

"Ah," he grunted, looking down at the ancient stone beneath his feet. "I reached beyond the threshold to save her."

She nodded slowly. "You have left me no choice, Ayan-Dar, priest of the Desh-Ka." She paused, and he could sense a wave of great sorrow in her heart. "You both must be punished upon the *Kal'ai-Il*."

CHAPTER TWENTY

In the midst of battle, Kunan-Lohr felt Ulana-Tath die. The heart of the woman, the warrior, who had loved him, and whom he had loved with all his soul, was stilled. A shudder of anguish ran through him as her soul passed from this world into the Afterlife. His hope had been that she would survive to care for their daughter, and that she could carry the warning of the blight the Dark Queen was bringing to the land. A tingling sensation crept down his face as the mourning marks appeared beneath his eyes.

In that moment, the burden in his heart became too much to bear. Managing to disembowel the latest of the endless stream of warriors the queen had sent against him, he staggered back from the battle line for a moment as one of his warriors moved forward to fill the gap. He allowed himself a moment to grieve, for that was all he could spare. The cycles he had spent with his love, so many memories, flashed through his mind. It was all he could do not to cry out in anguish from pain in his heart that was far worse than any wound a sword could inflict.

Even now, so near the end, he could not allow himself that luxury. He was the master of a city that was likely doomed, the leader of valiant warriors who stood and fought beside him, and the father of a child who was a miracle by virtue of her very existence.

A child who, through yet another miracle, had survived. He could hear her song in his blood, as clear as if she were in his arms, crying in fear and loss. He focused on Keel-Tath, hoping that she could sense and understand his love.

Then he focused on an entirely different emotion: hate. A black, raging hatred for the queen washed over him for all she had done. The bloodlust in his veins, which had been a guttering flame sapped by the exhaustion, hunger, and thirst that was killing him and his warriors, spread fire through his soul.

As he stood there, recovering his strength while imagining his hands wrapped around Syr-Nagath's neck, he surveyed his surroundings. The mouth of the pass was completely sealed by a mound of bodies that rose to a height of at least three warriors, head to toe. The bodies at the front of it, facing the queen's forces, had been stacked in such a way that the wall was nearly vertical, and they had to climb to the top. Once there, they had been easy pickings for Kunan-Lohr's warriors, who waited on a parapet of the dead just behind the wall's edge. He had long since stopped noticing the smell, the stench of voided bowels and blood, overlaid with the unmistakable smell of decaying flesh. Thousands of carrion eaters, some winged, some constrained to the ground, had flocked to the feast.

While the wall had provided an excellent defense, as more of the queen's warriors died, the vertical face had become a slope, somewhat easier for the attacking warriors to climb. They still died by the hundreds at the hands of Kunan-Lohr's warriors, but there was no end to the queen's minions. When Kunan-Lohr had last dared look over the wall at what lay on the far side, he counted the banners of five full legions. The entire approach to the pass was covered in black-armored figures in tight formations, ready to force themselves into the abattoir he had created for them.

While he had taken a grievous toll of those sent against him thus far, his warriors were totally exhausted after a full three days of non-stop combat.

More and more of his own had fallen as fresh enemies had attacked over the wall, day and night. There remained fewer than a hundred now, nearly all of whom were wounded. Kunan-Lohr, miraculously, had escaped serious injury. The only trophy he had to show for this battle thus far was a gash on his forehead he had received after tripping over a body.

"My lord."

He looked up at the words gasped by one of his warriors. Covered in blood and gore, Kunan-Lohr was not even sure who it was. "What is it?"

The warrior pointed to the wall, which for the first time in days was empty of live enemy warriors.

"Perhaps the Dark Queen wishes to surrender." Kunan-Lohr gathered what little moisture he had in his mouth and spit on the blood-smeared road.

His attempt at humor elicited a few tired grins, but that was all. They had no energy left even for a laugh. Nor did he.

"Kunan-Lohr!"

A chill ran down his spine as he recognized her voice. Syr-Nagath.

"I have no time for you, unless you wish to offer your head in surrender." His shout echoed from the walls that rose above them, making his voice sound as if it had been spoken by one of the ancient gods.

He was shocked when she suddenly appeared at the top of the wall of the dead. Behind her came a line of warriors, but like none he had ever seen. They were all large males whose faces were different, and whose armor was segmented, serpentine. He recalled that the queen had summoned builders from Ka'i-Nur. Now it appeared that she had summoned warriors, also.

"Despite your treachery, you have fought bravely and well, Kunan-Lohr," the queen told him as she made her way down the terrace of bloody bodies, never losing her footing. The brutish warriors followed close behind her. "But the time has come for this to end."

"The treachery is yours, Syr-Nagath." Kunan-Lohr felt the rage that had ignited a few moments earlier exploded into a roaring flame. "You tried to kill my daughter, and somehow had a hand in killing my consort. You have no honor, and I can only hope that you shall face eternity in the cold and dark."

Syr-Nagath laughed. "If your words are for the benefit of my warriors, you need not bother. They do not speak in this tongue, and their lives are mine in a way you shall never understand." She stopped and stared at him. "Surrender your lives to me now and I will spare your city. I would have offered this to you earlier, but they," she gestured to the warriors on either side of her, "only arrived this morning."

"And you would not have any of your other warriors hear these words."

"No. They would not understand." She regarded him for a moment. "The Way as you know it is coming to an end, Kunan-Lohr. The Homeworld will soon be mine, and the Settlements not long thereafter. One day what was," she raised her arms and looked up at the feat of engineering that was the pass at Dur-Anai, "will be again. We will return to the greatness of the days of old, before our race was corrupted into the stasis it suffers through the Way given by the priesthoods after the Second Age."

"You would lead us all to destruction and death. The Way has preserved us. And we will not surrender to your lies. I know you have no intention of sparing Keel-A'ar. Otherwise you would not have brought forth so many legions."

"As you wish."

She gave a brief command in words that Kunan-Lohr could not understand. With an ear-splitting roar, the warrior brutes bounded forward toward him.

"*Ready!*" His warriors formed up on either side of him in a perfect line. Exhausted and injured, they would no doubt die shortly, but they would die well, and with great honor.

Taking a brief moment for himself, he sent a thought to Ulana-Tath, hoping she could somehow hear it beyond the veil of the Afterlife. *I shall join you soon, my love.*

And then the enemy was upon them.

* * *

Ayan-Dar stood silently as Ria-Ka'luhr was released from the shackles of the *Kal'ai-Il*. He regretted that the young acolyte had to suffer, but he silently thanked T'ier-Kunai for the modest punishment of three lashes. And, truth be told, while recovering from the wounds would be agonizing, the punishment had granted Ria-Ka'luhr more respect in the eyes of his peers. He had not cried out, had barely even flinched as the *grakh'ta* whip, wielded by T'ier-Kunai, flayed the skin from his back.

Other acolytes unshackled Ria-Ka'luhr after the punishment was over, and as the first gong struck, he made his way unsteadily toward where T'ier-Kunai had taken her place, at the threshold of the entrance. He had twelve rings of the gong to make it to the stone marker that signified his acceptance of the atonement. One who was punished, but who could not make it that far would die by the sword of the high priestess.

"For that is the way of the *Kal'ai-Il*," he said softly to himself.

As he watched Ria-Ka'luhr make his way toward T'ier-Kunai, Ayan-Dar thought back to the young acolyte's tale of his remarkable quest, which he had told immediately after his shocking return.

"I knew that you had completed your quest," Ayan-Dar had told Ria-Ka'luhr and those gathered to hear his tale after his shocking return to the temple, "for I took this from a band of honorless ones." He handed Ria-Ka'luhr the sword he had taken from the young honorless warrior who had been among those who had attacked Ayan-Dar during his search for Keel-Tath. "This is the sword that you were to return from the mountain temple."

Ria-Ka'luhr's eyes were wide as he held out his hands, accepting the sword. "I was sure it had been lost."

"So the tale, or part of it, that one of the honorless ones told me was true," Ayan-Dar mused. "She said that they had killed an acolyte." He flicked a glance toward T'ier-Kunai. "She also said that she was bound in spirit to the Dark Queen, and I saw the mark of *Drakash* on her palm."

T'ier-Kunai's mouth dropped open with disbelief as Ayan-Dar looked expectantly at Ria-Ka'luhr.

"I never saw the Dark Queen." Ria-Ka'luhr shook his head. "The honorless ones overwhelmed me as I came down from the mountain. I killed a ten or more, but one of them was lucky with a war hammer." He pointed to a recent scar over his right temple. "I regained consciousness some time later, bound and gagged. They had me in a wagon and were taking me east. None of them ever spoke to me or in earshot, and I had no idea what their plans might have been. But thanks to one of them being inattentive for a moment, I was able to make good my escape. Along the way back to the temple, villagers were kind enough to see to my needs."

T'ier-Kunai frowned, wondering aloud. "But why all this time could we not sense you?"

He shook his head. "That, my priestess, I do not know."

The healer mistress, whom T'ier-Kunai had invited, spoke. "It is rare, but head injuries have been known to affect the song of the spirit." Her eyes were fixed on the scar on Ria-

Ka'luhr's head. "It is not unlike a temporary loss of memory that may be suffered in such a case."

A silence descended for a moment, and then T'ier-Kunai asked, "And why, on your way home, did you interfere with Syr-Nagath's warriors who were in pursuit of the mistress of Keel-A'ar?"

At that, Ria-Ka'luhr was clearly uncomfortable. Ayan-Dar had been watching him closely, and could clearly sense him now. But it was as if he was sensing someone...different, as if Ria-Ka'luhr were indeed standing before him, but his emotions were those of another. It was strange, and he had never experienced the like. He made a point to ask the healer mistress about it later.

"I can offer no excuse, my priestess, except that I felt compelled to. I could not stand by and allow her to be slaughtered. And her child..." He bowed his head lower. "She was bringing her child here that she might be kept safe. I volunteered to escort her, and could not simply stand by and do nothing when the honorless ones ambushed her party."

"I can understand, acolyte of the Desh-Ka," she told him. "But if you are to become a priest, you must learn to stand above the everyday world, the pleasures and the tragedies alike." T'ier-Kunai spared a pointed look at Ayan-Dar. "Beyond the *kazhas* and protecting the Homeworld from the Settlements, we are bound to constrain ourselves to the temple, and nothing more."

"Yes, my priestess..."

The last sound of the gong shook Ayan-Dar back to the present. Ria-Ka'luhr now stood at the threshold, his back covered in sterile cloth. That was all the healers could do for one punished on the *Kal'ai-Il*.

The acolyte nodded as he caught Ayan-Dar's gaze.

Naked, the many scars criss-crossing his body visible to all, head held high, Ayan-Dar strode to the center of the platform. Because he was a priest, only other priests could be involved in his punishment. As they shackled his feet, he cast his eyes about the stone wall that surrounded the dais, searching for the last priest or priestess who had been punished here. He grinned without humor when he finally found the name. It was one he did not recognize, over three-hundred cycles ago. "The time is overdue for another, then."

"Ayan-Dar?"

The young priestess who had shackled his feet looked up at him, wondering if he had spoken to her.

"Just the mutterings of an old fool. Complete your task, child."

With a bow of her head, she rose and fitted the oversized shackle to his wrist.

"I suspect I may be the first one-armed priest to be punished here. Please make sure not to pull my arm off when you tighten the chains."

"Yes, Ayan-Dar." She looked at him, and he could see the marks of mourning on her face. She was not the only one.

"Mourn for the evils in the world beyond our walls, child," he told her softly. "Not for me."

She only nodded, not trusting herself to speak as she tightened the wrist cuff.

As the wheels in the mechanism below the dais began to turn at the hands of yet more of the priesthood, Ayan-Dar took a final look around him. The *Kal'ai-Il's* huge central dais was surrounded by three concentric rings of massive stones supported by pillars. Each ring rose higher, creating a raised amphitheater so that all could see the punishment. On the stones stood all the priests and acolytes present in the temple, everyone but a few wardresses in the creche. Over a thousand sets of eyes were fixed on him now.

He could not help but smile at the thought of the creche. Despite the tragedy of Ulana-Tath's death, Keel-Tath had settled in quickly, accepting her new home. While he wished that Kunan-Lohr could live, that the girl would at least know her father, he knew that the master of Keel-A'ar would soon come to his end of days. Syr-Nagath would allow no other fate for him. Ayan-Dar made a silent vow to Kunan-Lohr that he would do the best he could in his stead, and that the girl would know everything Ayan-Dar could tell her about her parents. He would speak to the keeper of their Books of Time, and teach her the *Ne'er-Se*, the lineage of her family, when the time came.

As the chains tightened, suspending him in the air, Ayan-Dar for the first time in a long while felt as if his life had a purpose. Born from chaos as she might have been, Keel-Tath had given him a reason for being.

"Why do you smile?"

It was T'ier-Kunai, standing on the stone block just in front of him that put her face level with his. He noticed the mourning marks had run their course down her face and neck to disappear beneath her armor, and a tide of painful emotions swept over her soul at what she now had to do.

"Because I am happy, high priestess of the Desh-Ka."

"I will never understand you," she whispered as she held up a thick strip of leather to place between his teeth. It would help focus the pain and prevent him from biting his tongue.

He shook his head. "I appreciate your kindness, my priestess, but I will do fine without."

With a solemn nod, she stepped down. Taking the whip from a waiting priest, she walked to the edge of the dais, facing Ayan-Dar's back. Unfurling the barbed tendrils behind her, she stepped forward and snapped the *grakh'ta* with all her strength.

Ayan-Dar exhaled slowly as the metal barbs of the whip ripped into his back. Pain was an old and dear friend, and while the *grakh'ta's* sting could be excruciating, he had suffered far worse in his many cycles. The truly aggravating thing, he thought as the whip's tendrils flayed him a second time, was that he would not be able to spend much time with Keel-Tath while he recovered.

The whip cracked against him a third time, and he greeted the pain with a quiet sigh. He had to endure three more. Six lashes to some may have seemed a draconian punishment for what was outwardly a minor transgression, of reaching beyond the threshold to take Keel-Tath. But it was symbolic of Ayan-Dar having repeatedly pushed beyond the boundaries of acceptable behavior for one of the priesthood. He knew that he would have been called to task much earlier had anyone other than T'ier-Kunai been high priestess. He also knew how much it was costing her to drive the barbs of the *grakh'ta* into his flesh. At that, he felt more than a passing sense of guilt, for it was probably hurting her more than it was him.

But he also felt a degree of relief at the severity of the punishment, for it would show the others of the priesthood that T'ier-Kunai was strong, and that all would be held accountable for straying from the Way.

He held onto those thoughts as the whip hammered against him three more times. By the last strike, despite the control he exerted over his body, the pain was leaking through his mental defenses. T'ier-Kunai was not the largest among the warriors, but she had a powerful arm, and had put every bit of her strength into the whip.

After the final blow, the chains lowered him to the dais with a great clanking sound. He swayed unsteadily on his feet as two priests released him from the shackles.

"Make sure you carve the runes of my name deep into the stone," he told them, nodding to the wall around the dais where the list of those who had been punished was inscribed.

Then he turned and, after drawing himself up to his full height, moved slowly toward where T'ier-Kunai and Ria-Ka'luhr awaited him.

With the eyes of the priests and acolytes upon him, he took the steps that led down from the dais at a measured pace, ignoring the trickles and drops of blood that fell from his ravaged back to spatter on the smooth stone walk.

When he reached T'ier-Kunai, he bowed his head and saluted. "With your permission, high priestess, I would go to the creche once my wounds are dressed."

"You may, Ayan-Dar," she said, returning his salute.

"May I go, also?"

T'ier-Kunai looked at Ria-Ka'luhr, whose voice was tight from the pain, his body shivering. "Yes, acolyte. But do not stay overlong. You will need to rest. The full weight of the pain has not yet set in."

After the healers quickly dressed Ayan-Dar's wounds in sterile cloth, the two of them hobbled toward the creche, which stood nearby.

T'ier-Kunai watched them go, swallowed up by the throng of priests and acolytes who filed out of the *Kal'ai-Il* behind them.

Waiting until none could see her, she took a deep, shuddering breath before gathering up the bloody *grakh'ta* whip and following the last of the warriors out.

* * *

In the creche, Ayan-Dar cradled Keel-Tath with the greatest of care, one of the wardresses standing close by. The child looked up at him with wondering eyes before reaching out with her tiny hands, her crimson talons glinting in the soft light. He wished he had his other arm and hand, that he might let her grasp one of his fingers while he held her. Her white hair had already grown considerably, and was now like a pure white cloud framing the deep blue of her face.

Without thinking, he began to recite the ancient prophecy that he was more convinced than ever spoke of her birth:

> "*Long dormant seed shall great fruit bear,*
> *Crimson talons, snow-white hair.*
>
> "*In sun's light, yet dark of heaven,*
> *Not of one blood, but of seven.*
>
> "*Souls of crystal, shall she wield,*
> *From Chaos born, our future's shield.*"

Smiling, he added, "That was written for you, dear child. Long, long ago."

Ria-Ka'luhr stood quietly beside him. He had made no move to hold or touch the child, but had been content to watch Ayan-Dar hold her. His eyes flicked occasionally to the three warrior priestesses, standing at intervals around the creche, who stood guard over the temple's children. Their eyes stared toward the center of the creche's single room, as if they were in a trance. But they watched the children with their second sight, which was far more powerful than any senses of the flesh. Nothing so small as a microbe could enter this room without their knowledge and consent. It was not a task assigned to junior priests or priestesses. Those who served here had to pass the most rigorous trials by the high priestess herself, for it was one of the highest responsibilities of the temple, and among the greatest honors.

"Someday you may serve here, as well, young Ria-Ka'luhr."

"Of that I may only dream, Ayan-Dar." He managed a weak smile. "I must first pass the trials of the Change."

"That day shall come soon enough." With a sigh, Ayan-Dar handed Keel-Tath back to the wardress. His heart almost broke as the child began to cry, her tiny hands grasping for him. "I will be back soon, little one," he told her. "But first, I must take this battered old body and rest. Come," he said to Ria-Ka'luhr, who was looking quite ill. "Let us get you to your quarters."

* * *

At last in his own room, Ayan-Dar sat on a simple stool, overcome with weariness and the painful throb of pain from his lacerated back. The next few days, he knew, would be most unpleasant. What he felt now was akin to holding his hand close enough to an open flame to distinctly feel the heat. But soon it would be more like his hand resting on glowing coals. He would have to lay down at some point, on his stomach or side, of course. But once he did, he would not be able to get up very easily.

A soft knock sounded at his door.

"Come in, high priestess of the Desh-Ka," he called. He had felt T'ier-Kunai approaching from the song in her blood.

The door opened, and she entered, bearing a tray. On it was a mug of ale and some strips of meat.

"And what should the peers think," he said, smiling, "of their high priestess serving food and drink to such a ne'er-do-well?"

"That I am nearly as much of a fool as you," she said as she closed the door behind her and set down the tray on the low table beside him.

"You looked in on Ria-Ka'luhr?"

"Yes." She handed him the mug of ale, which he gratefully accepted. As he drank, she told him, "Having more sense than you, he has already taken to his bed to rest."

Ayan-Dar looked at her. Something in her voice told him there was more. "And?"

She shook her head, a look of frustration on her face. "I do not know. There is something about him that I cannot explain. I only sensed it for a moment, when he was in great discomfort as he lay down. It was as if I was looking at him through a glass, a prism, perhaps, and for just that brief moment saw two images of his spirit. One was what I expected to see. The other..."

"What? What did you sense?"

"The other image of him was one of torment, of madness."

With a grunt, Ayan-Dar set down the mug and said, "Being punished on the *Kal'ai-Il* is a traumatic event. I can accept it more easily, but for an acolyte it would be far more difficult. While there is no stigma among us after the punishment is rendered, it would be a brutal blow to a young warrior's honor and ego. Especially for an acolyte who is a mere step away from joining the priesthood." He shrugged, realizing too late the pain it would cause. Baring his teeth, he added, "And he had already suffered at the hands of the honorless ones. If I only knew what role Syr-Nagath played in this affair."

"We can discuss that later." She reached over and took his hand in hers. "Vow to me, Ayan-Dar, that you will never, ever force me to do such a thing again. Every strike of the whip tore at my heart."

"I seem to recall making a similar vow to you not long ago that I managed to break," he said, lowering his eyes. "I meant you no dishonor, T'ier-Kunai. But I would have suffered such punishment a thousand times over to save that child's life."

"I know." She squeezed his hand. "That is why I respect you so, you old fool."

With a wistful sigh, he looked into her eyes. "If I were but thirty, perhaps forty cycles younger..."

She smiled and shook her head. "You would be three or four times the fool you are now, and I would have nothing to do with you at all. Now lay down. You have an unpleasant time ahead of you and you need your rest."

"As you command, my priestess." Suppressing a groan, he lay down on his thick bed of hides on his stomach.

He felt a hand on his shoulder. "I shall look in on you from time to time." Then he felt her lips kiss his cheek.

Ayan-Dar only nodded as the pain in his back began to hammer against him. As he focused his mind on blocking it out, he wondered about what T'ier-Kunai had said about what she had seen in Ria-Ka'luhr. Torment and madness.

The thought followed him into a deeply troubled sleep.

CHAPTER TWENTY-ONE

Kunan-Lohr knew that he was beaten. The Ka'i-Nur warriors were beasts. A group contained him while the others fell upon his warriors, whose last defiance lasted only a few minutes. He had managed to kill two of the brutes, but he suspected that had been more by sheer chance than anything else, or perhaps they had simply underestimated him. They were unimaginably quick, extremely skilled in a form of swordcraft he had never encountered, and brutally powerful. If Syr-Nagath could raise an army of such warriors, she would indeed be able to make her grand designs come true.

"*Kazh!*" Her voice broke through his thoughts. "Stop!"

The warriors surrounding him backed away, wary and with swords held at the ready should Kunan-Lohr try to attack her. The other warriors had formed a larger circle around them, a solid wall of serpentine armor and strange, alien faces.

They parted to allow Syr-Nagath to step forward.

"You would challenge me, would you not, Kunan-Lohr?"

"Yes," he said fiercely. "I would challenge you, Syr-Nagath."

She drew her sword, but then handed it to one of the warriors. "You cannot challenge a female with child." She stepped closer, holding her arms wide. "I am unarmed, master of Keel-A'ar."

He backed away, fearing some sort of trick. "You are lying." He tightened his grip on the sword, preparing to strike. He knew that the massive warriors behind and to either side of him would kill him before he could take her head, but he would gladly die in the attempt.

"You would not kill your own child, Kunan-Lohr." She stepped even closer.

The words rooted him to the ground in shock. He remembered with sickening clarity mating with her, her price for letting him depart for home to see Keel-Tath born. It had not been an impulsive demand, as he had thought at the time. He realized now that she had planned this. *But why?*

Without fear, she walked up to his sword and gently pushed the tip aside. She took his free hand and placed it against her belly, just below the armored breastplate. "Tell me now that this is not your child, growing in my womb."

Kunan-Lohr closed his eyes as he sensed the child. It would be months before it was born, but he knew in that moment that what she spoke was the truth.

"No," he breathed, consumed by this horrible twist of fate. He could not imagine what dark plans she had for the child. "Oh, no."

She stepped away, holding his gaze as she did so. "Take him!"

Two warriors grabbed Kunan-Lohr's arms. The one holding his sword arm forced his hand open, and his weapon clattered to the bloody ground.

"I know you would take your own life, if you could, but there is much yet that I wish you to see before you die."

Knowing that he could not slash his own throat with his talons, Kunan-Lohr closed his eyes and fought to relax his throat. He sought to swallow his tongue and suffocate himself.

"His tongue."

He heard the queen's words, and instantly a pair of huge hands was prying open his mouth. He fought as best he could, struggling in the grasp of the giants who held him. Another one took hold of his head, holding it steady.

With his jaw held open, he felt a finger stab into his mouth, the talon lancing into his tongue. He struggled even more, but to no avail. The brute pulled his tongue out past his lips, and then shoved a spike through the end so he could not pull his tongue back into his mouth.

Kunan-Lohr did not scream, for he would not give the Dark Queen the satisfaction. He glared at her, his hatred a raging torrent in his soul.

That was when he saw two more warriors coming toward him, bearing two metal plates. The plates were a hand's breadth in diameter, glowing red and smoking with heat. The warriors held them by means of a handle that was wrapped with thick cloth to insulate their hands from the heat.

"We have far to go for you to see what I wish to show you." Syr-Nagath spoke softly, having stepped closer. Her lips brushed his ear. "I can never trust you not to somehow escape and slash your throat with your talons, or take your life with a dagger or sword."

Knowing in that instant what she planned, he screamed. Not in fright, but in fury and helplessness.

The warriors holding his arms shifted their grip to his forearms. Two more stepped forward, swords at the ready.

With a nod from the queen, the warriors with the swords sliced off Kunan-Lohr's hands.

He shrieked in agony.

Then the warriors bearing the red-hot irons stepped forward and pressed them against the stumps of his wrists, searing the flesh and closing the wounds.

The last thing he would remember was the sight of Syr-Nagath, watching him with cold detachment.

Then, mercifully, he passed out.

* * *

When he awoke, he found himself staring down at the floor of a wooden wagon. It was moving, bobbing side to side and rattling as the wheels turned over the cobbles of the ancient road.

Lifting his head, pain surged through him. His tongue was aflame and his wrists throbbed. It took him a moment to remember what had happened, that his tongue had been spiked and his hands taken at the wrists.

Fighting against a wave of nausea, he opened his eyes. He was naked, held upright by a thick metal collar bound to a rough wooden post. His arms were held out to his sides, strapped to a crosspiece attached to the post.

Ahead of him marched a legion of the queen's warriors. Turning his head, he could just see more legions behind him, trailing away into the distance. The air was filled with the sound of tens of thousands of marching feet.

He recognized this stretch of the road, and knew that they must have been on the march for at least three days. That was how long he had been unconscious.

"You are awake, I see." Syr-Nagath had appeared beside him, riding a nimble *magthep* with an immaculately groomed coat. "You do not look well, master of Keel-A'ar."

The only thing he could do was to fix her with a glare of venomous hatred.

"Just imagine, Kunan-Lohr." She swept her hand around, indicating the legions around them. "All of T'lar-Gol is now mine. The southern kingdoms have already pledged their honor to me after sending emissaries to challenge me to ritual combat." She glanced at him. "Even though I am with child, I accepted their challenges, and sent the heads of the emissaries back to their lords.

"Along the shores of the Eastern Sea, my builders are preparing a fleet of craft that will carry us to the continent of Urh-Gol. After that has fallen, I shall take the continent in the south, Ural-Murir." She paused, her eyes focusing on something far beyond the deep purple mountains in the distance. "By the time Ural-Murir has fallen, the builders will have the first of the great ships ready, ships that will carry us again to the stars to begin the conquest of the Settlements." Turning to him, she said, "In a way, I wish that you could be there to see it. You would have made a worthy consort. But that is not your Way, is it?"

Kunan-Lohr, of course, could make no response.

Baring her fangs in a smile, the Dark Queen laughed and then rode ahead.

He watched her go, his heart heavy and his spirit crushed.

* * *

While Syr-Nagath had not told him directly, Kunan-Lohr had no doubts as to the destination of her army: Keel-A'ar. For him, it was a long, agonizing journey, strapped to the crucifix in the cart. He quickly lost weight, for he was fed only gruel and water that the alien Ka'i-Nur warriors forced down his throat in a tube. They left him in his own filth until they could no longer stand the smell. Then they would douse him with buckets of freezing water.

He had no idea how many days the agony had gone on before they finally emerged from the forest to the east of the city.

There, looking as if it had the day he had last left it, was Keel-A'ar.

The sight would have lifted his spirits, save that the city was surrounded by more of the queen's legions, no doubt sent from the nearby provinces to the south.

It was, he had to admit with a leaden heart, an impressive sight. The city was ringed with orderly formations of warriors, their glossy black armor glistening in the sun.

But what caught his eye were the strange machines that were placed at intervals around the city. Each sat on a wheeled chassis, and at the apex of the roughly triangular base was a long arm on a pivot, offset with a massive counterweight. The machines were huge, with the arms as long as fifteen or more warriors were tall.

"I have never seen one of these war machines in action," Syr-Nagath was again riding beside him, enjoying his reactions, "but the builders assure me the results will be spectacular."

They continued forward, the newly arrived legions deploying off the road to take their place on the eastern side of the city, facing the main gate. The warrior driving his accursed wagon continued forward until it was at the head of the legion and Kunan-Lohr had an unobstructed view. The warrior silently dismounted and stood there, holding the *magtheps* still.

Kunan-Lohr could see the figures of warriors along the parapet behind the walls. Some of them pointed at him. Then, as one, they saluted him.

"They recognize you, I see." She spared him a glance. "Say your farewells to them, Kunan-Lohr."

With a nod to her First, a set of horns sounded.

Behind the war machines, Kunan-Lohr saw warriors with torches move forward. They set them against giant spheres that sat in metal chain slings that, he saw now, were attached to the end of the long arms of the war machines.

Throwing arms, he realized with a sick sensation at the pit of his stomach.

The giant spheres caught fire. When they were fully ablaze, the queen nodded.

The horns again blared.

As one, the war machines surrounding the city fired. The counterweight at the front of each machine pitched the throwing arm up and forward. The flaming spheres were snatched upward and thrown in high, graceful arcs toward the city.

Moaning in horror, Kunan-Lohr wanted to squeeze shut his eyes, but did not. The fire bombs rained down upon his city, upon his people. He could sense their terror in his blood, and he cried out in anguish as they began to die.

In mere seconds, Keel-A'ar was wreathed in flames within its protective walls, walls that could do nothing against these weapons. While the builders would do what they could to assist the warriors in protecting the city, they had no defense against this type of attack. The only thing that saved the city from rapid immolation was that most of the structures were built of stone and roofed with metal or ceramic.

The Dark Queen had taken that into consideration, of course. The next volley fired by the infernal machines comprised huge rocks that smashed through the walls and roofs, allowing the liquid fire of the spheres to spill inside.

The air was filled with flames, smoke, and the terrified screams of the dying or those who were about to die.

That is how the day wore on, with the machines alternating between the burning spheres and rocks. None of the tens of thousands of warriors who ringed the city ever took a step forward.

By early afternoon, Keel-A'ar was a caldron of flame that soared above the walls. Kunan-Lohr, his heart utterly broken, stared as the main gate finally flew open. Thousands poured out, all of them of castes other than warriors. They, he knew, would never surrender. But they had hoped that Syr-Nagath would show mercy upon those who did not live by the sword.

They were wrong. Every last one of the robed figures who fled from the conflagration was slain right before his eyes, even the children from the creche, carried in the arms of the wardresses and wet nurses.

Every one of their cries for mercy and screams of pain and fear echoed in his dead heart as he watched them die, cut down by the merciless warriors of Ka'i-Nur.

After the last of them had been killed, the queen had their bodies hauled back to the gate and thrown into the flames. Still, the infernal war machines fired into the city, even though Kunan-Lohr was certain that not a single soul remained alive.

Tens of thousands of people, dead. Beyond the roaring flames that soared into the sky, a huge pillar of smoke rose above the dead city, bending away to the west as it met the winds aloft.

"This shall be the new Way, Kunan-Lohr." Syr-Nagath's eyes were alight with the flame that burned within her own twisted soul. "This is the power of the future, that I shall bring from the distant past."

Kunan-Lohr stared through the main gate at the huge pile of ash and glowing embers that had once been living people. His people. In their deaths he saw the fate of his race under the rule of the Dark Queen.

He closed his eyes. There was nothing more in this world to see.

Beside him, Syr-Nagath spoke the last words he would ever hear.

"Cast him in."

* * *

Standing before what had once been a great city, Ayan-Dar stared through the blackened gates into the smoldering pile of ash that was all that remained of Keel-A'ar. He had watched them die through his second sight, after sensing the terror wrought by the queen's weapons upon the helpless population.

He had been a mere thought away from coming, hurling himself through space and time to stand before the Dark Queen, sword already swinging to take her head from her body. It was a fantasy he had imagined a thousand times as he watched the people of Keel-A'ar burn.

But of course, he could not. He already owed T'ier-Kunai a great debt, and he could not dishonor her again. To do so would be to forfeit his life, and he no longer had such a luxury, with Keel-Tath in his care.

T'ier-Kunai stood beside him, aghast at the scope of the tragedy. Both of them were long inured to the horrors of war, for that was why they lived. But the Way dictated that warriors fought other warriors with and for the sake of honor, and that the other castes and children, above all, were sacrosanct.

In this, clearly, the Dark Queen did not believe, Ayan-Dar thought grimly. The Way that had preserved their kind for long millennia was about to be undone. And yet none among the priesthood, even T'ier-Kunai, were willing to see, let alone act, on what to him was clear as the mountainous pillar of smoke that rose from the ravaged city.

The queen's army had marched away while the fires were still roaring, a pyre that could be seen that night from many leagues away. He had to wait until morning, for he could not have restrained himself from killing any of her warriors who might have still remained.

Ignoring the acrid smell of the smoke and the burning sensation in his eyes, he stepped closer to the still-hot debris near the threshold of the gate.

There, at the edge of the pile of burned bodies, lay a charred husk with a metal collar around its neck. He winced at the sight of the stumps at the body's wrists.

Kunan-Lohr. There was no trace of armor or weapons on his body. The queen had withheld even that small dignity from Keel-A'ar's last lord and master.

"How many cities will suffer this fate?" He considered the pitiful remains of what had once been a great warrior and leader. "Keel-A'ar shall certainly not be the last."

"Keel-A'ar is not unique," T'ier-Kunai told him. "Cities have been destroyed in the past."

He turned to face her, wincing at the pain from the wounds in his back, which were still healing. "Indeed, they have. But when was the last time one was reduced to ash, with every inhabitant, even the children, slaughtered? When surrender was denied to the defenseless. Even the builders, a caste that she covets, were massacred!" He could not suppress his anger as he demanded, "Tell me, when was the last time such an abomination occurred? A thousand cycles ago? Ten thousand? More?"

T'ier-Kunai looked away, unable to meet his gaze.

"I do not believe this has happened on the Homeworld since the end of the Second Age. Even the honorless ones, if given the opportunity, would not have committed such an abomination. In past cycles, when they have sacked cities, they did not murder every living inhabitant." Something tore in his heart as he stared at a tiny, blackened form not far from Kunan-Lohr. It had been an infant, perhaps one who had briefly shared the creche with Keel-Tath before her mother had taken the child to the temple.

Unable to look anymore, he turned away.

Outside the wall, a short distance from the gate, was another pyre, not yet lit. On a carefully prepared bed of wood lay Ulana-Tath's body. They had originally planned to give her a funeral of honor at the temple. But after what had taken place here, Ayan-Dar had convinced the high priestess that this would be more fitting.

Beside the pyre stood one of the priestesses who was among the guard of the creche, cradling Keel-Tath in her arms. The child had begun to cry when the assault on the city began, and had continued until a healer had finally sent her into a deep sleep.

T'ier-Kunai had originally been vehemently opposed to bringing the child here, but Ayan-Dar had insisted. "This is part of her world now. This was her city, where she was born. Her parents died for it, and for her. Even if she does not yet understand these things, there will come a time when she will, when she must. All she may retain of this is fleeting images, or the smell of charred flesh and bone. But we cannot insulate her from what she will eventually have to face when it is time for her to take up her sword and fulfill the prophecies appointed to her. You may not yet believe, T'ier-Kunai, but you will."

With one last look at Ulana-Tath and the expression of peace on her face, Ayan-Dar took a torch that he had prepared for the purpose and lit the tinder at the base of the pyre.

After tossing the torch into the rapidly growing fire, he came to stand beside the priestess who held the child.

As Keel-Tath always did when he was near, she reached out for him. The priestess gently placed the girl in his hand, and he cradled her against his chest.

Together, priest and child watched the roaring flames reach toward the sky.

EPILOGUE

The most celebrated event that ever took place at any of the ancient temples was the ordination of a new priest or priestess. It was also an event most rare, for very few who started the long path that led to the priesthood completed the journey. Surviving the rigors of the *kazha*, the school of the Way, was only the first step. Beyond that lay long cycles of far more difficult training in the art of war, and great challenges that each novice had to successfully accomplish. Then, and only then, would they finally receive their first Collar of Honor.

Unlike those worn by the priests and priestesses, the collars of the acolytes were bare of the sigil, a device at the throat that bore the rune of the order to which the wearer belonged. The acolyte's collar also did not have the first five pendants worn by all who ascended to the priesthood, and which proclaimed the name of the wearer.

Ria-Ka'luhr wore the collar of an acolyte as he knelt before T'ier-Kunai on the dais of the temple's main arena. As were all the warriors here, she was resplendent in her gleaming black ceremonial armor, the rune of the Desh-Ka a cyan flame on her breastplate. Her black cape billowed in the light breeze, the silver piping around the edges glinting in the noonday sun.

Above them shone the great moon, in full splendor in the magenta-hued sky.

In the white sands that surrounded the dais knelt all of those who called the temple home. The priests and priestesses, acolytes, the non-warrior castes, the children, all were here. Even Keel-Tath, the youngest child of the creche, was there, cradled in the arms of one of the wardresses, her wide eyes transfixed by the spectacle.

Ayan-Dar felt the child's presence. He wished that he could have held her, but as one of the most senior members of the priesthood, his place was in the first ring of those who knelt before the dais. The others who lived in the temple were arrayed in concentric circles that expanded outward across the sands.

The gong at the *Kal'ai-Il* sounded once. Twice.

When the echo of the last deep ring faded, T'ier-Kunai began to speak.

"The greatest honor accorded to us, and the most worthy task, is to welcome another into our fold. To have had a hand in shaping a life over many cycles, to have taken a child who would become a warrior, to see him rise above that most noble form to become something far more. To see him become a teacher of the Way, that our race may be preserved. To entrust him as a defender of our race in the ancient balance with the Settlements." She paused, looking down at Ria-Ka'luhr. "To all these things did this acolyte aspire. He rose to each challenge of blood and honor that was placed before him, and has proven himself worthy of the priesthood."

Looking up at those assembled around the dais, she said. "Today again the Crystal of Souls shall shine upon another, and it shall purify with fire. Each of us who wears the Collar of Honor with the sigil of our order knows the pain of the flesh this brings, and the powers it bestows upon those who survive the crucible of the Change."

She again looked down at the acolyte kneeling at her feet. "Ria-Ka'luhr, do you accept your responsibilities as a priest of the Desh-Ka, and consign yourself to the sacred fire that shall sear your body and soul?"

"I do, high priestess of the Desh-Ka." He spoke clearly, his voice carrying across the arena to the most distant listener. "My life and my honor are yours."

"Very well."

The six senior priests and priestesses, Ayan-Dar among them, rose to their feet. T'ier-Kunai turned and began to walk in a slow, measured pace toward the largest structure in the temple, a massive domed coliseum. Ria-Ka'luhr fell into step behind her, followed by Ayan-Dar and the other five senior members of the priesthood.

The gong again sounded from the *Kal'ai-Il*. As one, the other members of the temple rose to their feet and joined the procession.

The entrance to the dome was a massive wooden door, taller than three warriors stood tall and as thick as one, head to toe. T'ier-Kunai opened it with a brush of her hand and proceeded into the darkness that lay beyond.

Ria-Ka'luhr paused as the other six priests and priestesses filed past him on either side, disappearing into inky blackness as they stepped past the entry threshold.

The others of the temple gathered behind him in a semicircle. Many of the acolytes had never before witnessed this ceremony, for it had been over ten cycles since the last priest had been ordained.

Before Ria-Ka'luhr, the darkness was banished by a soft glow. With a deep breath, he stepped into the light.

The door closed behind him.

He found himself in a massive arena. It was the largest structure he had ever seen. Unable to help himself, he looked up to find the walls filled with carvings. Runes that told of the ancient history of the Desh-Ka and scenes of glorious battles rose to the apex of the dome high above him.

Around the great arena, a series of thin windows rose from the ground toward the top. While magenta light streamed in, Ria-Ka'luhr could not make out any of the other buildings of the temple that should be outside. It was as if the coliseum was floating in the sky.

He moved to the central dais, itself a work of art as much as that which adorned the walls of the dome that soared above him. He knelt on the smooth stone and waited.

In addition to the door through which he had entered, there were six others, evenly spread around the arena. Seven doorways. Seven priests and priestesses. Seven Crystals of Souls. Seven ancient orders. It was a form of symmetry that had survived for hundreds of thousands of cycles.

How much longer it might survive was a question that was never asked.

All seven doors opened. T'ier-Kunai, Ayan-Dar, and the other priests and priestesses of his escort stepped into the arena. He assumed they had used their power of teleportation, for there was no hallway or room from the door to the outside through which they could have reached them.

They approached the dais, then knelt in a circle to his left and right. T'ier-Kunai knelt opposite him.

"Now," she told him, "shall your true training begin."

* * *

The storm raged beyond the mouth of the cave. Dara-Kol huddled against the far wall, shivering from the cold as a barrage of lightning and thunder tore the night sky. The rain fell in sheets, so heavy that she could not have seen beyond the length of her arm had it been daylight.

She would have given anything to be able to build even a small fire, but to do so was to invite death. Her two companions, one of them the fierce young spear-carrier, had been killed through similar desperate recklessness in the months that had passed since Kunan-Lohr had tasked her with taking his sword to his daughter. Dara-Kol had known from the outset that it would be a difficult journey, but she could never have imagined the nightmare it had become.

The three had made their way south as Kunan-Lohr had instructed, and they had been welcomed in the southern kingdoms. They were making good progress in traveling west, taking a long roundabout path far from Keel-A'ar before swinging north toward the Desh-Ka temple.

One night, while they rested at an inn in a small village in the south, they were set upon by the very people who had given them shelter. She and her companions had not known that the Dark Queen had sent word to the far corners of T'lar-Gol that any survivors of Keel-A'ar were to be handed over to her, lest those who sheltered them suffer the same fate as their home.

Dara-Kol and the others had known, of course, that Keel-A'ar was gone. She had felt them die, and Kunan-Lohr, as well, through a wave of agony through the song in her blood. The three of them had curled up, unable to move, so blinding had been the pain.

While the trio had claimed they were from another city when asked, Dara-Kol knew that some folk they had encountered had recognized Kunan-Lohr's sword. Just like the dagger he had given her as proof of his words to Eil'an-Kuhr to pull his warriors out of the queen's encampment, his sword was unique. It was a Sign of Authority, a signature that was easily recognized by any who had encountered him. She would have covered it up, tried to conceal it, but that would have made it stand out even more, for warriors never hid their weapons.

Good fortune had favored them the night the villagers had tried to take them, and they had escaped with their lives. But they had lost their provisions and all but the three *magtheps* on which they rode.

That night had been the start of the nightmare. Word had spread that there were fugitives from the queen in the southern lands, and it was a matter of honor for every warrior to find them, and to avoid the queen's wrath.

Dara-Kol was not sure now how long she had been running. The first of her companions, a female warrior whom she had not known before setting out on Kunan-Lohr's quest, died within the first month. The young spear-carrier, whom she had come to greatly admire, and would one day have loved, died a few months later as they finally escaped the southern kingdoms and entered the Great Wastelands.

She cringed at the memory. Both of them had thought themselves safe, for very few ventured where the great *genoth* still reigned and every creature that crawled or flew had its own unique way to kill the unwary.

In the end, he died because of a simple fire they had built to keep warm during the frigid nights. She did not even know who had attacked them. She had been roused from a deep, exhausted sleep by the sounds of fighting. She heard his war cry and a wet thud as his spear found its target, then the sound of swords on metal, of screams. All she could see were shadows dancing at the edge of the fire's light, the glint of metal blades. He never screamed for her to run, and she knew it was because he hoped they had not yet seen her.

Never before had she felt such deep shame as she had that night when she fled, slipping away quietly, leaving him behind to die.

How alone she felt, as if she were the last of her kind.

In a sense, she realized, that was true. Aside from Kunan-Lohr's daughter, if she still lived, Dara-Kol was probably the last survivor of Keel-A'ar.

As the rain poured outside, she cradled the sword of her dead master to her breast. It was the only reason for her existence now, and she would not fail in her quest.

She would not fail.

* * *

Deep beneath the brooding fortress of Ka'i-Nur, Syr-Nagath grunted with pain and the effort of bringing forth the child from her womb. Aside from two healers who were acting as midwives, the birthing chamber was empty, although the order's greatest warriors stood outside, on guard.

Like the rest of Ka'i-Nur, the birthing room was made of stone, although this stone was warm to the touch, its temperature determined by the will of the healers to keep the birthing mother in comfort.

Not that Syr-Nagath was concerned with such things. Comfort had never been a part of her life, and never would be. She thrived on violence, on chaos. And the child she was bringing into the world, she knew, would help her with both.

With a scream, she pushed, sloshing warm water over the lip of the birthing pool. Her talons scored the stone where her hands gripped the edge.

Between her legs, one of the midwives watched intently. "I can see the child's head."

Syr-Nagath took in several deep breaths, then pushed again, grunting with the effort. With a scream of release, the enormous pressure and pain in her belly subsided.

The midwife leaned forward, scooping up the child as it emerged into the world. "It is a male-child, my mistress."

The midwife closed her eyes, holding the child under the water for a moment to let it become accustomed to its new environment. The other midwife leaned over to spread a film of healing gel over the water, and the midwife holding the child raised him up until it enshrouded him.

Syr-Nagath waited, bringing her breath under control as she watched the healing gel disappear into her son's flesh.

After a few moments, it oozed out the child's mouth, and the second midwife took it into her arm. She closed her eyes, focusing on the symbiont that was now joined with her. She opened them again and quietly announced, "He is completely normal, my queen."

The first midwife lifted the child from the water, placing him into Syr-Nagath's trembling arms as he took his first breath of air and began to cry.

"I name thee Ka'i-Lohr," his mother, the Dark Queen, whispered. "Welcome, destroyer of worlds."

DON'T MISS THE NEXT BOOK OF THE FIRST EMPRESS SAGA: *FORGED IN FLAME*

Keel-Tath, the child who would unite her people, as foretold by an ancient prophecy, has grown to be a young warrior in the confines of the Desh-Ka temple, where she has been sheltered by her old friend and mentor Ayan-Dar from the clutches of Syr-Nagath, the Dark Queen. But when Keel-Tath is forced to choose between sanctuary and her honor, she goes into exile, leaving behind a broken-hearted Ayan-Dar.

Captured and bound in chains by those who serve the Dark Queen, she is rescued from an unspeakable fate by a warrior from the shadows. Thus begins Keel-Tath's perilous journey to the ends of her war-ravaged world, through deadly wastelands and even deadlier seas, unaware that some of those she holds most dear stand ready to betray her...

For details, visit http://AuthorMichaelHicks.com!

DISCOVER OTHER BOOKS BY MICHAEL R. HICKS

In Her Name: The Last War Trilogy
First Contact
Legend Of The Sword
Dead Soul

In Her Name: Redemption Trilogy
Empire
Confederation
Final Battle

In Her Name: The First Empress Trilogy
From Chaos Born
Forged In Flame
Mistress Of The Ages (Coming Fall 2013)

In Her Name **Trilogy Collections**
In Her Name: Redemption
In Her Name: The Last War

Harvest Trilogy
Season Of The Harvest
Bitter Harvest
Reaping The Harvest (Coming Summer 2013)

To learn about upcoming releases, visit
AuthorMichaelHicks.com!

A SMALL FAVOR

For any book you read, and particularly for those you enjoy, please do the author and other readers a very important service and leave a review. It doesn't matter how many (or how few) reviews a book may already have, your voice is important!

Many folks don't leave reviews because they think it has to be a well-crafted synopsis and analysis of the plot. While those are great, it's not necessary at all. Just put down in as many or few words as you like, just a blurb, that you enjoyed the book and recommend it to others.

And thank you again so much for reading this book!

ABOUT THE AUTHOR

Born in 1963, Michael Hicks grew up in the age of the Apollo program and spent his youth glued to the television watching the original Star Trek series and other science fiction movies, which continues to be a source of entertainment and inspiration. Having spent the majority of his life as a voracious reader, he has been heavily influenced by writers ranging from Robert Heinlein to Jerry Pournelle and Larry Niven, and David Weber to S.M. Stirling. Living in Florida with his beautiful wife, two wonderful stepsons and two mischievous Siberian cats, he's now living his dream of writing novels full-time.

CPSIA information can be obtained at www.ICGtesting.com
Printed in the USA
BVOW032307060513

320055BV00001B/100/P